MW00479848

Step Bride

B. B. Hamel

Other books by BB Hamel

City Series:

Undersold
Kinged
Filmed
Honored
Jerked
Taught (Novella #1)

Stepbrothers:

Based
Rock Hard
Cocked
Raging Hard
Smash
Stiff

Find out how to get a FREE book at www.bbhamel.com!

This is a work of fiction. Any similarities to real people, places, or events, are entirely coincidental.

Copyright © 2016 B. B. Hamel
All rights reserved.
ISBN: 1523816589
ISBN-13: 978-1523816583

CONTENTS

Step Bride

Prologue

I went to college to get away from drama.

But in Vegas, with my mom's new crazy antics swirling in my mind, I was ready for a little trouble. I must have lost my mind.

Because when I saw *him*, I knew what sort of trouble I was about to get into.

Cocky and muscular, wearing an expensive suit, he swept right into my life like a hurricane. In the back of his limo, right before making the dumbest decision of my life, I felt his breath hot against my neck.

I want to see you wearing only diamonds, he whispered.

I couldn't help but laugh. Did that line work on other girls?

It's not a line. I want to taste that soaking pussy while you're wearing millions.

Sex and money. Was that all he thought about?

Sex, money, and violence, girl. Get used to it.

His fingers roamed down along my body, and I felt a chill run down my spine. I gasped when his lips found my throat, his rough hands along my thighs. Maybe it was the champagne, or maybe it was the excitement of all the wealth, but I couldn't help myself.

Truthfully, it was just him. His cocky smile, his body, his lips.

I wanted him to touch me. I wanted him to explore me.

He pressed my legs open, almost roughly, his hands suddenly on my soaking pussy.

I knew you were begging for it, he whispered in my ear.

His fingers did things I'd never, ever forget. My hands pressed against the glass of the limo, sweat rolling down my back, I bit my lip and stared into his eyes.

Good, girl. Watch while I get you off. I want to see your pretty face say my name.

He had me. In that moment, he had me completely.

"Lucas," I said, over and over.

His wicked grin. So violent. So damn sexy.

I'd never forget that smile, even when it started to mean something completely different.

Chapter One: Natalie

I never wanted to be famous.

But when your mother inherits a fortunate, loses it over the course of a few years, and then goes on a string of awful reality TV shows, it's hard to avoid the cameras, at least to some degree.

Truthfully, I'm not famous, not really. My mother, on the other hand, is a minor celebrity and appears in gossip rags pretty regularly. Headlines like "Socialite Mother Snorts Coke for Days" or "Camille Taylor Seen Stripping for Cash" were not unusual. Sure, most of it was bull, but still, it was not exactly healthy trying to grow up a normal teenager when your mom was out running around all the time.

Which was why I got out of her house as soon as humanly possible. I got accepted into the University of Texas, packed my bags, and tried to pretend like I had never lived in Chicago and had never heard of Camille

Taylor.

The thing about the past, though, is you can never escape it. Especially when it's your mom.

"Don't let it ruin your trip," Pacey said.

"I'm not," I grumbled, tossing the magazine across the room.

"Come on, look outside." She walked over to the opened the curtains. "We're in freaking Vegas!"

I sighed, nodding. The school year had just ended, and Pacey and I had decided we were going to treat ourselves for getting through another brutal semester.

Really, neither of us wanted to go home. Pacey didn't get along well with her dad, and I intensely disliked my mother. So instead of heading right back to another rough summer of being trapped in our respective parental homes, we'd decided on a few days of debauchery.

Although debauchery wasn't really my thing. I never thought I'd end up in Vegas, let alone dressed up in one of the sexiest dresses I owned. The plan was to hit the strip, maybe go to a casino and see where the night took us.

Instead, I had to be an idiot and buy a gossip rag. I knew I might find something about my mother in there, and I knew that might ruin my good mood, but I did it anyway.

And of course, there she was: Camilla Taylor, big-time socialite, laughingstock of the world.

I was so embarrassed that I could die.

"Don't let your asshole mother ruin this," Pacey said again.

"Okay, okay," I said, taking a deep breath. "Let's do it."

"Hell yeah!" Pacey poured us both another shot, and we knocked them back. I made a face, shaking my head.

I was nothing like my mother. Where she loved to party, I preferred quiet nights. Where her whole job was acting like an idiot on television, I hoped to be a lawyer one day. I liked stability and normal, serious things, whereas she was only interested in frivolous parties, cute clothes, and rich boys.

I followed Pacey out into the hallway and down the elevator, giggling as we went. I had never been to Vegas before, and it was totally not normally my thing. The flashing lights, the seedy underbelly, it all was another world. I thought of myself as a serious student trying to get out from under an embarrassing mother. Getting caught doing something stupid in Vegas was the last thing I needed.

But I worked hard and I deserved a little fun. Or at least that was what Pacey said. Without her, I would have probably ended up right at home as soon as the semester had ended, hiding up in my room.

Instead, Vegas. We moved through the streets, gaping at the hotels, at the action. It was amazing, and I had to admit that I was already beginning to forget all about my mom.

"Come on," Pacey said, grabbing my arm. "Let's gamble our meager savings away."

I laughed. "Maybe not all of it, okay?"

"Nope. Every penny. I'm putting it all on black."

"I am not bailing you out, Pacey."

"Good! I'll become a lady of the night."

I laughed, shaking my head. "You don't have the tits for that."

She frowned, looking down at her chest. "They may be small, but they're proud."

"True. You have very proud boobs."

We laughed as we stumbled into a casino. Pacey led the way, taking us over toward the blackjack table.

"Now," she said softly, "we have to act like we belong, okay? Try and be serious."

I nodded. "Serious. Got it."

We bought some chips and then sat down at the table. Pacey seemed to know what she was doing, and I was mostly watching. She was the image of a serious player, keeping a straight face and nodding respectfully to the other players.

And as soon as she won her first hand, she started screaming with joy.

"Hell yeah!" she whooped. "Getting rich tonight, baby!"

An older man at the end of the table gave her a dirty look. She flipped

him off.

"So much for being serious," I said to her, laughing.

She shrugged. "We're here to have fun, remember?"

I watched her gamble like that for the next hour or so. I didn't bother

putting any money down since Pacey was doing enough for the both of us.

She was up and she was down, and by the end of the second hour, she was

back to being about even.

Finally, Pacey walked away from her third different poker table. "Let's

get out of here," she said.

"Tired of losing money?"

She shook her head. "Never tired of that. No, I just want to dance."

"That's the most cliché girl thing ever. You just want to dance?"

"Ugh, girl, listen. I just want to dance. That's all."

I laughed as she began to shake her ass. "Okay, stop it. People are

staring."

"Come on, we're supposed to be loosening up, right? Twerk with me

girl."

I laughed and shook my head, backing up. She did have a point,

though. We were supposed to be having fun, loosening up. We were

supposed to be forgetting about all our troubles. So why couldn't I relax

like Pacey could?

Eventually she stopped twerking and we were off, trying to find a club. It didn't take long, considering Vegas is literally covered by them. We got lucky and the bouncer thought Pacey was hot, so he let us skip the line and head right in.

The place was booming. People in expensive clothes were all over the place.

"Looks like we chose wisely," Pacey said.

"I feel underdressed."

"You look hot as shit. Come on."

We went to the bar and ordered drinks.

"You almost ready to loosen up?" she yelled over the music.

"Fine, okay? Fine!" Our drinks appeared and Pacey held hers up.

"To having a good time."

"And to forgetting about my insane mother."

"Cheers to that." We clinked glasses and I drank.

The music was deep and loud, filling the space. We finished off our drinks and headed out to the dance floor.

Pacey was right. I needed to relax, to have some fun. I lived so much of my life trying not to be like my mother, always saying no to things, always trying to be responsible. For once in my life, I was going to be reckless. I was going to say yes to everything that happened, and I was going to have a good time.

Pacey and I hit the floor, dancing. It felt good to finally decide to let my guard down, to finally relax. I was a little buzzed, but definitely not drunk. Some guys came up and hit on us, but Pacey chased them off with some seriously targeted dirty looks.

"No grade D beef," she yelled in my ear. "We're looking for a filet."

"Why the meat metaphor?" I called back.

"Do you really need to ask?"

I made a face and shook my head. She laughed loudly and twirled me, giggling. I could feel the music getting into me, making me feel loose and good. Everyone around us was dancing wildly, couples grinding, everyone young and sexy. Most people had a drink in their hand, and I felt like I could finally blend into the crowd.

Pacey grabbed me and twirled me again, sending me stumbling a few steps away.

She yelled something, but I didn't hear her. It was lost in the music.

I looked across the floor.

That was the first time I saw him. I caught his eye, completely by mistake, and that mistake would change my life.

It felt like a chill ran down my spine. His face was chiseled and his eyes were a slate blue, his dark hair cut short. He was wearing a suit tailored perfectly for his muscular body, and his full, perfect lips turned up into a slight grin as he returned my look.

Then Pacey was back, dancing with me again.

I shook my head, getting the man's image out of my mind. There were hundreds of people in the club, so I figured I'd never see him again.

I was so, absolutely wrong.

Five minutes later, I felt someone's hand at the small of my back. I saw Pace's face begin to contort into her normal dirty look, but she suddenly stopped. I turned and looked.

It was him, the man in the suit. He smirked down at me. "Dance?" he asked.

I looked at Pacey. She just stared, dumbfounded.

I knew I had already made the decision as soon as I felt his hand on me. It sent shivers along my back, and one glance in his eyes only confirmed it. He was stunning, handsome, and serious looking, the kind of guy I always imagined but never actually met.

And I had decided to say yes. No more avoiding fun because I was scared of being like my mother.

"Okay," I said.

He pressed his body against mine. Pacey melted away into the crowd, disappearing from view. For some reason I didn't care, though, and I began to dance with my handsome stranger.

"I saw you staring at me," he said in my ear.

"I wasn't staring."

"You were. It's okay. I like that you want me."

"I don't want you." He was being so forward, so cocky.

"What's your name?"

"Natalie."

"Natalie. I'm Lucas Barone."

"It's nice to meet you."

I could feel his cocky smirk against my ear. "I know it is."

We kept dancing, our bodies pressed together.

I had no clue what I was getting myself into. I didn't care, and I refused to think about it. Instead, I was letting myself have fun, letting myself finally relax.

And Lucas seemed nice.

Handsome and confident, maybe even cocky, but nice.

Boy was I so wrong about that.

"You know you're the sexiest thing in here?" he said to me. "That dress makes me want to tear it off. It makes me want to taste you," he said. As we danced, he said things to me that nobody had ever said before, things that made my knees feel weak and my body feel electric.

Finally, after what felt like forever, when he asked if I wanted to see more of the strip, I knew I should say no.

He was a total stranger. I didn't know him. But he was so confident, so cocky, and he had that irresistible swagger and body.

So instead of doing the responsible thing, the right thing, I said yes. I sent a quick text to Pacey, and then I let him take me by the waist and lead me out into the cool Vegas night.

I didn't expect the limo. Or the bodyguards.

I didn't expect anything at all.

How could I have known?

Chapter Two: Lucas

"You've been a liability for this family for too long, Lucas."

I stared at the old man, keeping my face passive, trying not to let him know how much he disgusted me. The room smelled like polished wood and cigar smoke, just like he did.

"You think you can take over the business the way you've been behaving?"

"I'm efficient." I smiled slightly.

"You're brutal and violent. That's what the captains say, at least. Yes, you get your job done, and you often do it very well. But you bring far too much attention to the family and you know it."

It was the same argument I had heard time and time again.

My father was old. He was part of the old guard, and he was getting up there in years. No matter how many young girlfriends he had, he was still an old man.

"You need to settle down," he said. "You need to become a respectable man."

"I have respect," I said softly.

"Not the kind that I care about."

I wasn't interested in my father's respect. I had the respect of the bosses, of the muscle, of the captains. And if not their respect, then their fear. I ran my operation seriously and brutally, and nobody questioned me.

Nobody except my father, the head of the Barone Crime Family.

"Son, you cannot take over my position the way you've been acting. It simply cannot happen."

I sneered at him. How dare he tell me that I couldn't take over the business? I'd been running the business essentially single-handedly while he grew fat on his lazy ass. I was out in the streets hustling for hi, for the business, day in and day out. Maybe he disagreed with my methods, but the results spoke for themselves.

"You can't stop this, old man," I said.

"I can," he answered, his anger rising. "And I will. Unless you do as I tell you."

"And what do you want me to do, father?"

"Get married."

I stared at him, surprised. "Married? Are you joking?"

He sighed. "You're too wild, Luca. You're running around as if you're invincible. You need a family to soften you, to make you into a true businessman."

I laughed out loud at the absurdity and the hypocrisy. "You've been single for years, father, and you think I need a wife?"

"Your mother passed, God bless her soul." He paused, smiling. "But I'm not single any more."

That gave me pause. "What are you talking about?"

"This has not been made public yet, but it will soon. Do you remember Camilla?"

I nodded. "Of course. That two-bit reality TV star you were banging."

The anger returned. "She's your stepmother now, and you'll respect her."

I gaped, not sure whether I wanted to laugh or yell. How could the old man be so fucking stupid? Camilla Taylor was a notorious party girl and socialite, despite being a mother and in her forties. Despite her being twenty years younger than my father, she had also already inherited one fortunate and had completely spent it all on expensive clothes, houses, and cars.

She was a gold digger. Everyone knew that. Everyone except my father, apparently.

"Now that I am married, you will be too," he continued. "If you wish to inherit my position, you will be married soon."

I stood up, shaking my head in disgust. "I can't believe you'd fall for a vapid gold digger like Camilla Taylor."

He pounded a fist on his desk. "Do not speak of her that way again, Luca. Do you hear me?"

"I hear only the blustering of a dried-up old man."

"You will get married!" he yelled after me as I left his office. "You will settle down or get cut out!"

As I walked through the halls of our family estate on the affluent outskirts of Chicago, his words kept ringing in my ears.

The old fool wanted me to get married. He thought marriage could settle me down, but he was wrong.

I didn't care about marriage. I took the women I wanted and moved on, always a new one. I'd never met a woman that could slow me down for a single second.

I simply possessed what I wanted. I couldn't imagine tying myself down with marriage.

And yet, the old man still was in charge of the Family, as much as I hated to admit it. One day he'd be too old and infirm to do much, but he was still respected enough to keep control.

A wicked idea came into my head, and I could feel myself already beginning to smile.

If father wanted me to get married, then I'd get married. That was his only order, wasn't it? All I needed was a marriage certificate and I will have done as he asked and bought myself some time.

What is marriage, anyway, but an empty promise made to some woman that only wanted your money?

Not even marriage could slow me down. I was Lucas Barone, heir to the Barone Crime Family.

As I booked my flight to Vegas, I laughed.

I'd find my wife. I'd take her and make her mine, and then I'd take control of the Family.

Vegas was the perfect place to find her.

~~~~~~

I climbed out of the limo and looked at the line in front of my favorite club. It was exclusive and tough to get into, but the bouncers all knew me. Plus, they were good about letting in attractive women, exactly the sort of thing I was looking for.

Time to find a wife, I thought. I gave a nod to my second in command and he grinned back.

"See you inside, Vince."

"Yeah, boss."

I didn't need a bodyguard or anything like that, but I liked Vince. He had been with me for a long time and was basically my number two. It was good to have people around, especially loyal and armed people.

I walked toward the entrance and the bouncer nodded to me.

"Mister Barone," he said.

"Jimmy." I flashed him a smile. "Talented in there tonight?"

He grinned hugely. "Very talented. You'll be pleased."

I slipped him a twenty as I walked past.

Once inside, I let the beat wash over me.

I didn't love clubs. I didn't like the crowds, the assholes, the vapid girls, the annoying staff. But there was nowhere in the world better for picking up the sort of empty-headed club girl that I needed.

I quickly went into the VIP area and got a drink. It was quieter but still packed. I wondered briefly if they were lowering their standards, but it didn't matter. I wasn't like all the other rich, spoiled assholes around me. I worked for what I had. Even if my father weren't the boss of the Family, I'd still be hustling on the streets. I had a better mind and a stronger arm than any other goon out there.

Soon I found myself scouting out the dance floor. Talented, like the bouncer had said, but nothing was interesting me. I skirted around toward the bar again.

"How's it going, boss?"

I looked over and nodded to Vince. "Not the best in the world."

"Really?" He looked around. "Seems like plenty of ass in here."

"I'm looking for a specific kind of woman here."

"What type?"

I cocked my head at him. "Dumb and easy." I paused and laughed. "The kind of woman that would marry a fucking mobster like me without getting to know him."

"I think you'll find that, boss."

"We'll see."

He leaned back up against the bar and crossed his arms. Good old Vince. I hoped he got laid tonight.

I moved back toward the dance floor, letting the waves of music and motion wash over me.

That was when I spotted her.

Full lips. Green eyes. Long brown hair. Pale, but in a fucking pretty way. She looked way too gorgeous for the club, almost normal, like she wasn't fucking trying so hard.

For some reason, I felt my cock starting to stir. At a single glance I was already getting hard for her. There was something in her look that drew me toward her. She quickly looked away, but it was way too late.

There was no turning back. I was way too curious.

I moved through the crowd and finally found her. She was dancing with a friend, a perky little blond chick who stopped and stared at me as soon as I rolled up behind them. I put my hand on the small of the girl's back, and she slowly turned to look at me.

I knew the expression on her face.

Her name was Natalie. And it didn't take too much dancing before we left the club, heading out to my limo.

"Nice car," she said, smiling uncertainly.

"Can't travel Vegas any other way," I said.

"What are you, rich or something?"

I smiled suggestively at her. "Or something, yeah."

She bit her lip. "Where are we going?"

"I'll tell you," I said, moving closer to her, "but you have to get inside first."

"I don't know. I don't usually take rides from strangers."

"Oh, I'm sure you're used to riding," I said. "In fact, you can show me exactly how you ride it."

She shook her head. "I don't know."

"You can get out any time you want, but I think this will be fun."

For a second, I thought she was going to say no. I could see it in her eyes. But suddenly her expression changed, hardened, and she nodded. "Okay. Let's go."

We climbed into the limo and I poured us some champagne. The driver rolled down the window.

"Sir?"

"Drive around for a bit."

"Yes, sir."

The divider went back up, and I looked at Natalie. "To you and me, Nat." We clinked glasses.

"Okay, now, tell me where we're going."

"What's Vegas best known for?" I asked her, sitting close.

"Sin," she said, laughing.

I grinned at her. "Sure, sin. What else?"

"Hmm. Gambling. And quick marriages."

"Did you gamble already tonight?"

She nodded. "Pacey did. She's bad at it."

"So you gambled."

She nodded again. "Yeah."

"How about you get married then?"

I watched the expression on her face change. "What do you mean?"

"Listen, sweetheart. In Vegas, marriage is quick and cheap. It doesn't have to be for real, but I've never done it before. Have you?"

She laughed uncertainly. "Have I ever been married before?"

"Sure."

"No, never married."

I put my hand on her thigh, sipping my drink. "Let's get married."

She laughed, shaking her head. "No way. That's crazy. Are you serious?"

"Dead serious." I moved a little closer. "I'd love to see what you're like on your wedding night."

"We can't get married. I don't even know you."

"You know my name. You know what I look like. What else do you need?"

She ran her finger around the rim of her glass. "I don't know. What do you do for a living?"

"I run a few businesses."

"Sounds shady."

"It is."

She laughed, not sure if I was joking. "Okay, but you don't know anything about me, either."

"I know enough. I know you were the sexiest girl in the club back there. I know you're smart, honest, and I'm betting you're wet as hell."

"I am not wet," she said quickly.

"Sure you're not. I bet you're also wondering if I'm totally crazy, and I'm telling you I'm not."

"But why?" she said softly.

"Because I want a new experience, and you're it." I kissed her neck gently, and she let out a soft moan. "I want to experience you, Natalie."

"I don't know."

My hands moved up her thigh. "I know."

She wrapped her arms around my neck. "Why me?"

"The second I saw you, I knew I wanted you."

I found her pussy, warm and wet. I knew she was practically begging for it, but I had no clue just how soaked she was going to be.

"Say yes," I whispered as I gently rubbed her.

"I don't know," she moaned.

"Marry me, Natalie."

She paused as I slipped my fingers down her panties and touched her clit, rubbing softly.

"Okay," she said.

I kissed her hard on the lips, losing myself.

Chapter Three: Natalie

I woke up with a start.

For a second, I thought I was hungover. But I quickly realized that I hadn't really drunk that much the night before. I looked around my hotel room and smiled at Pace's snoring face.

And then what had happened came flooding back to me.

Lucas, the limo, the ceremony. He was mysterious and sexy and incredible. I couldn't believe I did it, but it was beyond the most exciting night of my life.

And it started with his fingers on my clit, rubbing me in agonizingly incredible circles. He kissed me hard and I kissed him back, hungry, hungrier, as he pressed against me, his fingers working my pussy. I spread my legs wide for him, letting him take me, and I couldn't believe it.

I couldn't believe I was kissing a man like Lucas, letting him touch me, following his lead. As he pressed a finger deep inside me, I felt the sweet pleasure rock my spine. I kissed him hard as he worked me.

"This is just a taste, Natalie," he whispered in my ear as he rubbed my clit. "This is just a little bit of what I want to make you feel."

The pleasure was overwhelming. My pussy was soaked, had been ever since we'd started dancing. I didn't want to say no, couldn't say no. What he was suggesting was crazy though. Marry him? It couldn't be real; it definitely couldn't be.

But the way he made my pussy feel, the way my head spun when he whispered dirty words in my ears, I just couldn't stop myself.

I was saying yes.

The orgasm rocked through my body. I came on his fingers, his practiced fingers. He whispered in my ear the whole time, dirty words, as I came and came hard.

"Come on my hands, Natalie. I love this slick pussy. Come for me now and I'll make you my bride. Then I'll make you feel things you didn't know you could feel. I'll slide my thick cock between your legs, fuck you until your knees shake."

The orgasm rocked through me, rolled up my spine. I was spinning on an incredible cloud.

The orgasm. From only his fingers. My only orgasm of the night.

I shook my head, looking at the window. I wasn't sure what time it was. Part of me couldn't believe what had happened.

I still didn't know his last name.

"Nat?" I looked over and Pacey as awake. "Where did you come from?"

"Hey, Pace."

She sat up, her head in her hands. "I feel like fucking shit."

"I know. I saw the puke in the toilet."

She made a face. "Oh god. I'm so sorry."

I laughed. "It's okay. It's Vegas, right?"

"Speaking of which." She looked up at me, grinning. "What happened to you last night?"

I opened my mouth but stopped. How could I explain it to her? *Well, I married a guy, but I freaked out after the ceremony and made him take me home.* I couldn't say that, but I didn't want to lie.

"Nothing really happened," I said, telling a half-truth. "We didn't sleep together or anything."

"Seriously?" She looked genuinely surprised. "That guy was gorgeous, Nat. Why not?"

"Well," I said slowly, "it got a little weird, I guess. Freaked me out, moved too fast."

She sighed. "Typical," she said, grumbling. "A guy wants to do more than kiss you and you're suddenly freaking out."

I nodded sheepishly. "That's right. Silly old me."

"Ugh, I need to wash this vomit taste from my mouth." She stood up and walked into the bathroom unsteadily.

I felt bad about keeping the truth from her, but it was just all too soon and too strange. I kept thinking about the way he got me off, so confidently and seriously, and then about what had happened afterward.

I kept thinking about the Elvis preacher. About the vows, the ceremony, the kiss. It felt fake, but I knew that those things really were legal in Vegas. Afterward, I asked him to take me home. He only nodded and dropped me off, disappearing as mysteriously as he had appeared.

And yet I couldn't stop thinking about his kiss, his touch. It was addictive and incredible, and I had never felt like that before, not with any other guy I'd been with.

Lucas wasn't a guy; he was a man. A totally different breed of man than I'd ever been around before.

I heard Pacey brushing her teeth in the other room, so I quickly checked my phone. As I'd left the limo last night after the ceremony, I had given Lucas my number.

No calls or texts from any unknown numbers. But there was a voice mail from my mother.

I felt a little disappointed, but what did I expect? I had let the guy get me off, married him, and then freaked out and ran away all within like a few hours' time.

"You ready to get out of here?" Pacey said, leaning against the wall.

"I am, but you definitely don't look like you are."

"I just need breakfast," she said. "An enormous breakfast. And vodka."

I laughed. "No vodka for you. We're going back home now, remember?"

"Don't remind me."

She disappeared back into the bathroom and I heard the shower go on.

Curious, but also dreading it, I tapped on my mother's voice mail and held the phone up to my ear.

"Natalie? Ugh, I hate leaving messages, but this is important. You're coming home, right? You may have seen some stuff in the gossip rags. It's very important that you call me back immediately. Love you!"

I frowned at the phone and listened to the message again, a stone growing in my gut. Mom didn't normally even talk about the gossip rags, so it was a little unusual that she mentioned them specifically. I tapped her name and called her back.

"Hello? Natalie?" She answered on the second ring.

"Hi, Mom," I said.

"Where are you?"

"I'm in Las Vegas right now. I told you that."

"Oh." I could hear the annoyance in her voice, but I had told her. I'd texted and called and emailed my itinerary, but obviously she hadn't paid attention to it. "Well, I have some important news."

"What happened?"

"Nothing happened," she said. "Not everything is bad, you know."

"Sorry, but the last time you said that you had gotten arrested."

"That was just one time," she grumbled. "And anyway, that's all behind me now."

"What do you mean?"

"The drinking, the partying. Hell, even the TV. It's all done with."

I felt that little stone of dread blossom into an enormous boulder. "What's going on, Mom?"

"I got married, sweetie."

Worst nightmare confirmed. "To who?"

"A very nice man. His name is Arturo. He's a Chicago businessman, and we've been seeing a lot of each other lately. Oh, I'm so sorry you couldn't be at the wedding, but it was a spur-of-the-moment type thing. You understand?"

I was barely listening. My mother tended to ramble when she was uncomfortable, and she began to tell me all about the wedding. I had stopped listening when she'd told me that she had gotten married again.

I couldn't believe it. After Dad had died and left her his fortune, I never thought she'd move on to anyone else. She seemed so heartbroken, so upset. I always thought that her acting out and being a reality TV star was just a way to run from her grief.

And yet here she was, married again.

I felt angry and betrayed.

But I shouldn't. She was a grown woman who could make her own decisions. And besides, Dad had died a long time ago. Even though Mom made plenty of very bad decisions, she wasn't really a bad person.

"I'm very happy for you," I said finally during a very brief pause.

"Oh I'm so happy to hear that," she said. "There's one more thing."

"What?"

"Well, I'll be moving into his estate."

"His estate?"

"Yes. It's right outside the city, and it's so, so lovely. Lots of land, animals, all of that. You'll really love it, sweetie."

"Wait, what?"

"He says you can have an entire wing to yourself if you like. There are hiking trails and a little pond."

"What about our house?"

There was a pause on the other end. "Well, I sold it, honey."

"What?"

My childhood home. She had sold my childhood home?

"I'm sorry, but Arturo said that it wasn't appropriate for me to own my own house anymore. We don't need it, honey."

"How could you?" I blurted out, anger finally winning. "How could you get married again and sell the house without even talking to me?"

"Sweetie," she said slowly, "I know this is a lot to process. It just happened so fast."

"No, Mom," I snapped. "You messed up big time. You have been an irresponsible train wreck for years, one of the worst parents imaginable. I thought it was bad when you got arrested for drugs, but this? This is way, way worse. This is a betrayal."

"Sweetie," she said more firmly, "we can talk about this when you're home. When you calm down."

"I won't calm down," I said.

"I'll have Arturo's people get you at the airport."

"Mom—"

"Goodbye."

She hung up.

I stared at my phone, my mouth hanging open.

In a single moment my life had suddenly been thrown into chaos. Everything I thought I knew about my life had suddenly shifted. I didn't have my home anymore, and my mother had gotten married to a man I knew absolutely nothing about.

"You okay?" Pacey asked.

I looked at her, my face ashen. "She sold my house, and married some guy."

"I heard your side. I'm sorry."

She walked over and threw her arms around me.

"This summer is really going to suck," I said after a minute.

Pacey laughed. "Yeah. This summer is really going to suck."

Chapter Four: Lucas

I woke up groggy in my huge Vegas bed and rolled onto my side. I was conspicuously alone and had spent my wedding night drinking good scotch with Vince.

My wedding night. I, Lucas Barone, had gotten fucking married. I chuckled to myself at the thought. Of course, the girl didn't really think it was real, or maybe she did and she just didn't care. But I had the marriage license to prove it.

That wedding, although cheesy and stupid, had been very real.

I was a little disappointed about how the night had ended, though. Natalie was fucking sexy, all cute and innocent-seeming but a fucking pro when you got under her panties. She'd been moaning my name and had come like a wave as soon as I'd gotten my fingers on her soaked little pussy. I had assumed she was good to go and wanted more.

But as soon as we finished the ceremony, she freaked, said she wanted to go home. I wasn't the type to force a lady into anything, and I actually did have some respect for her, so I dropped her off as promised.

But fuck did I want her still. My cock was hard against the soft sheets as I thought about her body dancing against mine in the club.

I knew I wanted her the second I saw her. Those full lips looked like they were made to suck my cock, and I wanted to come deep down her throat.

The mere thought of that made me fucking crazy. I reached down beneath the sheets and began to stroke myself.

Natalie had no clue what she was missing. I could have fucked her sweet pussy for hours in my luxurious suit. I'd love to take every stitch of clothing from her body and watch her blush as I talked dirty in her ear.

I imagined letting her ride my face as I jerked myself off. After I got her nice and fucking wet, on the verge of coming again, I'd slide my cock deep into her slick cunt and fuck her so rough but slow.

I wanted her to beg for it, after all. When she finally came a second time, I wanted it to completely take over her body, make her have the shakes. My job wouldn't be done until she came so hard she practically forgot her own name.

That would happen, like it always happened. I'd work her sweet fucking body over and over again, make her sweat, make her beg. She'd never been with a man like me before, insatiable, always fucking hard, and always ready to make her come.

I wanted to see that ass back up against my cock. I wanted her to beg me to finally come. She'd want me to fill her tight little pussy up.

Natalie seemed so fucking innocent, but she'd be my slut in the sheets. I felt myself getting close as I jerked my cock, thinking about fucking her hard from behind, slapping her thick ass, making her mine.

Finally, I finished, shooting my cum into a tissue.

Fucking tissues. That would have been much better if it were Natalie's tight, warm little pussy.

I cleaned up and rolled out of bed, heading into the shower.

I had Natalie's number, but why bother? She had made it clear that she wasn't interested the night before. I wasn't the type to give second chances, anyway. Plus, I had gotten what I needed out of her. No reason to push it any further.

I climbed into the shower, still thinking about the way she came in the back of the limo. Maybe I was missing out on something, too, if I never got a chance to fuck her.

But oh well. You couldn't fix the past. You could only move forward.

~~~~~~

Hours later, the Barone manse was practically empty. It was about eight at night, and most of the guys had left already. Staff still lingered around, plus the usual armed guards, but they practically blended into the background.

I felt fucking good. Sure, I didn't get to fuck Natalie, but who cared? There were plenty of other women in Chicago that I could sleep with. It wasn't like I ever had a problem finding a willing and attractive partner to suck me off.

Best of all, I had my marriage license to shove in my father's face. He'd be forced to back off based on his own absurd logic.

Just because he finally married one of his many whores didn't mean we all needed to get married. He was simply obsolete, and I just needed to play along with his silly games for long enough to make my move and finally take control of the family.

I walked down the dimly-lit hallways, idly looking around. The Barone house was huge, three wings, three floors, and filled with all the gilding and opulence that came with having way too much fucking money.

We were old-school mafia. Maybe we didn't call ourselves the mob anymore, or at least not openly, but we were. And we'd been one of the most successful families in history. We were definitely the oldest still-operating family left in the Chicago area, and we had control of the most profitable turf all throughout the city and the suburbs.

I didn't necessarily have expensive taste, but I understood the reason

44

for it.

We needed to exude power. And nothing said power like an absurd use of wealth. Everything about the Baron manse screamed money, sex, and power.

I fully intended to uphold that tradition when I was in power.

My father's study was in the east wing, second floor, all the way in the back. I stopped and knocked on the door.

"Enter," I heard him call out.

I pushed open the door. "Evening, Father."

"Luca. To what do I owe the pleasure?" he said, distracted. He was looking at something on his desk and didn't even bother to look up.

I shut the door behind me as I walked inside. I sat down in one of the armchairs and crossed my legs, relishing the moment.

"Nothing special," I said. "Just thought I'd pay you a visit."

"Good," he mumbled. "Good. I'm glad you're here."

That had me curious. "Why?"

"Your stepmother and new stepsister are moving in tomorrow," he said. "Have I told you about them?"

"You mentioned the new wife," I said, annoyed. Had he already fucking forgotten our conversation?

He glanced up. "Yes, I did." He paused. "Well, I expect you to be respectful of her as she is part of the family now. She has full privileges of the estate, as does your new stepsister."

"Stepsister," I said, laughing. "What's she like?"

"Can't say I know for sure," he said. "Her name is Natalie. Cute girl, goes to college." He grabbed his phone and pulled up a picture. "Here. This is her and her mother."

My heart nearly fucking stopped in my chest as I took the phone from him.

Staring back at me was a picture of my wife.

The picture was probably a year or two old, but it was definitely her. I could hardly believe it. The Natalie I had met the night before certainly was nothing like her infamous mother. Where Camille Taylor was brash and loud, Natalie had been quiet and demure, almost shy.

"Luca?" my father asked. "What's wrong with you, boy?"

"Nothing," I said quickly, handing the phone back to him.

The marriage license in my back pocket was suddenly like burning fire.

"So, what did you want to see me about?" he asked.

"Ah," I said. "I wanted to check on the Carosi job."

He narrowed his eyes. "You know that's going fine."

"Good," I said, nodding. "Well. Have a good night."

"What's wrong with you?" he asked again. "You're keeping something from me."

I shook my head. "Still hungover, I guess. Just got back from Vegas."

He made a face. "Still wasting my money, I see."

"My money," I said. "Every dime, I've earned."

"Yes, well." He went back to whatever he had been looking over before. "Be kind to your new stepsister."

"Of course." I paused, grinning. "She's family now."

I turned and left as quickly as I could. I walked down the hallway, turned a corner, and leaned up against a pillar.

Laughter erupted from my body violently. A nearby guard glanced in my direction like I had suddenly grown a second head.

What an absurd turn of events. My new stepsister was the same woman I had met in a club completely at random, and the same woman I had married to piss off my father.

But I couldn't tell him about it now. Not yet, at least. Maybe I could use it one day down the line, but right now it would be a waste.

Most important of all, though, was that Natalie was coming to live with use. In just a few hours, my stepsister, no, my wife was going to be staying in our home. I'd be able to see her whenever I wanted to.

"This is going to be a great summer," I said to the guard.

"Of course, sir," he mumbled.

I walked away, grinning madly.

Chapter Five: Natalie

Home again. Or at least what was left of it.

"Can you help me with this box, sweetie?"

I dropped my own bag onto the ground as my mother shoved a box into my arms.

"Good to see you too," I said to her.

"Welcome home." She smiled and kissed my cheek. "Now, in that truck over there."

I carried the box to where she was pointing, and a tired-looking guy took it from me and loaded it in.

My childhood home was in chaos. Two trucks were parked out front and men I'd never seen before were crawling in and out, carrying things and loading them into the trucks. I watched as two men carefully hoisted my dresser up into the back of a truck.

Meanwhile, my mother was guiding the whole affair with the precision of a military commander. She was directing, commanding, and yelling, all while managing to make the poor movers' lives more difficult.

And I didn't know anything about it. She told me she had sold it, but not that she hadn't moved out of it yet. Of course she chose the day I was coming home to get it finished when she probably had weeks, or maybe even months.

"Mom," I said to her, "why are you doing this today? You knew I was coming home, right?"

She gave me a haggard smile. "Yes, sweetie, I know. But this all happened so fast, and the buyer wants to move in tomorrow. So here we are."

I sighed. "And all my stuff?"

"Sweetie, you're going to love the new house. It's absolutely enormous, and the grounds are incredible."

I knew that arguing or complaining was going to get me nowhere. She quickly moved away, already harping on a pair of movers that weren't treating her precious coffee table with enough respect.

I couldn't imagine where we'd be keeping all of our stuff. Probably in some storage shed in a barn out back behind the main house. From what I could tell, I was moving into this enormous mansion, an absurdly expensive piece of property with pretty much every amenity I could ever imagine.

And I hated it. I hated that my mother had made this decision for me, and I hated that she had waited until the last possible moment to do the move. At least the guys that had picked me up from the airport were nice, even though they had instructions to drop me off with my mother.

Apparently we were supposed to head to the grounds together to get "checked in" or something like that. It seemed incredibly strange, but I was going with everything for the time being.

Frankly, I had nowhere else to stay.

The day moved on like that as the trucks slowly filled up. I helped out where I could, but mostly I just stayed out of everyone's way. Mother was bossy enough, and the guys didn't need another distraction.

Finally, the trucks were packed. I was basically thrown into the back of a black SUV, my bags taken from me and stowed somewhere else. "You won't need these," the guy said as he carried them off.

What the hell was happening to me?

"Are you ready, ma'am?" our driver asked my mother as she climbed in next to me.

"Yes. Let's head out."

"Great." He pulled out into traffic, and the two trucks followed close by.

"Mom, why didn't you tell me about any of this?" I asked her, finally ready to go on the offensive.

She shook her head. "I know, I'm an awful mother. But listen to me." She took my hand and looked more serious than I had ever seen her before. "This is a great opportunity for both of us. Arturo can take care of you and me. He's a wonderful man."

"I don't know him," I said. "And why do we have to get 'checked in' or whatever?"

"Well, he runs a very strict household. Lots of security."

"Why?"

She looked at me dubiously. "You don't know?"

I shook my head. "What the hell is happening, Mom?"

She glanced at the driver and then back at me and quickly plastered a smile on her face. "Nothing. Nothing at all. We're just moving into our new home. You're going to love it, I promise."

I could tell I wasn't going to get anywhere new with her. The fake smile was there, which meant she was ready to act however she needed to get through the conversation.

I wanted to throw her out of the moving car. Instead, I put on my headphones and listened to music as we drove through the city, out toward my new home.

It felt like my whole life had shifted. Lucas kept breaking into my thoughts, despite the huge stress I was under. I kept thinking about his delicious cocky grin, his taste, his hands on my body. I kept thinking about the way he made me feel.

He made me ravenous and starving for more. And that scared me. It scared me that I had gone through the wedding ceremony with him, and it scared me that I couldn't wait for him to peel off my clothes and to fuck me absolutely senseless.

I always had control of myself. I tried very hard to be the opposite of my mother in almost every way imaginable. But around Lucas I'd felt myself acting totally outside myself, like I almost wasn't in control anymore.

And it had felt really, really good. That was what scared me the most.

The city slipped past the window, and the tight streets turned into wider avenues as we transitioned into the suburbs. It took about forty minutes to get out of the city, and another ten before we were finally at the absurdly ornate gates of the house.

The car stopped in front of a guard booth. I'd never seen one outside a residential home before, but there it was. The driver had a brief conversation, and then we were waved inside.

My mouth hung open as we wound up along the driveway. Manicured lawns, croquet courts, fountains, beautiful trees and flowers and bushes, and the house itself. It was all enormous, incredible, amazing. I'd never seen anything so expensive and beautiful in my whole life, even back when my mother hadn't spent all of my father's fortune yet.

We stopped outside a small wing of the house, and the driver climbed out. He opened my door. "If you'll follow me, ladies."

We got out and walked behind him. I couldn't help but look around.

"Where is Arturo?" Mom asked the driver.

"Mister Barone will be here shortly," he said. "I'm supposed to get you two situated first."

Barone? Why did that name sound so familiar? I didn't have time to think too much about it since I was too busy gaping around me.

We were led inside the house. It was richly decorated with plush rugs, statues, lovely plants, and paintings that were each probably worth more than my entire wardrobe. We followed the driver into a small side room, where he sat down at a desk.

"Okay," he said, "have a seat. I'm going to go over the grounds with you, make you both sue badges so you can get in and out easily, and basically answer any questions you may have."

What followed was one of the most surreal experiences of my life.

It was like an orientation at a hotel resort. The driver, whose name turned out to be Franklin, explained all about the grounds. He showed us a map and pointed out the pool, the hiking trails, the horse stables, the animal barns, the grape vineyard, the hedge maze, and much more. He printed us both plastic cards that would unlock any doors and said that if a door didn't unlock, it was considered off-limits.

Mother didn't seem to bat an eye at the off-limits comment, but that struck me. What sort of businessman had off-limits parts of his home, especially for his new stepdaughter and his new wife? It seemed strange, but no stranger than anything else.

After maybe a half hour, Franklin finished our little orientation. He asked if we had any questions, but I was far too overwhelmed to ask any.

"Okay," he said, standing. "Follow me. Mister Barone and his son are waiting to greet you."

We followed him out into the hallway. I could tell that Mother was practically bubbling with nervous energy. She kept fixing her hair and nervously playing with the hem of her expensive and revealing dress. Meanwhile, I felt mainly dread and awe, in that order.

Franklin took us down a series of hallways that made no sense to me, and by the time he knocked on an ornate wooden door, I was completely lost.

"Enter," someone said from inside.

Franklin opened the door. "Go ahead in. I'll be out here if any of you needs anything."

"Thank you Franklin, dear," Mother said.

He smiled at her. I noticed for the first time that Franklin was actually pretty young. In the car I had assumed he was an older guy, but he had a baby face up close. I didn't have time to dwell on that, as Mother swept me into the room.

What I saw next nearly put me on the ground.

Sitting behind a large, oak desk was an older man. He was older than Mother by a few years, but he seemed fit regardless. His dark hair we thinning but cropped short, and although he was certainly soft in the middle, he held his weight like he was once a football player. He stood up, smiling. His suit was expensive and fit him well.

"Ladies, welcome."

"Arturo!" Mother said, walking toward him. He came out from behind the desk and they kissed.

But that wasn't what had my full attention.

No, it was the grinning bastard standing next to the desk.

He was as handsome as I remembered, if not more so. Everything that had happened the night before came flooding back to me in that moment as his cocky grin burned right into my face.

Lucas Barone. The man from the night before. The man I had married on a whim. The man I had been thinking about nonstop since I'd laid eyes on him.

"Lucas," Arturo said, "this is your new stepsister, Natalie."

"Natalie," he said, his smile delicious and so infuriating. "It's lovely to meet you."

My jaw dropped.

What was I supposed to say?

There were no words. My emotions were a bomb inside me, a roiling mess of conflicting desires.

I wanted to slap him. I wanted to scream at him. I wanted to strip him down and finally feel his hard cock between my legs.

I was so fucked, so deeply screwed.

Instead of doing any of that, I turned and left, slamming the door behind me.

Chapter Six: Lucas

I watched, unable to hide my amusement, as my wife stormed out of my father's office.

Arturo and Camille looked confused, and I couldn't help but laugh.

"What's funny?" Arturo asked, annoyed. "That's your stepsister."

"I know that, Father."

"Well, if she's uncomfortable, make it right."

I nodded, grinning like mad, which only served to piss Arturo off even more.

"And don't forget what I said to you the other day," he added. "Settle down or else."

Camille looked at him. "What do you mean? Luca seems like such a sweet boy."

If only you knew, tramp, I thought to myself as I walked past them.

"Nothing, darling," Arturo said. "Now, let's talk about our plans for later . . ."

I left the room, not interested in listening to some inane discussion of their celebration feast or whatever they had planned.

I jogged up ahead, turning right at the hall, and stopped as I saw Natalie leaning up against a wall, looking down at her phone.

"Hey, sis," I said to her as I approached.

Her head snapped up. Her expression was pure hatred and anger, and it almost made my cock hard. I loved how strong-willed she was, how interesting and smart. It was dangerous, but I wanted so badly to tame her.

"You knew," she said softly.

I held up my hands. "I promise that I didn't."

"You knew. You had to have known. That was why you picked me, why you wanted to marry me. It was all some elaborate prank."

I couldn't stop myself from grinning hugely at her, which only made her even angrier.

"This isn't a joke," she snapped.

"I know, I know," I said. "Look, I promise I didn't know who you were. Truthfully, I only found out about your mom and my dad yesterday, just before I left for Vegas."

"So you did know." Pure disgust. I wanted to tip her head back and bite her lip, press her up against the hardwood door and slip my fingers down against her tight cunt. I wanted to make her say my name.

"I knew about your mom but not about you."

She bit her lip. "I don't believe you."

"Nat, why would I marry my stepsister? Do you have any clue how dangerous this is?"

She cocked her head, suddenly unsure. "Why would it be dangerous?"

"You don't know what we do," I said softly, laughing. "You haven't heard of my family."

Uncertainty passed across her expression, and I knew it was the truth.

The Barones weren't exactly famous, or at least not famous in the conventional sense. But if you had any money or power in the Chicago area, or really anywhere, you had likely heard our names whispered in some dark corners. We worked hard to keep our name out of the national media, and so it didn't surprise me that Nat had no clue who we were. But still, it was almost adorable how naïve she was.

"Mom said your dad was a businessman," she said after a second.

"He is, in some ways." I leaned up against the wall next to her. "But you have to be wondering about all the security."

"I thought it was weird."

I cocked my head at her. "Do you want to know what you're mother dragged you into?"

"Not really," she said, breathless, "but tell me anyway."

"The Barones are mafia, sis. Old, powerful mafia." I paused, grinning hugely. "Welcome to the mob."

She stared at me for a second and then began to laugh. "Yeah, right. Come on."

I smirked, shrugging. "It's the truth. You're part of the family now, in more ways than one, so you have a right to know."

"You have to be joking."

"Wish I were, sis. But the truth is, we're all a bunch of violent fucking criminals around here."

I loved watching the tiny little crack in her certainty begin to spread as she realized that I wasn't making a joke. Finally, she looked completely defeated.

"This is crazy," she mumbled.

"Now you understand why it's so dangerous?"

She looked up at me fiercely. "Now I understand why you're such a jerk at least."

I moved closer to her, touching her hair. She didn't flinch or move away. "Come on, Nat. I had a good reason for marrying you last night, and it had nothing to do with your mother."

"What reason?" Her lips were slightly parted.

I wanted so badly to take her then and there. She looked like she was begging for it, her lips parted, not moving away from me. I could have easily kissed her in the shadows of the old hallway and eventually dragged her into one of the hundreds of empty rooms. But for some reason, I held back. Probably because there was a staff member lurking not too far away, and I couldn't risk word of my relationship with Natalie getting back to my father.

"Because of this new marriage," I said, "Arturo suddenly thinks I need to settle down. I decided to marry someone in Vegas to appease him, or at least to rub the absurdity of the whole marriage sham in his face."

"Marriage sham?" The anger began to return. "So you married me to get back at your dad?"

I shrugged, smirking at her. "Maybe, in a way."

"This whole thing is just a coincidence," she said softly. "And you're a total asshole."

"I think that about sums it up."

"And now I'm stuck here."

"You can leave any time you want, sis."

"Stop calling me that." She looked down the hall. "Where's my room, anyway?"

"See the guy in the suit lurking over by the window?" She nodded. "Ask him. He'll show you."

I could see how angry she was, but she was doing a great job of holding it back.

"So what now?" she asked. "We pretend like it never happened?"

"We can't do that," I said, "because you're my wife, and I intend to keep it that way."

She screwed up her face. "It wasn't actually for real, right? I mean, you're worried that your dad will find out what happened in the, uh, the limo, right?"

I reached into my back pocket, my grin practically tearing a hole in her. "Here." I held up the marriage license. One glance and her face turned white.

"You've got to be kidding," she said. "No way it was for real."

"Sorry, sis. I mean, sorry, wife. We're married for real."

She shook her head, pushed off from the wall, and walked away without another word. I watched her approach the staff member, and he led her away, farther into the house.

I stayed standing there, my cock absolutely rock hard, excitement swimming through my veins.

I didn't know what it was about her. I had no clue why she got my blood up so hot, why she made me so absolutely fucking thirsty for her soaked pussy. But I loved teasing her, loved pushing her buttons, and I found that I didn't want to stop, even if it was a very, very dangerous game.

My stepsister. My fucking wife. What a fucking wonderful mess.

As I moved to head back to my rooms, I caught a commotion back down toward my father's study. I moved down the hall and watched

Camille get hustled from the room as a few mob captains rushed in.

Frowning, I headed that way. Something bad had just happened; I

could feel it right in my gut.

Natalie was still in the back of my mind as I pushed open the door and

joined the meeting.

Chapter Seven: Natalie

I was living with mobsters.

Real, actual, live gang members. Violent criminals. Thugs.

The security suddenly made sense. The insane wealth made sense, too.

I had no clue how they could live so openly the way they did, but I believed

Lucas. I didn't think he had been lying about anything he'd said.

Even though he was an absolute and total asshole.

Still, what were the chances of that? Of all the clubs in Vegas, and all

the women, he picked the one I had gone to, and he chose me, the one

person he absolutely never should have gone after and definitely shouldn't

have married.

Marriage. Part of me had known that it was real. Part of me

understood that happened in Vegas. But most of me just wanted to deny it

all, to pretend like the night was just one meaningless moment of total insanity and that I hadn't really gotten married. But as soon as I saw that certificate, I knew it was real. I knew it had happened.

I had married my stepbrother. My very rich, very attractive, very dangerous, and very off-limits stepbrother.

What the hell was I going to do?

~~~~~~

My room was huge.

It was probably the size of the entire first floor in my old house. I had a small sitting area complete with couches and a nice television, a full set of old wooden furniture that all looked like it belonged in a museum, flowers and plants everywhere, paintings on the walls, and this enormous four-poster bed. An entire family of four could have slept in that comfortably.

It was without a doubt the most absurd room I had ever seen. My things had already been carried up, including most of what had been in my bedroom at home. The Barones moved pretty fast and clearly ran a tight ship. I was impressed, although still pretty pissed off. Everything had happened so fast, and suddenly I was stuck in this cavernous room.

I was totally exposed. I had no clue what kind of people I was now living with. Maybe I didn't even have any real privacy at all, and they were standing in the walls behind the pictures, watching me at all times.

But that was just paranoia. Arturo seemed to genuinely love my mom, at least based on the very tiny interaction I had seen and what she had told me. I had to think that he would treat his new stepdaughter well, even if he was a dangerous mobster.

Then again, there were so many people at the house. I'd only seen a tiny fraction of it, too. Who knew how many rooms there really were, and how many secrets.

Overwhelmed, I flopped down on the bed and blew my hair out of my face. I scrolled through my phone and found Pacey's number.

She answered on the second ring. "Hey!"

"Hey, Pace. How's home?"

"Fine as usual. Dad is being a dick and Mom is pretending like he isn't. How's your new life?"

"It's insane, Pace. Seriously insane."

"What's it like?"

How could I explain it to her? "Words won't do it justice."

"Try."

"It's like an enormous mansion. Like a castle almost. And the grounds are so, so huge, and there are so many people. They're super paranoid about security, too."

"Really? That's weird."

For a second, I wanted to tell her about the Barones. I wanted to tell her that I was living with mobsters and married to the son of the leader. But I knew I couldn't. Pacey didn't need to know, and it was a huge risk anyway. If she told anyone and it somehow got back to Arturo and the others, who knew what he would do to my mother and me.

"Yeah," I said quickly. "He's just a little odd, I guess."

"So what's your room like?"

"Basically a cavern," I said, and I proceeded to explain it to her. Of course, she wouldn't understand just how expensive everything seemed and the sort of luxury that surrounded me until she saw it.

"I'm almost jealous," Pacey said.

"Honestly, Pace, I want to get the hell out of here." I paused, an idea hitting me. "Listen, is there any way I could come stay with you for the summer?"

There was a long pause. "You know I'd love it if you did, Nat."

"But?"

"But it's not a good time around the Harris household. Dad isn't doing too hot at work, so things are pretty tight. Tempers are high and all that."

"Okay. I understand."

"I'm really sorry. I hate to say no to you."

"It's okay, really. I just hate this house already. It's so cold and impersonal. I miss my old room."

"I bet. I still can't believe your mom just sold the house without telling you."

"Can't you, though? This sort of shit is endless with her."

"Tell you what. How about I come visit tomorrow?"

"I would love that."

"Text me the address."

"Okay."

"I gotta go. Mom is calling."

"See you tomorrow, Pace."

"Later."

She hung up the phone, leaving me alone in the vast room again.

~~~~~~

It took me twenty minutes to get outside the house.

Wandering through the halls, I couldn't believe how absolutely huge the place was. It felt like a maze, with the same hallways constantly popping up, but I was totally unable to find any way out. My key worked on most doors, though some remained locked. Most of them were just empty bedrooms, anyway.

I had to ask directions twice before I finally found the stairs down and the door out onto the grounds. I passed a ton of people wandering around the house, though none of them paid me any attention unless I directly spoke to them. I figured they were paid staff and were used to treating the guests that way.

For my part, though, I wasn't used to having staff. I distantly understood that I could ask them for things, but I mostly just wanted to be left alone. I felt embarrassed and uncomfortable simply being in the house, let alone bossing some poor staff member around.

Once outside, though, I began to feel a little bit better. The cool summer day was sunny and comfortable as I followed a path down through the grounds. I saw open stables with horses grazing, pens with farm animals, rows and rows of flowers, and even what looked like a small vegetable patch. I couldn't imagine mobsters as farmers, and so I just assumed someone else had installed it all before the Barones took over the grounds.

Farther along, I came into a wooded area. The path stretched around a small lake, and the woods were very peaceful. It felt great to finally be away from all the people and the bustle. For the first time all day, I felt halfway okay.

As I walked, I found my mind suddenly straying back toward Lucas. The way he looked at me, that devilish smile, it screamed of sex and desire. He seemed like he couldn't get enough of me. The way he reached out and touched my hair and spoke so close to me sent a rush down my spine. Despite being such an asshole, I still found myself inexplicably drawn to him.

Just like that night in Vegas. I didn't understand it then, and I didn't think I ever would. But he was my stepbrother now, and a dangerous one. I just needed to get along with him for the summer, and then hopefully I would never have to see any of them again.

Oh, and I needed a divorce. But one thing at a time.

I came to the end of the woods and found myself at the end of a large lawn leading back from the house. I noticed someone coming toward me, wearing an expensive suit.

I recognized him as he got closer. Lucas waved to me, and I wanted to run away.

"Hey, sis," he called out. "Lost?"

"Not lost," I said. "Just looking around."

He stopped a few feet away from me and crossed his arms. "Well, how about a tour?"

"No, thanks," I said, and walked past him.

He fell into step next to me. "What are you interested in seeing?"

"I don't want a tour," I said. "Just looking for the pool now."

"Come on," he said, taking me by the arm. "This way."

"Hey," I protested, but he was already walking off the path. He dropped my arm and I fell into step behind him. "You can't just drag me around like that."

He grinned back at me. "Sure I can."

We moved between some buildings, and I stopped in my tracks. Spread out in front of us was an enormous pool with two hot tubs and plenty of chairs set around it. Nobody else was around.

"Wow," I said. "This is really nice."

"It's fine," he said, walking over to the water. "Doesn't get much use."

"Seriously?"

"Seriously. Gangsters aren't really the type to lounge around a pool all day."

I shook my head, annoyed. "So why even have something like this?"

He began to loosen his tie. "Because it shows off our wealth and power."

"Seems like a huge waste to me."

He took off his tie and dropped it over a chair. He slipped his jacket off next, draping it over his tie. "It's not a waste. Not in our line of work anyway. Image is everything."

He began to unbutton his shirt. "What are you doing?"

"I thought you wanted a swim."

"I never said that."

He shrugged, stripping his shirt off. I stared his at chest, muscular, defined, and covered in tattoos. I remembered that body well and had the crazy urge to walk up to him and touch his skin.

Or maybe I wanted to push him into the water. I wasn't sure.

He began to unbuckle his belt.

"Stop," I said quickly, blushing.

"What? We're stepsiblings now. It's not weird." He pulled off his belt and then slipped his pants off.

I stared at him standing in front of me, wearing nothing but his tight black boxer briefs. He took his pants and laid them out over his other clothes, and then he turned back to me.

"Image is everything, Nat. Don't forget that. We have all of this because we don't want anyone to forget who we are and what we can do." He stepped up to the edge of the pool and then dove in.

I stared at his clean, incredible lines, his handsome body, and I felt the heat between my legs spike.

He surfaced in the middle of the water. "Come on it, sis," he called. "It's nice today."

For the second time that day, I turned and walked quickly away from him.

As I retreated toward the house, his laughter was ringing in my ears.

And the image of his body, nearly naked, his cock slightly hard against his thin boxer brides, stuck in my brain and made my skin tingle.

Chapter Eight: Lucas

"What happened earlier, boss?"

I looked at Vince as I toweled off.

"Bad news about that, Vince."

He smirked. "It's always bad news in this business."

I laughed, nodding. I slipped my wet underwear off and tossed it aside. Vince turned away, looking out across the lawn as I pulled my clothes back on.

Damn Natalie. I wasn't sure why I kept pushing the girl, why I couldn't let her be, but she was still very much on my mind.

I loved the way she looked at me, the way she bit her lip. It was almost too much, the way she acted as if she hated me while her body screamed how badly she wanted me.

Dressed, I began walking back toward the house. Vince fell into step next to me.

"Roddy got pinched," I said. "And our shipment was confiscated."

"Fuck," Vince said. "How did that happen?"

"I don't know, but Arturo tasked us with finding out."

"Shit luck."

"Yeah. We'll start on that tomorrow."

"Any ideas?"

"I have a few."

We stopped outside the back door. "Anything you feel like sharing?"

I grinned at him. "Not yet. Do some digging on your own tonight if you can."

He nodded. "You got it."

"See you later."

He turned and walked off. I watched him disappear between some buildings and sighed.

Damn shit luck. Nobody knew why Roddy got pinched and why the shipment got confiscated. We'd been planning that deal for months, and now the Russians were pissed we weren't delivering.

It had been one of the biggest deals with them in a long time. We didn't usually work with the Russians since the crazy bastards were so unpredictable, not to mention they were on the decline, but Arturo thought it was time we started being friendly again. And so I had worked my ass off setting up a nice little exchange of goods for cash.

The whole thing was very, very secretive. I could only name a handful of people that even knew about it, and I couldn't imagine any of them ratting to the cops. I'd suspected that someone was being tailed by the feds for a while, but I had no real proof of that.

I walked into the house, shaking my head. I didn't have to deal with that problem just yet. Father demanded that the whole family show up for a special dinner he had planned for Natalie and her crazy mother, which meant a ton of important mob captains would be there.

I moved through the hallways, nodding here and there to the staff. Some of the people that worked for my father treated them like garbage, but that never felt right to me. Really, they had the most power in our house. They knew it better than anyone else, and they were the ones that cooked our food and cleaned our rooms. It felt like madness to be an asshole to them. Besides, some of them were decent people.

I moved up to the third floor and followed the winding hallways to the very far corner of the southeast wing. I stood outside a blue, ornate door, grabbed the knocker, and banged it.

There was no answer. I knocked two more times, but nothing.

"Louisa," I called out, "you either open up or I'm going to barge in."

The door opened a crack. "What?" Louisa said.

"I need a little favor."

"Not in the mood for this, Luca."

"You don't even know what it is," I protested.

"Doesn't matter," she said. "I know our new stepmother and stepsister are here, and I know you like to be a dick."

"All of that is true," I said.

"So go away."

"Sorry, kid. I need a favor, whether you want to help or not."

There was a short pause, and then she sighed. I knew she couldn't say no to me. "Fine. Come in."

The door opened and I smiled at my younger sister. "You're looking spry today."

She gave me a look and closed the door behind me as I entered her room.

Really, it was more like an apartment. Louisa was father's little princess, but she was admittedly incredibly odd. A few years younger than me, Louisa had dropped out of high school early on and had decided that she wanted to help with the family business full time. When Arturo told her that wasn't happening, she turned into something of a spinster, living in a remote corner of the property and not going out very often.

Her rooms were large and covered in electronics equipment. Louisa plopped down on a couch and grumbled at me.

"What's the favor, Luca? I'm busy."

"You're never actually busy, kid."

"Sure. I got a raid in ten minutes."

I rolled my eyes. "That doesn't count as 'busy,' you know."

"Maybe not," she said, shrugging, "but you need something from me and I'm already bored, so get talking."

I laughed as I sat down across from her. Louisa was slight and pretty, with thick dark hair and dark eyes. She looked just like our late mother, in a lot of ways. She was thin and always has been, and I was always worrying that she didn't eat or exercise enough.

I was like my father in some ways. We were both too protective of Louisa.

"I need a dress."

"Changing sides, are we?"

"It's not for me."

"Who then?"

"Natalie. Our new stepsister."

Louisa gave me a long look. "I'm not sure I like where this is going."

"It's just a little prank. She's a tad nervous, and I thought this could break the ice."

"What kind of dress?"

I grinned at her. "The sluttiest thing you got."

She laughed, but I could already tell that her interest was shifting. She was like that, always getting distracted, always moving on to the next thing. I loved her fiercely, and she was really the only person in the world that I trusted.

"Do whatever you want," she said, getting up and walking over to a computer. "You now where the closet is."

I stood. "Much obliged."

"Tell Stumpy I won't be at dinner." Stumpy was her nickname for our father, something he absolutely loathed but would never reprimand her for.

"He'll figure it out on his own."

"Sure," she muttered, already in a new world.

I walked away, back toward her bedroom. Once you left the main sitting area and entered her private room, the only place where the staff was not allowed to enter, the place was a mess. I threw open her enormous closet and was greeted with row after row of dresses, coats, shirts, pants, and more.

"For a recluse, you have a ton of clothes," I muttered as I picked through her things.

Ten minutes later, I had the perfect thing. It was probably from Louisa's old life, back before she had locked herself away.

I carried it out and back into the main hall. "See you, kid."

She gave me an absent wave. I doubted she really even noticed when I walked out of her room.

I paused in the hallway, admiring the dress. I imagined Natalie wearing it and felt my cock stir, and I knew it was the right thing.

Smiling to myself, I went to find a staff member to help.

Chapter Nine: Natalie

The warm water washed down my body. I had to admit, although the day had been totally crazy and I was dreading dinner, I loved my new shower.

The bathroom was connected right to my room, and it was large and modern, clearly having been renovated recently. The shower was a large walk-in right next to a big white tub, and the water pressure was incredible.

I stood there letting the water run down my body as I thought about Lucas. I couldn't believe he was willing to strip down in front of me like that right in the middle of the backyard. Anybody could have walked in on it; anybody could have seen it. He was definitely acting brash and inappropriate, and I could barely understand why.

But I had to admit that his body was incredible. Lean and defined, the tattoos only served to make him look that much more intense.

And Lucas was intense. Everything he said, every move he made, it all had an edge to it, like he was on the verge of throwing me down and fucking me senseless. I'd been soaking wet since the moment I met him, and I couldn't get him out of my mind.

Which was why my hand slipped down between my legs. I pressed my back against the cool tile wall and began to gently rub myself, thinking about him.

The way he handled me in the limo. His confidence, his cool calm, the way he teased me. It all drove me absolutely wild.

He was an arrogant asshole, but I couldn't deny that he made me feel something. I wanted to know what it would be like to slide down along his cock, to let him sink himself deep inside me.

I was sure he could handle me. He could throw me around if he wanted. I would let him do what he wanted, take charge, show me the sort of man he was. Like in the limo, I wanted to feel his fingers again, but more. I wanted to feel his mouth roam my body, touch my skin, lick and suck my clit until I couldn't stand it anymore.

And I wanted his cock in my mouth. I felt so dirty for thinking it, but I wanted to taste his cock on my tongue, to suck him until he groaned. He made me hungry for it, and although I knew it was completely wrong, I wanted to suck him off in a dark corner of the house.

I rubbed myself faster, my fingers working my slick clit as I imagined what I'd let him do to me. I knew I couldn't, because if we were caught things could be very bad, but I wanted it anyway. He could fuck me in the pool, slide his thick cock between my legs from behind. I was sure he'd make me beg for it first, and although it would drive me wild, it would only make it that much sweeter when he finally pushed himself deep inside me.

I could only imagine the dirty things he'd whisper in my ear and the shiver that would run through my body as I felt him fuck me deep. I wanted that shiver, wanted those dirty words. I wanted to ride his tongue, or maybe bend forward and suck his cock while he licked my pussy.

I could feel my orgasm coming on as I pictured him fucking me from behind, holding my hips tight between his hands. He'd slam himself deep inside me, tell me how dirty I was, how much of a slut I was for giving myself to him.

I came, saying his name softly, my fingers working my clit.

My body wanted him so, so badly. I felt a rush of excitement as I finished my shower. At least I'd gotten off, and he probably wouldn't bother me so much at dinner.

I climbed out of the shower and began to towel off. Suddenly, I heard a knock at my door.

I quickly wrapped the towel around myself and ran over to the door. "Just a second!" I called.

I pulled on a pair of sweatpants and a sweatshirt before pulling the door open.

Sitting on the floor was a simple white box with a small red bow. Curious, I bent over and grabbed it, carrying it into my room. I shut the door behind me and locked it.

"What are you?" I said out loud to myself. I placed the box down on a table. There was a card with my name on it written in a hand I didn't recognize.

I opened the card and read it.

Dear wife, I thought you might like something to wear for tonight. Don't worry, I borrowed it from my sister. I hope it's your taste. Yours, Lucas.

Frowning, I opened the box.

Inside was a gorgeous black dress. I pulled it out and held it up. It was light and beautiful, probably more expensive than anything I ever wore, and probably my size, too. I frowned at the card again. I hadn't even realized that I had a stepsister now, too. Nobody seemed to mention her.

I took the dress into the bathroom and finished drying off. Once I was finished, I pulled the dress on and looked at myself in the mirror.

It was tight and revealing. The neckline plunged down, showing off my breasts, and it was tight around my hips. I was afraid to even walk in it in case my ass suddenly fell out.

There was no way I was wearing it, but the message was clear: Lucas wanted to see me in it. And the mere thought made my pussy wet all over again.

Stop it, Natalie, I thought to myself. *Get yourself together. He's just teasing you.*

I pulled the dress off and carefully draped it over a chair. I couldn't wear it, but maybe I could use it for revenge someday in the future.

More importantly though, I was very curious about this stepsister I hadn't heard of. I made a note to make sure I met her at dinner, or at least asked about her.

Shaking my head, I started to get dressed in something a bit more appropriate. Damn Lucas. I didn't care if he was let down. I wasn't about to show up in that dress in front of my new family, even if I wanted to get the hell out of here.

He could go tease someone else. I wasn't going to fall for it anymore.

That was what I told myself, at least. I didn't want to go to this dinner, but I also didn't feel like making a scene with my mother and my new stepfather. I might as well try to get along with them, at least until I figured something else out.

A knot in my stomach, I finished getting ready, trying not to think about the dress draped over the chair and what it meant.

~~~~~~

"Thank you for coming, everyone," Arturo said. He stood at the head of a long stable in the middle of a large banquet hall. At least twenty other people, mostly other men, sat at the table, and everyone held up their glass of wine.

"As you all know, I have not taken a new bride in a very, very long time, which is why my marriage to Camille is very important and dear to me. I hope you all welcome her and her lovely daughter into our family. To Camille, my love, salute."

Everyone repeated "salute" and clinked glasses.

I avoided Lucas's look. I was seated next to my mother at the one end of the table. Arturo was at the end, one place setting was empty to Arturo's right, and Lucas was seated across from me.

"Thank you, darling," Mom said. "That was lovely."

"I meant every word." Arturo looked at me. "I hope you'll feel welcome here, Natalie. I'm very glad you're a part of my family."

"Thank you," I said.

Camille kissed him. "You're too kind, Arturo."

"Nonsense," he said, and the two of them began talking quietly to each other.

I felt like I was going to retch, so I looked away.

Lucas caught my eye. "What do you think?"

"Of what?"

"This." He gestured around him. "Pretty absurd, right?"

I laughed. "A bit much, yeah."

The room was enormous, and the table was set right in the middle of it. Staff came and went with the food, placing fine wines and other delicious things on the table in front of the guests. I didn't know who anybody was, although Arturo had briefly introduced them all at the beginning.

They were all "business associates," which clearly meant they were all important mobsters. Nobody was saying that out loud, of course, but the implication was pretty clear.

The first course came, and I started eating. I avoided Lucas's eye, although he became embroiled in a conversation with the portly man next to him. I kept wondering about my stepsister and why she hadn't shown up yet. I assumed the empty seat was meant for her.

After the salads were cleared, I leaned in toward Lucas. "So," I said, "where's this famous sister?"

Lucas paused and glanced at his father. "In her rooms, I expect."

"Why isn't she here?"

He gave me a strange look. "Louisa is busy. That's all."

He seemed to be avoiding the question entirely, and I could tell by his expression that I shouldn't press.

"Did you get my gift?" he asked.

"Obviously," I said.

"Not obviously since you aren't wearing it."

"That wouldn't be appropriate." I felt myself blushing, wondering if anyone was listening to us.

"Just a simple gift, Natalie." His smile was so disarming, so handsome. "Nothing more than that."

I felt his foot suddenly move up my leg.

What an asshole. I kicked him away and he grinned even larger.

"Natalie," Arturo said suddenly, "what are you studying at school?"

"Computer science," I said.

"Computers!" Arturo exclaimed, laughing. "You would get along well with Louisa."

I glanced at Lucas and he looked surprised. "I'd love to meet her," I said.

"Ah, well, soon enough," Arturo said.

"I would too, Artie," Mom said.

Artie? I wanted to fucking vomit.

"Soon, very soon."

"Louisa keeps to herself," Lucas said quickly.

"What do you mean?" Mom asked. "I'm her new stepmother. I should at least meet her."

The look on Arturo's face was strange. "Mother," I said quickly, "maybe you should tell Arturo and Lucas about your last show."

"Well, I'd love to." She launched into a description of her last reality show.

Mom was always good for a quick distraction, especially if you asked her about herself. But I could tell there was something weird about Louisa, something that strained Arturo and Lucas's relationship.

The night wore on slowly, and I began to get bored. As the main course was removed, I felt my phone vibrate in my bag. I reached down to the floor and pulled it out.

One text from an unknown number. *Having a good time?*

Who is this?

Look up.

Lucas had his phone out and was smirking at me. "How—"

"Lovely wine, right?" he said quickly, interrupting me.

"Sure," I said. My phone vibrated again.

You know why I sent you that dress?

Because you're an ass?

Because I wanted to fuck you while you wore it. I'd slip it just up above your hips and sink my cock deep into that tight, wet pussy.

Too bad that isn't happening.

It is too bad. Just think, if I got you off with only my fingers, imagine what I can do with my tongue?

I felt a deep, scarlet blush come onto my cheeks.

"Darling?" my mother said to me. "What's the matter? You look a little warm."

"Ah, nothing," I said. "I'm just feeling tired. It was a very long day."

"Say no more, dear," Arturo said. "Go. Don't let us old men keep you here."

"Thank you, Arturo." I stood up quickly. "Good night everyone."

I quickly turned and left the table, heading back toward my room.

As I got out of the hall, my phone vibrated again. *My cock is hard just thinking about you in that dress. Come to my rooms and wear only that any time you want.*

I leaned up against a wall, breathing heavily. Lucas was such an ass, but I didn't know why I let him get to me so easily.

I turned off my phone and put it into my pocket. How the heck did he get my number? Probably some mafia crap that I didn't even want to know about.

I shook my head, getting myself together. I really was exhausted from the long day.

It only took one staff member to give me directions this time before I locked my bedroom door.

What a day. I flopped down into my bed and tried not to think about my stepbrother, my husband.

Chapter Ten: Lucas

My mind kept ranging back over the day before as Vince drove the car out into the city.

Natalie's body, her questions at dinner, everything about her drove me insane. And I loved teasing her more than anything, especially since she was so easy to rile up. All it took was a little dirty talk and she was running away like it terrified her to even consider.

Vince headed deep into the city, and I knew I needed to get my mind right. I couldn't be distracted on a job, especially not on an important job. We were out scouting the locals for any information on what happened to our shipment for the Russians.

Vince turned into a seedy neighborhood toward the very heart of the city. This was my neighborhood, my turf, and even though it was a little run down, it was still one of the best-earning areas in the city. Arturo gave it to me a long time ago, and I had turned it from a piece-of-shit patch of run-down land to a profitable business in only a few years.

I knew the place like the back of my hand, and I knew the guy we were looking for liked to spend his time at a piece-of-shit crack den at the end of a dead end street. Vince turned the car toward it and parked.

"You don't need to be doing this, you know," Vince said.

"I know that."

"We got guys. We can send them."

"I know, Vince." I climbed out of the car and he followed me. "I like doing shit like this. People need to see my face, know that I'm for real."

"I know, boss. Just saying."

We walked down the block, and I watched a pack of locals quickly move inside their houses. I smiled to myself, satisfied with their reaction.

I was known. I was feared by many and loved by many. I tried to take care of my people the best I could, but there were a lot of shitty asshole living in the slums, and I did not abide by their garbage. If they crossed me, I killed them. If they injured my business, I injured their bodies. It was a pretty simple way of operating. I wasn't going to win a ton of best friends, but I was going to run a tight operation.

We walked to the end of the block and Vince climbed up the steps. I saw his hand was on his gun as he kicked open the door.

I followed him in, making a face. The place smelled fetid, like body odor and rotten plants. The windows were blocked with blankets and the rooms were littered with detritus. I kicked aside some empty cans and followed Vince farther into the house.

"Rodney White," Vince called out, "we know you're in here."

People were looking at us curiously. Some of them I recognized, but most of them were strangers, showing up with some cash to score and hang around for a while.

Rodney ran the joint. He was also part of the squad that was responsible for security on the Russian drop.

"Rodney," Vince yelled again, "get your ass out here before we start hurting people."

I leaned up against the door and caught sight of two people lying together on a dingy mattress in the room next to us. They were staring at me, afraid but curious. I sneered at them and they quickly looked away.

"Vince," Rodney said, coming down the stairs. "Lucas. Hey, guys." He looked nervous.

Of course he did. The shipment he was supposed to guard got fucking pinched, and now we were showing up at his place unannounced. Anybody could put that together.

I stormed past Vince and walked up to Rodney. "Hi, Rod. Tell us what happened."

He held up his hands. "I don't know, I swear. One second we was watching out, all clear, and the next the cops were swarmin'. I barely got out."

I hit him in the nose with the palm of my hand. He fall backward onto his ass, groaning and clutching his nose.

People were watching, now more curious at the sight of violence than afraid. Vince drew his gun and people quickly disappeared back into their little holes.

I got into Rodney's face. "Listen, Rod," I said. "I don't feel like wasting time. It smells like fucking shit in here."

"Sorry," he muttered.

"You know I don't like hurting you, right, Rod?"

"Sure."

"But you know someone fucking talked, and you're on the list of suspects. So please, Rod, give me something I can use."

"I don't know anything, Lucas. Please believe me."

I sighed. "I'm starting to get annoyed. Do I work well when I'm annoyed, Vince?"

"No, you don't."

"I really don't," I said, shaking my head.

"I been listening for you, but I didn't hear anything."

I hit Rodney again, this time in the stomach. He doubled over. I saw blood drop from his nose onto the stairs.

"I don't believe you."

He groaned. "Please, man."

"Talk to me, Rodney."

"You got to believe me."

I took out my gun and hit him with the butt. He fell to the side and I hit him again.

"Okay!" he yelled. "Okay, please."

"Talk, Rod."

"It's nothing I heard, just something I saw."

"Tell me."

"Russians. That night. They backed off, just a minute before the cops showed up. Almost like they knew."

I looked at Rodney long and hard. "That's a serious accusation, Rod."

"I know, man. I didn't want to say nothing since I'm not so sure, but shit. It's what I saw."

I believed him. I wasn't sure why, since I had basically beat him until he told me what I wanted to hear, but there had been something weird about that night.

"Okay," I said. "Okay, Rod. You did good."

I patted him on the shoulder. He flinched away.

"We should go," Vince said.

I noticed the crack heads were all out and watching again. "Sure. Rod, you take care. I'll have someone come out and clean this place up, okay?"

"Okay, Lucas. Okay. Sorry I held that back."

"It's okay." I nodded at Vince and we walked back out the front door.

"What do you make of it?" he asked me.

"I believe him," I said.

"Makes no sense though. Why dime out their own shipment?"

"I'm not sure. But we need to get eyes on that truck again."

"It's impounded. Police custody."

I shrugged. "Police custody doesn't mean what it once did."

He smirked. "Yeah, guess not."

We climbed into the car together, and Vince began heading back toward the compound.

My heart was racing in my chest. Part of me loved the rush of violence, the thrill of it. I didn't want to hurt an innocent guy like Rodney, especially one that worked well for me, but I couldn't tolerate bullshit. I couldn't appear soft in front of his people or my own.

Plus, it almost got me as worked up as seeing Natalie blush. It got my heart beating and my adrenaline rushing, though it didn't get me off like Natalie did.

There I was, thinking about her again. It was like I couldn't go fifteen minutes without thinking about her again.

As we sped back toward home, I couldn't get her out of my head.

Chapter Eleven: Natalie

I woke up confused.

It took me a minute to figure out where the heck I was.

Still in the Barone compound. Still living in the shadow of my new mobster family.

Still thinking about Lucas, my gorgeous, asshole stepbrother slash husband.

I groaned, rolling over onto my side. I wanted to go back to sleep. Maybe then I'd wake up back in my old house, surrounded by my own things, and no longer married to my dangerous stepbrother. Maybe then I wouldn't be in such an awful situation.

Instead, I sat up and sent a quick text to Pacey. At the very least I could see her and let her experience the absolutely surreal turn my life had taken.

I tossed my phone aside when I was finished and climbed out of bed. I brushed my teeth and threw on some sweats. I wanted coffee and maybe a banana, but I realized I had no clue where the kitchen was.

I pulled open the door and saw a small pocket on the ground. I bent over and grabbed it.

Inside was a menu and a number.

Seriously? I thought. *They seriously just deliver food to your room like a hotel?*

Ten minutes later, they seriously delivered coffee and cereal to my room like a hotel.

Sitting on my couch, my television turned to some crappy but entertaining soap opera, I felt halfway decent for the first time in awhile. Frankly, who wouldn't want food delivered to their room whenever they waned it?

I could definitely get used to that.

~~~~~~

A couple hours later, I felt nervous for Pacey to show up. I felt like I hadn't fully prepared her for what exactly was going to happen. I checked my phone for the hundredth time when suddenly it started to ring.

"Hello?" I answered.

"Uh, Nat? I'm at the front gate and some guy is telling me that I'm not allowed inside."

I narrowed my eyes. "Seriously? Put him on the phone."

I heard some muted words and the sound of someone else taking the phone. "Hello?" the man's voice said.

"Hi. This is Natalie. I'm not sure what the proper procedure for this is or whatever, but can you please let my friend inside?"

"Sorry, ma'am," he said. "You don't have guest approval."

"Guest approval? Are you fucking kidding me?"

"No, ma'am. Sorry about that."

"I live here. This is my house now. Let my friend inside."

"Sorry. I can't do that. Please get approval."

I wanted to scream. Instead, I said, "Please put Pacey back on."

The phone was handed over. "What's happening?" she asked. "Am I about to get disappeared?"

I laughed. "No. It's fine. Just hold tight. I'll sort this out."

"Okay. This guy is very intense, though. He keeps giving me this dirty look like I'm a terrorist or something."

"I'm so, so sorry about this. I'll figure it out."

I quickly hung up.

For a brief moment, I felt dizzy and trapped. Anger flared through me. How dare they keep my friends out? I wasn't a prisoner, except maybe I was. They brought coffee to my room, but they wouldn't let me have a friend over. It was absolute madness.

Pissed off, I called my mom. I let it ring, but it went to voicemail. I tried to call another three times, but she didn't answer.

What was I supposed to do? I rifled through the packet they had left at my door, but there were no useful numbers. I checked the drawers and by the landline phone, but there was nothing.

I felt so damn powerless. I didn't even know how to find security, let alone how to find anyone that could help me.

And then I remembered.

I had his number. Lucas.

He had texted me the night before.

I looked at the messages, biting my lip. I really didn't want to ask him for help. I really, really didn't want to. But my friend was sitting out there like an asshole all because I was living in some mafia prison compound.

Taking a deep breath, I tapped his number.

"I knew you'd call," he said on the second ring.

"This isn't about that," I said.

"What's it about, then? I'm not sure I want to hear anything other than how badly you want me to come to your room and fuck your senseless."

"It's about my friend."

"We can invite her too, if you want. I'm open to most things."

I made a face. "No, listen, Lucas. I'm trying to have her over, but security won't let her in."

He laughed. "Not surprising. You've only been here a day. Nobody knows you yet."

"Can you help me?"

"Of course I can."

I paused. "Okay, will you?"

"What's in this for me?"

"The knowledge that you're not such a total asshole."

"Not interesting. Sorry."

I clenched my jaw. "Please. Make this easy for me."

"Wear that dress."

I paused. "No way," I said.

"Come to my rooms tonight wearing that dress."

"And do what?"

"Come inside, spine around once, and then leave."

"No way."

"Those are my terms. Take it or leave it."

I sighed, shaking my head. "That's it? I walk in, spin, and then leave?"

"That's it."

"Fine."

"Great. See you later." He hung up.

What had I just gotten myself into?

"You have got to be kidding me," Pacey said. "This place is insane."

"I know," I said. "I don't even know my way around it yet."

"How could you? It's freaking huge."

We walked along the halls back toward my room. I'd given her a brief little tour of what I knew so far, which basically consisted of us wandering the halls until someone pointed us in a different direction.

Finally we found my bedroom door, and I unlocked it, pushing it open.

Inside, it was covered in flowers.

Hundreds of flowers, all different shapes ad sizes, dotted the room.

"Whoa," Pacey said. "Did they put you in the green room?"

"No. I mean, these weren't here when I came to meet you an hour ago."

Pacey walked in and I followed her. There was a card propped up on the coffee table, and Pacey grabbed it before I could.

"'Enjoy the flowers, ladies.'" She looked at me. "'Lucas?"

My face darkened. "My stepbrother."

"Is it normal for a stepbrother to send his stepsister flowers like this?"

"No. There's nothing normal about him."

She laughed, tossing the card aside. "Well, whatever. This place is absolutely amazing, Nat."

I sighed, collapsing onto the couch. It was just too much. Between the whiplash of losing my family home and suddenly coming to live in a mansion, and my stepbrother wanting me, and me wanting my stepbrother, oh and marrying my stepbrother, it was all just too much.

"I can hardly believe it," I said.

But Pacey didn't hear me. She was too busy looking over the room, inspecting every little detail. She seemed more enthralled by the ornate display of wealth than I was.

"Your own bathroom?" she asked. "It's bigger than my bedroom. Holy shit."

I laughed. "And they bring food to your room."

She poked her head back out. "Seriously?"

"Sure. Want something?"

"Smoothie."

"I'll see what I can do."

Whole I ordered a smoothie sent up to my room, which apparently was a completely fine and normal thing to do, Pacey continued to explore the room.

Finally, her drink appeared, and we lounged on the couch together.

"I know I keep saying this, but I can't believe it."

"I am as surprised and overwhelmed as you are."

"Probably more, since you have to live here."

I laughed. "Yeah, true."

"Tell me about your new family."

"Arturo, my stepdad, he seems nice I guess. My mom and him seem to really like each other."

"What about Lucas?"

"He, ah, he's an asshole. I think the flowers are his version of a joke."

"Some joke," Pacey mumbled. "How old is he?"

"A little older than us."

"And what's he do?"

I paused at that. What did he do? Other than act as a gang member, of course.

"He works for his dad," I said.

Pacey nodded. "Okay, show me the rest of the place."

"Want to sit by the pool?"

"Sure!"

I stood up, smiling. Pacey had a way of cheering me up even when she wasn't trying. I had to dig through my stuff, but I found some bathing suits for the both of us to wear.

We changed and headed out.

My life had very suddenly gone from normal to totally crazy. But at least I had a pool.

Chapter Twelve: Lucas

It wasn't every day that I found two half-naked women sunning themselves next to my father's pool.

Actually, scratch that. I couldn't count how many times that exact scenario had played itself out and I'd ended up with both women back in my bed.

But I couldn't remember a time when one of those two was my stepsister.

Her friend was the same girl from Vegas, and I wondered if she would recognize me. I doubted it, considering how drunk she'd been, but I wondered how much Natalie had actually told her. I hoped nothing, and I knew Natalie wasn't an idiot. Still, there was always a chance, and so I decided to play it a little straight.

The two girls were lying in lounge chairs and wearing bikinis. "Ladies,"

I said as I walked over.

Natalie opened one eye. "Lucas."

Her friend sat up. "So this is Lucas," she said. "Thanks for the flowers."

I smiled. "Of course. Natalie told me about the trouble you had at the front gate. Consider the flowers an apology."

"Big apology," she said.

"Lucas, this is Pacey," Natalie said.

"Pacey, nice to meet you."

"Likewise." Pacey grinned at me as I slipped my shirt off.

I caught Natalie staring, and I stared right back. I loved the way her light skin looked in her dark blue bikini. It barely covered anything, leaving basically nothing to the imagination, and that was how I liked it. By contrast, her friend was thinner, almost stick-thin, with darker skin and honey-colored hair.

"What are you doing?" Natalie asked.

"Nat," Pacey said, "don't be rude."

"It's okay," I said. "I just thought I'd go for a swim."

Before Natalie could complain, I dove into the water. It felt good after a long day of breaking faces and pushing for information.

After meeting with Rodney, we had decided to take a quick detour through the Russian-controlled territory. I didn't go around aggressively breaking noses, but I did try and rustle up my contacts. I had a few guys in their mob that gave me reliable information in exchange for some decent cash, but I couldn't find any of them, strangely enough.

Almost like they had gone underground for some reason.

I surfaced and did a lazy little back stroke. I caught both of the girls watching me and smiled in return.

"Come on in," I said. "Water is decent."

"No, thanks," Natalie snapped, but Pacey was already getting up.

"Come on, Nat," she said. "I'm hot."

"Go ahead," Natalie replied. "I'm comfortable."

Pacey shrugged. She walked over toward the pool and dove in.

I laughed as she splashed over. She was fairly graceful in the water, but she was completely lacking something. For whatever reason, I had absolutely no interest in Pacey. Despite the fact that she was cute enough and obviously eye-fucking me, I didn't want the same thing.

For some reason, I wanted my wife. The girl that kept looking at me like I was the worst human being in the whole world.

"So, what do you think of the house?" I asked Pacey as she swam over.

"It's nice," she said. "Too big though."

I laughed. "Yeah, it is too big. Guess how many rooms are actually in use at any given time."

"Half?"

"Hardly. Less than a quarter of them, and that's being generous."

"Wow," she said. "Seems like a huge waste."

"It really is."

"What do you guys do that you have all this?"

I glanced at Nat and she gave me a look. Immediately I understood that Pacey didn't understand a thing.

"My father is in real estate. He owns a lot of buildings all over the country."

"Wow. That's really cool."

"I'll give you two a tour sometime."

"That'd be great."

She swam around me and I watched Natalie carefully. She studiously ignored my looks and tried to pretend like she was nodding off behind her sunglasses.

But I knew the truth. The second I had stepped out of the house and headed down toward them, Nat had been watching me like a hawk.

I swam over to the edge of the pool and climbed out, water streaming down from my muscular body. Pacey continued swimming laps.

I grabbed my towel and began to dry myself off.

"Can you do that somewhere else?" Natalie asked.

"Why? Distracted?"

"No. You're getting me wet."

"I know that. I can practically smell how badly you want me," I said softly.

"That wasn't what I meant." She was blushing like crazy.

"Come on, Natalie. Don't pretend like you're not dying for your friend to leave so I can tongue your tight pussy until you scream my name."

"Not in the slightest. Did you come out here just to mess with me?"

I grinned at her. "Yes. And to say that you make me fucking hard when you wear that bikini."

"Great. Thanks."

"Don't forget our deal."

"I haven't forgotten."

"Good. I'm sure you've been thinking about it all day."

"What are you two whispering about?" Pacey called out.

I smiled over at her. "Just an urgent family matter."

"Is anything wrong?"

"Not at all," I said, waving her off. I looked back at Natalie. "See you later, sis."

She ignored me as I walked away, my towel draped over my shoulders.

I loved the look on her face. It was half scorn and half desire, which only made me want her even more. I'd never met someone that resisted me so hard and yet so clearly wanted me like Natalie.

The issue of our marriage hadn't come up yet, though I knew I was gong to have to do something about it. Now that we had a rat in the family, times were extremely dangerous. It simply wasn't the best situation to have such a serious secret.

Vince was waiting for me just inside the house. I entered through the staff member door, a nearly invisible door that opened right into the kitchen.

"Swimming?" he asked me.

"Swimming," I confirmed.

"Not your usual thing."

I raised an eyebrow. "Got something to say?"

He grinned, holding up his hands. "Not at all."

"What are you doing over here?"

He shrugged. "Waiting for you. Admiring the view."

I followed his gaze and saw Natalie standing up, walking over toward the pool, and jumping in.

"Back off," I said fiercely, surprising myself.

Vince stared at me. "What?"

"My stepsister is off limits," I growled at him.

"Yeah, okay, of course," he said, taking a step back.

I didn't understand my reaction. I knew Vince was harmless, and we joked about women like that all the time. But suddenly I was pissed that he would look at Natalie like that. I knew the sort of shit he said, and I didn't want to hear it about her.

I calmed myself down and began to head back into the main portion of the house. Vince followed behind me.

"What did you want, Vince?" I asked him.

"Sent out feelers like you wanted, trying to find our Russian friend."

"And?"

"Got a response already."

I stopped and looked at him. "Really? This fast?"

"Yeah. That's what I thought, too."

"What did he say?"

"He wants to meet up."

"So the guy is invisible earlier, but as soon as we even ask around, suddenly he wants to meet."

"Suspicious."

I nodded at him. "Yeah, suspicious. Set a time and place."

"You sure?"

I narrowed my eyes at him. "You've been questioning me a lot lately."

He shook his head. "Sorry, boss. It just seems like an obvious trap."

"The Russians don't want a war. They wouldn't lay a finger on me. No, this is about something else."

Vince nodded. "Okay. I'll set the time."

He began to walk away. "Vince?" I called after him.

He looked at me. "Yeah, boss?"

"Cut the shit."

He grinned. "Got it."

I smiled back and he left.

I couldn't afford to lose Vince's loyalty. Of everyone in the mob, Vince was my closest advisor, my number two, my right-hand man. I trusted him almost as much as I trusted Louisa, and that was saying a lot.

I shook my head, heading over to my rooms. Things were getting more and more dangerous by the second. I couldn't exactly afford to be distracted by Natalie, but the thought of her in that dress got me hard as fuck.

For some reason, I knew she was going to uphold her end of the bargain. From there, anything could happen.

Chapter Thirteen: Natalie

I hugged Pacey hard.

"Thanks so much for coming," I said.

"Of course, Nat. I'll be back soon."

"Okay. You're the best."

She climbed into her car and drove off. I watched her wind her way down the long driveway, slip out past the gate, and merge into traffic. She disappeared over a hill.

I bit my lip as the weight of my reality came back to me. I was still very much stuck in the mob compound, and still planning on walking into my stepbrother's room wearing the tightest, most revealing dress I had ever put on.

I kept asking myself what the hell I was thinking as I headed back toward my room. I didn't even need to ask for directions and was able to find them all on my own. I went inside and hopped in the shower, cleaning myself off.

I checked the clock once I was showered. It was half past six, and I knew I needed at least an hour for my hair to dry. Lucas hadn't specified when he needed me to come by his rooms, and so I got on the phone and ordered myself dinner.

One delicious chicken dinner later and I was squeezing myself into the dress. My hair was dry enough, so I put on some makeup and chose a pair of heels that went well with the dress.

Looking at myself in the full-length mirror, I felt incredibly nervous. I didn't know why, since I was only going to walk in, spin once, and then leave. Still, the idea of him looking at me made me incredibly nervous, but also strangely excited. I could feel my hands shaking ever so slightly as I tugged at the hem of the incredibly short dress, trying not to think about the fact that his sister had worn the dress.

"Come on, Natalie," I said to myself in the mirror. "One spin and you're gone. Just do it already."

I took a deep breath, walked out into the main room, opened my door, and stepped out into the hall.

And realized I had no clue where I was going.

Embarrassed, I scurried back inside. I grabbed the phone and called up the kitchen.

"Excuse me," I said. "Do you know where Lucas's rooms are?"

The person on the other end paused. "This isn't a directory. It's the kitchen."

"I know," I said. "I'm so sorry. I just figured you'd know this place. I'm so new."

Another long pause. "Next time, ask whoever you're looking for first, okay?"

"Okay."

He proceeded to give me directions, which were surprisingly easy. Lucas was staying in my wing, only a hallway over.

I walked quickly out and headed in his direction, moving fast but nervously. Fortunately, I made it to his front door without running into anybody else.

I knocked once and waited.

No answer.

I knocked again, louder, and waited.

No answer again.

I was starting to get nervous.

On the third round of knocking, the door suddenly swung open.

"What?" he said, and then he stopped.

I stared at him, open-mouthed.

He was dripping wet and wrapped in only a towel. His tattoos snaked up his body and disappeared down into the area that his towel barely covered. His face broke out into a wicked grin.

"Well hello, wife," he said. "Please come in."

"You're in a towel," I said dumbly.

"Yes. I know."

"I can come back later."

"Come in." He stepped aside, so I walked past him. He shut the door behind me. "Well?" he asked, staring at me.

I blushed deeply. "Can't you put some clothes on first?"

"I didn't ask you to come while I was in the shower."

"I know, but—"

"But nothing," he said, coming nearer to me. "Don't you have a spin for me?"

"Uh, yeah." I slowly began to turn.

His hands grabbed my hips as my back was to him. I heard the towel drop to the floor.

"Lucas," I said. I felt something hard press against me and his lips graze my ear.

"You have no clue what you do to me, do you?" he whispered. "Just coming here drives me insane."

"Just one spin," I said.

"That's not why you're here."

I felt him kiss my neck, brushing my hair out of his way, I let out a soft gasp as he pulled me tighter against him.

"Why am I here, then?"

"Because you want another taste, Natalie. You only got a small bit of what you want, and you need more."

"More of what?"

I felt his hands begin to roam my body. "More of my fingers, more of my tongue. You keep thinking about how incredible it felt that night in the limo."

"I also keep thinking about how we're married. And you're my stepbrother."

"But you're here anyway," he whispered. His hands moved so slowly, so deliciously down my legs. I felt them slowly begin to lift up the hem of my dress.

My knees were shaking. And my pussy was dripping wet. I had a surprise for him, a surprise I wasn't sure he'd actually find.

"I am here," I agreed.

"Because you want to know. Does it really feel as good as I say it does? Can I really make you body feel things you didn't know about?"

His hands pulled up my dress.

"Fuck," I gasped.

"Natalie," he whispered, "you delicious, bad girl. No panties?"

"Surprise," I moaned as his fingers found my soaking spot.

"God, you continue to fucking impress me, Natalie."

"Good," I groaned and moved my ass against his clearly hard cock. "I want you to be impressed."

His fingers began to work my pussy and I tipped my chin back. His lips found mine, kissing me hard, as he continued to slowly work my soaked clit.

I reached behind me, finding his thick, hard cock. I began to stroke him slowly, feeling it on my back and my ass.

"Fuck, Nat," he said. "You're dripping wet. Your soaked little cunt is begging for it."

"And you're harder than I thought."

He spun me around, pulling me against him. He kissed me hard as I continued to work his cock, stroking him long and slow. He pulled away and I stepped back, admiring his body. His cock was hard and firm in my hand, his muscular chest covered in tattoos. I could see the desire in his eyes, starving for me.

I reached up and spit into my palm and then began to work it into his cock. He groaned as I began to jerk him, his hands working at my breasts.

"Is this what you imagined?" I whispered to him.

"Do you want to feel what I imagined?"

"Yes. Please."

He pushed me back and then grabbed my hips. He steered me toward a couch, tipping me back. I fell onto its soft cushions, laughing slightly.

He was on top of me in a second, his body pushing against mine, kissing me hard and rough.

I lost myself in his touch. Any thought of what we were doing was completely lost as I began to give myself over to him. His lips moved from mine and kissed my neck as I laced my fingers through his hair.

He moved farther down, kissing my exposed chest. His fingers and hands pressed my legs open and I gasped as he moved farther down.

"I've been dying to taste this pussy," he said, kissing my inner thigh. "You know I've been thinking about this every day since we met?"

"I can't get that night in the limo from my mind," I admitted.

"I think this might help."

I felt his lips kiss my clit ever so gently. Slowly, he began to lick and suck me, working my clit. Waves of pleasure built through my body.

I grabbed onto the pillows, trying not to moan too loudly. It was impossible though with the way he worked me. I felt his finger slide inside me, pressing deep into my pussy while his tongue and lips continued to work at my clit.

"Fuck you taste good," he said, looking up at me. His fingers continued to slide in and out of me.

"This is not what I expected would happen," I said honestly.

He smirked. "I think you're lying to yourself, then."

My witty retort was completely destroyed when his tongue began working my clit again.

He was absolutely ravenous the way he licked and sucked me. His hands fucked my pussy, pressing his fingers deep into me, sliding in and out of my soaked spot. I loved his naked body, the way he was still slightly damp from his shower. I tipped my head back, moaning loudly, beginning to completely lose myself.

His fingers pressed deeper and his tongue worked harder, licking and sucking. I began to move my hips, and I gasped as I felt him suck and lick. I reached down and grabbed his hair, feeling the pressure beginning to build.

"Come for me," he said as he continued to fuck me with his fingers. "Come for me, Natalie. I want to see your face while you fucking come."

"Keep going," I gasped. "Keep doing that."

His magic fingers kept pressing deep inside me. He went back to licking and sucking my clit, and I worked my hips, pressing his head harder against me.

Then I felt it begin to wash over me.

The orgasm started in my spine and rolled over my whole body.

"Oh shit, Lucas. Oh shit, oh shit," I said, over and over.

"Come for me, Natalie." He kept fucking me with his fingers. "Come on my mouth, come on."

His tongue licked and sucked as I came hard and fast, the orgasm rolling through my body, sending twitches down along my skin.

It was incredible and freeing. The only thing in my world was Lucas and his body, his fingers and mouth working me.

Slowly, so slowly, it began to subside. I stretched back on the couch, gasping, breathing deeply.

Lucas looked up at me. "That was what I wanted," he said. "That bucking face you make."

I blushed. "What face?"

"The face of someone in ecstasy." He moved up and kissed me. I kissed him back and felt his thick cock pressing against me.

"Still excited?" I asked.

"Still?" He laughed. "I'm harder than I've ever fucking been for you, Nat."

I reached down and felt him, stoking up and down.

"I can help with that."

"Can you? I'm not sure how."

I smiled. "What do you want me to do?"

"I want you to suck this cock until I come down your throat."

I bit my lip. "I can do that."

He grabbed my hair, whispering into my ear. "Are you sure you can take my thick cock?"

"I'm sure."

I pushed him back and dropped off the couch, down onto my knees. He smiled as I grabbed the base of his cock and began to stroke him. I licked the palm of my hand, getting it nice and wet, and began to slowly jerk him, stroking long and slow strokes.

"Ah fuck, that's good," he said. "I love looking at your pretty face."

I stared at his body, at his chest and tattoos. I didn't know what the heck I was doing, but I wanted to suck him off. I wanted it so badly, because he was so hard for me.

I slowly licked him from base to tip, and he grunted his approval. I tasted his salty pre-cum as I slowly slipped my lips around his tip and sucked it hard, pulled out with a pop, and looked him in the eye.

"I don't know," I said. "How badly do you want this?"

"Suck that cock, girl," he said, pressing my head back down. "Ah fuck, yeah. Like that."

I took him deep into my mouth and began to suck him for real. I worked his tip, using my tongue and lips, sucking back and forth. His hands pressed me down, sliding his cock into my throat, and I worked hard to take it.

He was huge and starving. I loved the grunts he made, the dirty words he whispered as I sucked him.

"I want to feel that pussy slide down my cock. I want to fuck you roughly until you can barely walk straight. You'll come on my thick cock and keep begging me for more."

I slid back and jerked him, catching my breath. I bit my lip and looked at him before going back to his cock, sliding it deep into my throat.

"Ah fuck, you dirty girl. Swallow that fucking cock."

I let him fuck my mouth, his hips sliding up, thrusting into my face. I used my hand to jerk him off as I sucked him, alternating between letting him fuck my mouth and doing all the work.

Suddenly he stood up, forcing me to slide back.

"Suck me off now. No hands. Just work that cock," he said.

I put my hands behind my back and smiled as I slipped his cock between my lips. I began to suck him hard and fast, not caring how messy it was, just wanting to make him come.

I wanted to taste him, already loved the way he tasted. I loved the feeling of his cock in my mouth, loved knowing that I was making him grunt with pleasure.

"Oh fuck yes, Natalie. Swallow that dick," he said. "I'm so fucking close."

He pressed my head down and began to fuck my mouth, grunting loudly.

"Oh shit. Swallow my cum," he said. And then I tasted him as he stiffened, grunting loudly. His cum filled my mouth and throat, and I swallowed every drop, just like he asked.

Finally, he finished, and I licked him nice and clean. He collapsed back down onto the couch.

"Holy shit," he grunted. "You've got one incredible fucking mouth."

I crawled up next to him, smiling. "You liked it?"

"Hell fucking yes." He looked down at me and laughed.

"What?"

"You have my cum on your dress."

I looked down at myself and turned beet red. "Oh no. Oh no!"

He laughed again, shaking his head. "It's totally fine. Don't worry about it."

"I can't walk back to my rooms looking like this, though."

"I'll give you something to wear."

"And what about your sister?"

"Louisa doesn't expect to see this dress again."

I sighed, shaking my head. "Lucas, what the hell are we doing?"

"Right now we're sitting here, enjoying our orgasms."

I nodded, going silent. I could hear his heart beating in my ear, and I loved the feeling of his hard body.

For the first time since I'd moved into the Barone compound, I felt completely safe and at ease. There had been this unspoken fear in my gut ever since my first day, but suddenly it was gone. I wasn't thinking about anything but Lucas and how he felt. My mother never crossed my mind, or any other problem.

"Come on," Lucas said finally. "Let's get you out of that dress."

"Again already?" I asked, teasing.

He smirked. "Ready when you are."

I glanced down at his cock and noticed that it was already starting to get hard again. I sat up, smiling. "Maybe later."

"Whatever you say, wife."

He stood and walked into another room. He came back a minute later with track pants and a gray hoodie. He tossed them to me.

"Thanks," I said, standing up. He was watching me. "A little privacy?"

"No." His grin was enormous.

"Don't be a dick."

He sighed. "Fine." He turned around.

"Don't peek," I mumbled as I slipped the cum-stained dress off.

I quickly pulled the sweatpants on and glanced up. He was peeking, but I just shook my head and pulled the hoodie on over my head.

"Decent?" he asked.

"Like you didn't already know."

He walked over and grabbed me by the hips, pulling me against him. He kissed me deep and hard. "You should get over this shyness of yours," he said.

"You should get dressed."

He shrugged. "I like being naked. Feels good."

"Yeah, well, it's distracting."

He laughed. "Good. I want you distracted." He walked across the room. "Drink?"

"I should get going," I said nervously. "Someone might notice me here."

"Whatever you want." He stopped in front of a dresser and poured himself some whisky.

"Listen," I said, "before I go: What are we doing about this marriage?"

He cocked his head at me and sipped his drink. "What about it?"

"Well, uh, we can't really stay married. We're going to divorce, right?"

He walked closer to me. "Why would we do that?"

I looked away. "Seriously, put some pants on."

He laughed again but complied, walking into the other room and then returning, wearing just some thin mesh gym shorts. "Better?"

"Yeah," I said, though it hardly was. I could still clearly see the outline of his cock. "So, uh, the divorce?"

"We can't," he said.

"I'm pretty sure we can," I said. "Whenever we want to."

"Things are complicated right now."

"I know, and divorcing will help them be less complicated."

"Actually, it's more about the business."

"You mean the mafia."

He grinned, nodding. "Yeah. We're having some trouble with, ah, informants."

"You mean you have a rat?"

He laughed. "Yeah, we have a rat."

"What's that have to do with us?"

"If we divorce right now, it'll potentially draw attention to us. Nobody knows about the marriage, so it's better if we just let it stand until this all blows over."

I nodded, understanding his logic but not happy about it. If it were up to me, we would have divorced already.

But I was beginning to understand the game we were playing. I wasn't happy about it, not by a long shot, but I'd been around my mother long enough to know that the men she dated were very often dangerous. I needed to learn to play along, or else things could get worse for me.

"Fine," I said. "When it blows over, we're divorced. Okay?"

"Sure." He walked toward me. "That is, if you still want to be divorced."

I laughed. "You're my stepbrother. That's just crazy."

He stopped inches away from me and reached out to touch my hair.

"Any more crazy than you sucking me off like that?"

"Yes," I said. "Maybe. I don't know."

"Face it, Natalie. You're desperate for what I have."

I turned away. "You're my stepbrother. This was just a one-time thing." I gestured at the dress.

"Sure. If that's how you want to play it, we can pretend you won't be back here begging for more."

"Good night, Lucas."

"Good night, wife."

I quickly crossed the room, opened the door, and walked out.

I knew I needed to get out of there quickly. Any time he came near me, I wasn't sure I could trust myself.

And I needed to get myself under control. What had happened back there was completely wrong; I couldn't believe I had let it get so far. I had planned on teasing him a little bit, not completely falling into his arms and letting him do whatever he wanted to me. It was bad enough that he was a cocky asshole, but he was also my stepbrother.

I couldn't risk my mother's marriage, or my own safety. As much as I disliked her, she was trying to be happy, and she was trying to provide.

I walked quickly back to my room, angry with myself but still thinking about his touch. The angrier I got, the more I imagined how it felt to touch him and taste him.

I was totally screwed.

Chapter Fourteen: Lucas

Chicago was beautiful early in the morning, especially in the summer. The bench was hard underneath me as I sipped my burning-hot coffee, waiting patiently.

Vince was on a bench within my sightline, but he was far enough away to be inconspicuous. Three other members of our team, plus three of Rodney's guys, were all standing around the park pretending like they weren't all watching me.

I hated waiting. It was part of the game we had to play, but that didn't mean I had to enjoy it. I had always been a man of action, someone that stood up and got done what needed doing, but I could force myself to be patient when I needed to be.

Still, this felt wrong for some reason. Vince had sent out feelers to some contacts we had in the Russian mob, and we got back one single bite.

He said we could meet, but only briefly, and only in public.

His name was Vasili Vladikovich. He was a low-level member of the Russians, basically a courier with no real power at all. We paid him pretty well in exchange for information every once in a while. I was pretty sure he was sick of being shit on by his bosses, and so I did my best to act respectful of him when I could.

But he was a real slime ball. There was a reason the Russians never promoted him. He wasn't stupid, but he was self-centered, slovenly, and rude. Basically, nobody liked him because he was an asshole.

I sipped my coffee, waiting. He was already fifteen minutes late, and I was getting ready to give up on the whole thing. I didn't need Vasili or any of the Russians; we could work the thing out for ourselves. But just as I was ready to stand up and walk away, I spotted him coming into the park.

Vasili was short, fat, and had a ratty beard. He was wearing a track suit, black and white, with white pumas. He looked like the most cliché Russian gangster in the world.

I nodded to him and he came over, looking nervous.

"Vasili," I said. "Thanks for meeting me."

"You know how dangerous this is for me?" he snapped.

"Why is that?" I glanced at one of Rodney's guys, who flashed me a quick "all-clear" sign.

"Our organization is on lockdown," he said. "You know why."

"The shipment. What happened?"

"You know what they do to rats, right?"

"Probably something similar to what we do."

"They cut off our balls and shove them into our mouth. They make us chew and swallow them. Then they cut our throat."

I raised an eyebrow. "Excessive."

"Scary, I say. So you calling me here, you could get me fucking killed."

"Okay, Vasili, but we're safe right now."

"Maybe. Only because I'm so smart."

"Why is that?"

"I lost my stupid handlers."

I raised an eyebrow. "Handlers? You're being followed?"

He nodded. "Idiots, though."

I flashed a quick sign to Vince. He nodded and stood up. They'd do another sweep around the area and make sure we were okay.

"Why are they following you?"

He snorted. "Because I know what's happening. I stupidly read a message, which earned me this." He held up his hand. It was wrapped in a white bandage.

"Finger?" I asked.

"Pinky. Clean off."

I nodded. That made sense. Vasili was probably pissed off about the

Russians taking a finger, which explained why he was willing to talk to me in the first place.

"Okay, Vasili, what did the message say?"

"Can't tell you that."

I clenched my jaw, willing myself to stay calm. "What can you tell me?"

"Just one thing."

"Enough dramatics. What?"

"We were involved, in the truck getting taken."

I let out a breath. I knew the Russians were involved, but I didn't know how or why. Vasili's confirmation helped a lot, though.

"I thought our organizations were friendly."

He shrugged, picking at his nails. "Friendly, not friendly, doesn't matter. We're all greedy fucks, right?"

I nodded. "Why have the police pinch the truck, though?"

He grinned at me. "Good question."

"Tell me, Vasili."

"Sorry, Lucas. Can't do it." He stood up.

"Wait. I'll pay more."

He looked at me for a second. "Check the truck," he said.

"It's impounded, with the cops."

"Check it." He held out his hand. "Pay me."

I made a disgusted face. "Vince is at the entrance. He'll pay you."

Vasili shrugged. "Okay. Good luck."

"Make sure you take care of that pinky."

He waved his bandaged hand and then walked quickly back toward the entrance. I saw Vince bump into him and place a package of money into his pocket. Vasili cursed but quickly realized what had happened.

He disappeared back into the city.

I leaned back on my bench and sighed, sipping my coffee. Still hot, but not hot enough.

"Well?" Vince asked.

I stood up and we began to walk back toward the car. I gave Rodney's guys the sign to disperse.

"He says they were involved."

"That it?"

"And to check the truck."

Vince frowned. "Not much new there, then."

"We know the Russians were involved. And I'm still pretty confident that we have a rat."

"Could just be on their end."

I nodded. I'd had the same thought. If the Russians were involved, then none of our people needed to betray us at all.

But something still felt off about the whole thing. That deal had been worked out over months, and it stood to benefit both of our organizations. Why would the Russians risk war? It just made no sense to me.

"We'll keep digging," I said to Vince. We rounded the corner and climbed into the car.

"Back home?" he asked.

I shook my head, "Quick stop downtown."

"What for?"

I grinned at him. "Just need to do some panty shopping."

He gave me a weird look but just shrugged. "Okay, boss."

We pulled back out into traffic, and I leaned back in my seat, smiling to myself.

Remembering Natalie, that dress, my cock in her mouth.

The taste of her pussy was still on my lips.

Chapter Fifteen: Natalie

When I woke up the next morning, I still couldn't get what had happened the night before out of my head.

Lucas's body, the way he touched me. His hungry look. The way I lost control and couldn't stop myself from touching his muscular chest, from kissing his grinning lips, from feeling his thick cock.

I ordered my usual breakfast, or at least the breakfast I'd been eating the last few days, and sat at the small table set in front of a window. The view was actually very lovely; I watched the grounds stretch out from my window and the cars that crawled along the road.

But my head was still stuck on the night before, which it really, really shouldn't have been. I needed to get myself together and move past him.

Frustrated, I stood up and quickly got dressed. I finish off my coffee and then stepped out into the hall.

Instantly I had no clue where I was going. I felt nervous wandering around the property without any destination, but I wanted to explore and I had nothing else to do.

So I began to walk. I started with my wing, purposefully avoiding Lucas's hall, and basically began trying doors at random. I quickly found out that a majority of them were locked.

But some of them weren't. I found a storage room with linens and bedding, another large bathroom with multiple toilets and showers, an indoor basketball court, a small gym, a bowling alley, and what looked like an old classroom.

All the while everything was covered in gilt and expensive fabrics. It was the most ostentatious place I had ever seen in my life, and the more I moved through it, the more I was convinced that it was huge.

I followed the stairway down to the bottom and pushed open the door. I found myself in the kitchen. The place was packed with workers, servants and cooks alike, some standing around and chatting, some hard at work on food prep.

"Lost?"

I turned and saw a young man standing to my right. It took me a second to realize that he was Franklin, the driver.

"Oh no," I said. "Just exploring."

He nodded, taking a drag on a cigarette. "Big place, huh?"

"It's crazy. How does anyone find anything?"

He shrugged and ashed his cigarette. "You get used to it, I guess."

"How many people are living here?"

He shrugged again. "Permanently? Supposed to be just Barone and his family, but there's probably fifty, maybe sixty people staying here at any given time."

I gaped at him. "Seriously?"

"Seriously."

"Why don't I see them?"

"Because they have orders to leave you alone."

I let that sink in. "Why?"

"You're the boss's new stepdaughter. He doesn't want you corrupted, I guess."

He was beginning to give me the creeps. "Well, thanks."

"Sure."

I turned and left the kitchen, walking fast. He had seemed nice at first, but the longer I saw him, the more awkward I felt. I wanted to get away from him.

I went up to the top floor and began walking again. Paintings lined the hallways, and I began to notice more people around. They all ignored me and walked quickly past, not saying a word. It began to feel a little strange, but I realized it was because they had been ordered not to bother me.

And that suited me just fine. I wanted to be left alone while I explored.

Another fifteen minutes of aimless wandering and I came to a dead end. The hallway I had just come down was strange, but I couldn't put my finger on it.

I had to walk to the other end and back again to realize that the hallway had only one single door.

The door was large and wooden. On a very small metal plaque, there was a name: "Louisa."

I cocked my head, looking at it. The name sounded very familiar, and then it hit me: this must be Lucas's sister's room.

Curiosity got the better of me, and I found myself knocking.

And quickly stopped myself, but too late. I had already knocked twice, loud and booming.

Why hadn't I met her yet? I realized that there must have been a reason why they were keeping me from her. Or why she had been keeping herself from me. Maybe she hated me? Maybe she despised my mother for marrying her father?

I took a few steps back away from the door. I was suddenly very nervous. But nobody was answering, and the silence stretched on. Maybe she wasn't in her room; maybe I was safe.

I turned and went to leave. I took a few steps quickly down the hall, trying to be quiet.

"Running away?"

I stopped. The voice was young, female, and coming from right behind me. I turned, a knot in my stomach.

She was pretty, slight, with big eyes, thick hair, and a slim face. I could see the resemblance between her and Lucas, though I guessed she took more after her mother than he did.

"Uh, I'm sorry," I said.

She cocked her head. "For what?"

"Knocking. I didn't mean to bother you."

"Sure you did," she said.

"Uh, sorry," I said stupidly.

"You're Natalie."

I nodded. "You're Louisa."

She stared at me for a second. The longer I looked at her, the more I realized that there were bags under her eyes and her clothes were all rumpled.

She looked tired.

"Come in then," she said, disappearing inside.

I hesitated. I should probably just leave, but she interested me. Curious, I followed her inside.

Her rooms were bigger than mine. I guessed they took up the entire wing and part of the downstairs. It was a total mess, with clothes and trash all over the place. There were several large screens set up and electronic equipment scattered all over the ground. I recognized a lot of it.

"Sorry for the mess," she said, sitting down cross-legged on a couch. "I threw a shoe at Rosita and she refused to come back."

I laughed nervously. "Rosita?"

"She cleans my rooms usually. But she showed up in the middle of a raid."

"Raid?"

"Yeah. Like, World of War Craft?"

I nodded. "Sure. Some of my friends play."

"It's fun."

She watched me as I stood there awkwardly. "So, uh, you're into computers."

"Sure."

"Me too. I go to school for computer science."

"Good for you."

I frowned. She seemed almost hostile one second and completely pleasant the next. I had no clue what to make of it.

"Uh, so. We're stepsisters."

"Sit down," she said. I walked over and sat on the couch. "Yep, stepsisters. I've never had a sister before."

"Me neither," I said, smiling. "I'm an only child."

"Must be nice."

"Lonely sometimes, but yeah, it's okay."

"Must be hard too, since your mother and all."

I laughed. "Yeah. You've heard of her, I guess."

"Camille Taylor. Hard not to hear about her." She paused, looking at her nails. "How much of that crap is true?"

"The shows?"

"All of it."

I shrugged. "Not much, but I honestly try to keep my distance."

"Not into the family business?"

"No, not really."

"Good for you." She looked at me seriously. "Why did my brother steal a dress for you?"

I turned beet red. I hadn't realized she knew about that. "Uh, he was just trying to be nice, I guess," I said quickly.

She laughed. "That doesn't sound like Lucas."

"No, it doesn't," I muttered.

"I don't care what you're doing," she said, shrugging. "I really don't."

"We're not doing anything," I said.

She smiled. "Sure you're not." She stretched her legs out, putting them in my lap. I was surprised but didn't move away. "Sorry I'm being weird. I'm just exhausted."

"I can come back later if you want."

"No. Stay for a bit. I want to get to know my new stepsister."

And so began the weirdest conversation of my life.

She began by asking about life at college. Evidently, Louisa didn't go to school and had opted to drop out of high school pretty young. I told her about class, about friends, and about partying, but she seemed most interested in asking about the computer lab.

Next, she wanted to know about past boyfriends. I was vague on this, and when I questioned her back, she completely ignored me. It was more like an interrogation than a conversation.

But she fascinated me. The way she jumped from topic to topic, her infectious laugh, her strange smile, it all drew me into her. I wanted to be her friend.

Finally, I decided to ask more about her.

"So, how come we haven't met yet?" I asked.

She cocked her head. "You haven't come here before now."

"Sure, but you missed that dinner."

She smiled. "I don't leave my room."

"I mean, I wouldn't want to leave my room for that either."

"No," she said, interrupting me. "I don't leave my room."

I stared at her. "Ever?"

"Well, no. I leave sometimes. I go for walks outside. But mostly, I'm in here."

I blinked at her. "Why?"

She shrugged, looking away. "You can ask my dad about that one day, if you want."

"I doubt I will."

She looked back at me, that smile returning. "He's not such a scary man, you know."

"I didn't think he was."

"Sure you did. Because we're mobsters."

I gaped at her, surprised. "Uh," I said, "what?"

She cackled at me. "Don't act dumb, Natalie. You're part of the Barone Crime Family now." She leaned closer to me. "We're all violent criminals here."

"You don't seem violent," I said.

"Not right now." She leaned back and yawned. "Okay, sister, I think bonding time is over." She moved her feet and I stood up.

"Well, uh, it was nice talking to you." I felt completely off balance.

"You too. If you see Rosita, tell her to stay away. I have more shoes."

I laughed, nodding. "Okay. I will."

She rolled over, pulling a blanket on top of her. I watched for a second and then turned and left.

Out in the hall, I shook my head. What a totally strange and surreal experience. As if my life weren't weird enough, now I had a stepsister that might have been totally nuts. Beautiful and very interesting, but nutty, without a doubt.

I headed back toward my room, shaking my head, wondering when the weirdness would ever end.

Chapter Sixteen: Lucas

I poured myself a whisky and stretched out on the couch, ready to try to think of a plan to deal with the Russians, when someone began banging on my door.

"Shut the fuck up," I yelled.

The banging did not stop.

"I'm going to rip off your balls," I growled, getting up, "if you do not stop."

I yanked open the door.

"Hi, big brother."

Louisa smiled in at me.

"What are you doing here?"

She moved into my room. I frowned at her but shut the door.

"Thought I'd pay you a little visit."

"You haven't been here in a while."

She walked over to my liquor cabinet and poured herself a drink.

"Things are different now."

I frowned at her. "Aren't you too young to drink?"

She knocked it back. "Probably."

"What's up, Louisa? I'm busy." I sat back down, stretching my legs out.

She poured herself another drink and then perched on top of the coffee table. I refused to take her bait; she was constantly doing strange things just to get a rise out of anyone. Usually it was the staff that had to deal with it, but every once in a while Louisa decided to make me the target of her games.

"I had a visitor earlier."

I raised an eyebrow. "People know not to bother you."

"She was very interesting. I can see why you like her."

I took a quick breath. "Natalie."

"My new sister. I like her."

I frowned. What the heck was she doing visiting Louisa? Not that there was any real rule against it, but I was willing to bet that my father would have preferred she didn't. Louisa could poke plenty of holes in the little illusion of power and control that my father had worked so tirelessly to build.

"What did she want?"

"I think she was just exploring, stumbled into the spider's lair."

"Well, I guess it's good that you two met."

Louisa nodded, sipping her drink. "She likes computers too."

"So you have something in common."

Her eyes narrowed. "Be nice to her, Lucas."

I clenched my jaw. "I am being nice."

"No, you're not. You think you are, but you're not."

"What do you know? You're too busy hiding in your room, throwing your little temper tantrum."

"Three years isn't a temper tantrum."

I stared at her, not responding. It was an argument we'd had many times since she had decided to lock herself away, and I wasn't about to have it again.

"Do you like her?" Louisa asked finally.

"We're not high school kids, Lou."

"Answer."

I sighed. "Maybe."

"I think she likes you, too."

"I know that."

She climbed off the coffee table and fell onto the couch next to me. "Just be nice, okay?"

"Okay."

We drank in silence for a few minutes. It actually felt nice to spend a little time with my strange sister. We used to be close, a long time ago, back before our mother passed away, back when we were children.

Then of course the business tore us apart, as it does to all families.

Before I could get too melancholy about it, my phone began to ring. I stood and walked over to it, picking it up. "Yes?"

"Luca, come to my study."

"Now?"

"Yes," Arturo said, annoyed. "Now."

He hung up.

I turned toward Louisa but she had already left.

Damn girl. Why did she seem to care if I was nice to Natalie or not?

Of course I was being nice to Natalie. Lou didn't want to know how nice I was being.

Shaking my head, I left and headed down toward my father's study.

～～～～～～～～～～～～～～～～～～～～～～～～～～～～～～～～～～

I knocked once and pushed open the door.

"Father," I said.

"Luca, come. Sit."

I shut the door behind me and sat down in one of the chairs facing his desk. He stood up and walked to his liquor cabinet. "Drink?"

"Whatever you're having."

He poured two whiskies and then handed me one, sitting down in the chair next to me. "Tell me, how did the meeting go today?"

"Vasili remains a little worm," I said.

"Good then." He smiled. "What did he say?"

"Good news and bad news there."

"Bad first."

"Bad news is, the Russians were definitely involved. But the good news is that Vasili says to check the truck that was taken into custody."

Arturo frowned. "Why check the truck?"

"I don't know. But he seems to think that will help us."

"Hmm." He leaned back in his chair, sipping his drink. "Luca, how are you getting along with your new stepsister?"

I sipped my own drink to mask my discomfort at the sudden change in conversation. "We get along fine," I said.

"Good, good. I haven't gotten much time with her. I had heard that you've been seeing her."

"Did you?"

"The staff talks," he said, waving his hand.

"Well, someone needs to try to make her comfortable. This is a strange life."

He nodded. "And what's your assessment of her?"

I frowned. "That's what you normally ask me when there is an asset in play."

"Is she not an asset?"

"She's family."

"Yes," he said, nodding, "family."

"Do you not trust her?"

"I fear her, more like. I don't know what she believes about us and our family. Her mother knows and is completely fine with it, maybe even smitten by it. But the girl I worry about."

I nodded. I understood his fears. I had shared them initially when I had heard that Camille's daughter was coming to live with us, back before I knew that I had married her.

We survived through loyalty and secrecy. If someone was disloyal, they couldn't live in the compound. Natalie was going to see and hear things that could potentially hurt us if they ever got out simply by living in the same building that we lived in.

And truthfully, I was still worried about what she thought. She never really said much about our business, which on the one hand was good, but it did show that she feared us. Fear was useful sometimes, but I didn't want her to be afraid. I wanted her to understand.

Still, I couldn't voice my fears to my father. I didn't want him to suspect or worry about Natalie. I knew that I could handle her, knew that she wouldn't do anything to harm us. Not yet, at least.

"I trust her," I said. "She doesn't talk about the business, but she knows."

He took another sip. "How sure?"

"I'm a good read, father. I'm sure."

He nodded. "Very well. I'll trust you, Luca, but don't disappoint me. Keep an eye on that girl."

"I will keep her close."

"Good." He stood up and walked around his desk, finishing off his whisky.

I stood. "Anything else?"

"Get into that truck. Keep me informed."

"I will."

He sat down and folded his hands. "One last thing, Luca. You were in charge of security the night of the exchange, and you failed. What happened?"

I stared at Arturo. It was the question I had been dreading. The truth was, I had failed that night, though it wasn't entirely my fault. Rodney's team was supposed to keep us updated and safe, but he could never have guessed that the cops would come in force and seize everything.

Rodney did what he always did. He survived. He had warned us that something odd was coming with just enough time for us to get out of there with minimal losses, but still, I had trusted Rodney.

"It was my failure," I said. "I take responsibility."

Arturo frowned. "Don't protect your people. If someone failed, punish them."

"If you want to punish someone, punish me. My people are my responsibility."

He didn't like that. I could see the anger twitch in the corners of his eyes, but he kept himself in check.

"Be careful, Luca. You're not above our rules."

"I understand that."

He stared at me and I kept my face impassive.

"Go. Get inside that truck."

I nodded, turned, and then left.

Out in the hall, I headed back toward my rooms, annoyance running down my spine.

Arturo was too controlling. He wanted to micromanage every single operation that I was involved with. I understood the impulse, and I didn't hate him for it, but he was going to get in the way.

I sighed, releasing my anger. I was glad that conversation was done and over with. Although I didn't love how it went, I felt like I had a weight off my back.

Back in my rooms, I smiled down at the package I had bought earlier in the day. It was the thing I had been looking forward to all day long. Lou had walked in just as I was about to put it all together.

But I was finally alone. My mind ranged back to my stepsister's body and the way her lips felt around my cock. I loved the way she swallow my cum greedily and licked me clean afterward.

The box held a nice little surprise for my stepsister, and I couldn't wait to deliver it.

Chapter Seventeen: Natalie

Another morning in the Barone compound.

Another morning having dreamed about my stepbrother all night.

About his lips against my neck.

About the feeling in my stomach every time he came around.

And about how angry he always made me.

Arrogant and cocky. But at least his sister seemed very nice. I had liked Louisa as soon as we had first started speaking, despite how strange she was. Or maybe because of how strange she was. Everyone in the Barone compound seemed so stiff and formal, but Louisa was the first person to actually treat me like a normal human.

I climbed out of bed, yawning. I had no clue what I was going to do all day, but part of me thought that it didn't matter.

Maybe I'd get a job. Or maybe I could work somewhere on the

compound.

Tough life. I lived in luxury and everything was provided for me. Anything I wanted, I could easily pick up the phone and get. So why did I feel so anxious all the time?

I pulled open the door, expecting my usual breakfast. It was there, but the tray was perched on top of a box.

I carried the tray inside and then grabbed the box. It was plain and unassuming and was wrapped in a red satin bow. There was a card attached, which I quickly opened.

Natalie, For old memories and for new ones. Yours, Lucas.

I frowned at that. What did it even mean? And why the heck was Lucas sending me presents?

I quickly tore off the paper and pulled off the lid.

Inside, I found underwear.

Black, lacy, sexy underwear. Bras and matching panties, and all of it my size.

Underneath them was the dress I had worn the night I went to his room. I put the underwear aside and pulled the dress out. There, staring me in the face, was the cum stain.

"Gross," I said, tossing the dress aside.

At least the note finally made sense.

What an asshole. Part of me felt angry as hell that he would send me something like that. What was he trying to do, rub my face in that dress? I'd already pegged him for an egotistical jerk, but I hadn't thought he was genuinely mean as well.

But as soon as I looked back at the underwear, I felt the other half of my emotions: pure, unbridled excitement.

Lust burned through my chest, and I felt my skin tingle.

I bit my lip, shaking my head. It was the exact response that he wanted. He wanted me to get turned on, to think about him stripping those sexy panties off my body slowly, about his tongue and fingers working me. He wanted me to remember the way his cock tasted, the way he came so hard, his grunts and groans.

He wanted me to get soaking wet. And as much as I hated him for it, I was reacting exactly as predicted.

I sat down on the couch, drinking the coffee that had been delivered on my breakfast tray. My last attempt at getting him back had completely backfired; I needed to think of something much better.

It hit me almost all at once. I looked at the underwear again, frowning. There were four pairs; I decided to choose two. Quickly, I stripped off my sweatpants and slid on a frilly black pair.

I sat back down on the couch and spread my legs wide, closing my eyes. I let my mind begin to wander.

I thought about the night in the limo, his fingers inside me. He was a gorgeous stranger back then, and the danger of it only enhanced my excitement. My pussy got soaking wet remembering how incredible it had felt to let him get me off.

And I began to rub my clit through the panties. It was so dirty, so dangerous to want him, to touch myself wearing the panties he had sent me. The danger only made me that much more aroused, though, as pleasure moved through me.

I continued rubbing myself as I thought about the way his cock tasted. I loved how he had taken control that night, grabbing my ass, moving me to the couch, fucking my mouth, sucking my clit.

I wanted him. God, I still wanted him so badly. I hated myself a tiny bit for that, since I knew that he knew it, that he had planned for all this. I was his secret wife, his stepsister, his sexual conquest, and I loved it, wanted more of it. I was drunk on him.

I moved faster, slipping a hand down my panties to slide a finger deep inside myself as I began to rub my clit. I was soaking, the panties themselves absolutely wrecked and dripping. I wasn't thinking about that, though. My plan was suddenly completely forgotten as I imagined what he could do to me.

Sliding his cock between my legs. Maybe I'd let him fuck me on the desk of the empty classroom. I wanted to feel him take me from behind, to fuck me roughly up against a wall. He could grab my hands and hold them down as he fucked me, whispering all those delicious, dirty words in my ear.

Pleasure bloomed through my whole body. It was so dangerous, so wrong, to want my stepbrother to fuck me roughly, to use me until I was begging for more. I'd never had a secret like him before, and I never knew that I wanted one. But I loved my secret marriage, loved how badly I wanted my secret husband.

I came, slowly at first, my body twitching, my muscles tensing, thinking about him. He made me smile. He made me wet. He made me feel things I'd never felt before.

And finally, the orgasm passed over. I lay back on the couch, slipping my hands from the panties. They were sufficiently soaked, and I was sufficiently tired.

I glanced over at the pile of underwear and frowned.

Only one more pair to go, thankfully. Maybe this would teach him for being such an arrogant asshole.

Fantasy was okay. Fantasy was fun, even. But me and Lucas didn't live in a fantasy world, and everything around us was so, so dangerous. As soon as the orgasm began to fade, my anger at him returned tenfold. He couldn't take such big risks like sending me underwear and a cum-stained dress. He couldn't be inviting me to his room.

And I probably shouldn't be sending him my used panties, but I couldn't help myself.

After all, he started it.

I stood up and walked over to the phone. I ordered some orange juice and a bagel.

I figured if I was going to get myself off again, I at least needed my energy.

Chapter Eighteen: Lucas

We spent the day planning.

Vince and I went around town, pulling in favors, dropping wads of cash, and basically bugging every single cop that we had on the payroll.

As far as a plan went, it was pretty simple. It came together a little faster than I was normally comfortable with, but I knew that speed was key here. We had to understand what had happened with the shipment, and we needed to find that rat as soon as humanly possible.

I was putting a lot on the line trusting Vasili. If we checked this truck and there was nothing but the shipment in there, no clues or any shit like that, then my credibility might be questioned. Granted, I'd have to hunt down Vasili and take the rest of his fingers, and he knew that.

Sometimes, being a violent, dangerous motherfucker had its perks. People tended not to lie to me, because it hadn't worked so well for others in the past.

Still, it was always a risk trusting a gutter fuck like Vasili. But I didn't

have any other choice.

Losing that shipment was probably the biggest blow our family had

taken in a long time. I knew my father mainly blamed me, though it was

clear that something completely outside the real of my control had

happened.

Still, it was my responsibility to fix that shit.

And so I found myself standing with Vince a block away from the

police compound lockup at three in the morning.

"Think he'll show?" Vince asked.

"Fucker better," I grumbled. "I'm tired and we dropped a lot of cash

on this."

Vince chuckled. "Who's money, anyway?"

"My own personal stash."

"You got that kind of dough lying around?" He whistled.

"I bury it in the backyard."

He laughed and I just shrugged. I sipped my coffee. He didn't need to

know that I wasn't kidding.

Ten more minutes of standing around, shooting the shit before we

heard steps approaching. Vince's hand twitched toward his gun, and I just

nodded at him.

The guy rounded the corner. He was tall and thin, almost like a giant stick. His dark skin almost blended in with his dark blue cop uniform.

"You the guys?" he asked as he stopped in front of us.

Vince nodded. "Are you Sanders?"

"Yeah, man," he said. "You got my money?"

I tossed him a small package. He caught it and quickly opened it, checking.

"It's all there," I said, a little annoyed.

"Hey, man, you can't blame me for checking. I ain't never dealt with you people before."

"We just want to look around. No trouble."

He shrugged. "Frankly, man, I don't give a fuck what you guys do in there. Just be in and out in ten minutes and we're good."

He began to walk back toward the compound and we followed him. Vince gave me a bemused look, and I just grinned at him.

We walked past the main entrance. Our friend Sanders glanced inside but kept moving. The guy sitting behind the desk looked like he was asleep.

We turned a corner and went down a narrow alley. Halfway down, we stopped in front of a side door that had been propped open with a brick. "In here," Sanders said.

We went inside. "Convenient," Vince muttered.

"Can't go through the front with you two gangster-looking mother fuckers," Sanders said.

I laughed. I liked him.

We moved through a series of short hallways.

"If anyone asks," Sanders said, "you just filed an ER-3481-C report, and I'm taking you to get your shit."

"What?" Vince asked.

Sanders just kept moving head.

We came up to a long hallway. Ahead of us was a large garage door. We stopped in front of it, and Sanders ran his I.D. badge through a small scanner.

The door began to open.

"Ten minutes," he said. "I'll open it again in ten. If you ain't here, it'll close on its own and I ain't opening it again. Got it?"

"Ten minutes," I said.

"Good luck." He turned and walked away.

Vince grinned at me. "Let's do it."

The door finished opening up into the outside portion of the lockup. The building was a simple square, with the center courtyard set up to act as the outdoor storage for vehicles. They kept smaller, more sensitive things inside.

The courtyard was packed with cars. We picked our way through, having to climb over a hood once or twice.

"How the fuck did they even get this shit in here?" Vince asked.

"Must be an outside entrance," I said.

Soon enough we made it to the other side. Sitting there in front of a large garage door that likely led to the street was the truck itself.

"Here we go," I muttered. "How are we on time?"

"Six minutes," he said.

"Shit."

I quickly moved forward, slipping a pry bar from my coat. I slipped it under the back of the truck's door and began to work it.

The damn thing was stuck.

"Give me a hand," I said. Vince slipped out his own bar and began to work it with me.

The thing didn't want to budge. "Fuck. We have to hurry," I said.

"Come on," Vince grunted. "Open, you mother fucker."

Finally, with a lurch, the door suddenly broke free of the lock and slid up. It opened with a loud, echoing bang.

We froze.

"Shit," I said.

But Vince was staring into the truck, wide-eyed.

"Boss, look."

I followed his gaze.

The truck was completely empty.

"What the fuck?" I said.

Vince climbed in and walked toward the back. I followed him inside.

"Nothing," he said.

"Think they moved it inside?"

"Maybe." He frowned. "We'll ask Sanders."

"Check the cab."

Vince hopped out and I heard him break open the front door.

I did a quick search of the back and didn't turn up a thing.

"Nothing," Vince said. "And we better move."

I nodded, hopping out of the truck. I pulled the door shut, and we began to jog back toward the other entrance.

Ahead, we saw the doors open. I jumped over a car, landing in a full-on sprint, Vince on my tail. We had to scramble over the hoods of cars, and we made one hell of a racket, but we made it, slipping under the door just in time.

Sanders stared at us. "You made a lot of fucking noise," he grumbled.

"Sorry," I said, catching my breath.

He began to walk back the way we had come. Vince and I followed.

"Hey, listen," I said. "Did you look up that truck for us?"

"Yeah, like you asked. Got the papers here." He held out a small packet.

Vince took it and began to look through the stuff. We kept walking and ducked back into the original room, weaving our way through shelves.

We stopped in front of a fire exit.

"The stuff in the truck," Vince said, "it's not kept in storage inside?"

Sanders shrugged. "Fuck if I know. What's it say in there?"

"Doesn't say. Just says a truck plus cargo was stored outside."

"Then the stuff should still be in there." He frowned. "Why? Was it empty?"

"Thanks, Sanders," I said, moving out into the alley. Vince followed me.

I heard the guy mutter something about damn mobsters, but we were gone, already heading back to the car.

We didn't say a word to each other as we walked back in front of the building again. The guy at the front desk looked as asleep as he had earlier, which was good. We probably woke up half the damn block running over those cars.

Once around the block, we stopped and leaned up against a stoop.

"Well?" Vince asked.

"Truck was empty," I said.

"Yeah, it was."

"I think that's what we were supposed to see."

"You think someone took the stuff?"

"Yeah, I do."

We were silent for a minute.

"Whole thing was a setup," Vince said finally.

"Yeah, it was." I shook my head. "But by who?"

"The Russians?"

"Makes no sense. They wouldn't risk a war with us, especially not over that deal."

"Maybe they didn't think it was as good as you did."

"Maybe," I said, shaking my head. "Or maybe their organization has a few leaks in it, too."

We climbed back into the car and Vince fired up the engine.

The drive back was full of silent plotting. My head was spinning through the possibilities, trying to figure out the players.

Everything felt like it was resting on a foundation of sand. Between the rat, the stolen shipment, and Natalie, I was torn in a hundred different directions.

And it made me feel so fucking alive.

I loved the stress. I thrived on it. I hadn't gotten to my position, my level of power, without being able to perform under pressure. That was what separated me from other men. I could do what was necessary even when the stakes were high as hell.

We got back to the compound around four, and I climbed out of the car. I waved to Vince as I headed back inside, and he went to put the car in the garage.

I stumbled up the steps, exhausted, ready to finally get some fucking sleep. But sitting outside my room was a small box wrapped in a bow, much like the one I had left outside Natalie's room.

A smile spread across my face. I grabbed the box and carried it into my room.

Inside, I poured some whisky and put on a record. I smiled to myself as I opened up the card.

Memory of me is all you'll ever have from now on. Here's a hint: Smell is the best trigger. Natalie.

I opened the box and my smile turned into a huge grin. Inside were two panties I had sent her earlier.

And instantly I knew what the card meant by smell. I picked up a pair and lifted it to my nose.

Unmistakable. It was her smell, her fucking delicious smell. I breathed her in deeply. The girl had clearly gotten off in these, and that made my cock instantly hard.

She was crazy. I couldn't believe she had responded that way. I mostly expected her to feel embarrassed and to maybe throw it all away. But instead, she sent me back this, the perfect response.

I smelled the other pair, smiling to myself. Scent really was the best trigger of memory, and the thought of her body came rushing back to me.

I wasn't sure what she intended with the panties, but it only made me want her even more. I took another deep sip of whisky, remembering the way she whimpered as my fingers did their magic, working her soaked cunt, making her mine.

I put the box on my nightstand, finished off my whisky, and climbed into bed. Maybe I'd have a nice dream of her sweet pussy wrapped around my raging hard dick.

Or maybe in the morning I could make that a reality. Maybe those panties were meant to be a challenge, but I saw them as a promise.

A promise that she was going to be mine, one way or another.

Chapter Nineteen: Natalie

The pool was surprisingly calm and empty as I sat there listening to music and paging through a magazine.

I kept thinking about my little prank that I had sent Lucas the day before. I hadn't heard anything from him, but I knew he got the box. At least, it wasn't sitting out in front of his door anymore.

I had a weird little feeling in the back of my head. What if he hadn't gotten it? What if someone else had grabbed it? I would be so, so embarrassed. Worse, it could cause some problems in his crazy family.

But I couldn't worry myself too much. He had started it, so I was assuming leaving presents like that was safe. Hopefully at least.

I sighed, looking up at the sky. I had been feeling so stressed out lately, but sitting by the water was calming me down a lot. I had always loved pools and never gotten to be near one when I was younger. Chicago was also not exactly the best environment for outdoor swimming, or at least outside of the main summer months.

Fortunately, it was a hot summer so far, which meant I could sit out by the pool in my bikini with absolutely zero discomfort.

I let out a breath, finally feeling relaxed.

"There you are."

I clenched my jaw, surprised. I looked over my shoulder and saw my mother walking toward me.

So much for feeling relaxed.

"Hi, Mom." I said.

She sat down in the chair next to me. "I haven't seen you in a while," she said.

"I know. You been busy?"

"I guess so." She stretched her legs out.

I hadn't seen her since the first night we moved in. Mom was like that, always disappearing. And I figured she had already taken over her part of the house, redecorating and ordering the staff around.

"How are you settling in?" she asked.

"Fine, I guess."

"Are you used to having a staff?"

I laughed, shaking my head. "Not at all."

"No, neither am I." She smiled and shrugged. "But people have been so nice, especially Franklin. He's really gone above and beyond to show me around."

I raised an eyebrow. "Who's Franklin?"

"Remember the nice boy that drove us here?"

"Sure."

"That's Franklin."

I remembered him well: the creepy guy from the kitchen.

"Well good. I'm glad you made a friend."

She laughed. "I wouldn't call him a friend, dear. He's still just part of the staff, after all."

"Right. Of course."

"He's a very smart boy though, speaks a few languages. Spanish, German, Russian, Italian, a few others."

"Are you taking language classes?"

She smiled strangely. "Trying to learn a little Italian for Arturo."

"How very nice of you."

"Have you explored the grounds much?"

I shook my head, looking out across the water. "I've tried, but it's so big."

"I know. Bigger than I would have guessed."

"What do they even need all this space for?"

"Oh, who knows? They have a lot of people in their organization. I think people stay here from time to time."

"Their organization," I said ruefully. "I wish you had warned me before we moved in."

"How could I have? You probably wouldn't have believed me anyway."

"I know, but, Mom, the mob?"

She frowned at me. "It's not what you think."

"It's exactly what I think."

"It's stressful for Arturo, you know. They lost some important shipment recently."

"I heard something about that, I think," I said, cocking my head. "Shipment of what, though?"

She laughed sweetly. "Who knows? Cocaine, heroine, probably something like that."

I sighed. "And that's okay with you?"

"It's a business, honey. There's a demand, so they supply it."

I shouldn't have been surprised, but I was. Truthfully, I wasn't exactly morally against everything the mob did. I knew they probably did some pretty awful things and broke some laws, but they were businessmen at the very core of things. But what really bothered me was the danger we were in just being in their family.

Camille had a knack for ignoring anything that was bad or wrong. She was incredibly single-minded when she wanted to be and would follow any path to achieve her goals.

And as I looked around, I knew that her goals had been pretty much achieved. She wanted wealth and power, and now she had some.

"Please try and get along with everyone," she said. "I hear you've been close with Lucas."

My head snapped over at her. "Who said that?"

She laughed again. "Calm down. It's okay. You're allowed to be friends with a mobster."

I took a deep breath. She didn't know anything, clearly. She thought I was freaked out because he was a mobster, not because I was married to him. And because of some very wrong and very exciting flirtation.

"I know that," I said. "He's just my stepbrother."

"Good. And did you meet your stepsister?"

I nodded. "Briefly, yes."

She frowned. "Well, good. I haven't yet."

"You will soon enough."

"I hear she's very strange." She leaned in to speak quietly, conspiratorially. "I hear she's crazy. Doesn't leave her room, talks to herself all day. Attacks the staff sometimes."

I frowned at her, annoyed. My typical mother, gossiping already. Fortunately I had already met Louisa, and I knew that most of that wasn't true. Sure, she never left her room, and she probably did attack the staff,

173

but she wasn't crazy.

"She's a nice girl," I said. "Just a little misunderstood."

Mom nodding knowingly, which only annoyed me more. "Well, I look forward to meeting her."

"I'm sure."

Mom stood up. "Okay, I'm off to do some work. Don't exert yourself too much today."

"Okay. See you."

She waved, oblivious to how annoyed I was, and headed back up toward the house.

I watched her disappear inside. Suddenly the pool didn't seem like a comfortable, relaxing place anymore. I was agitated and annoyed, and the last thing I wanted to do was sit around and stare at the stupid water.

I stood up, pulling on a T-shirt and a pair of jean shorts over my bathing suit. I tossed my magazine, phone, and headphones into my bag. I slipped my feet into my sandals.

My mind kept going back to Lucas and the mob. How did I feel about that? Camille had mentioned a shipment of some sort, and she even thought it was of drugs.

What did I think about that? Was I okay with being a part of a family that sold drugs?

I genuinely wasn't sure. It was all so complicated, so complex. I doubted Lucas was actually out there selling drugs to people, but his family did likely have dealings in it.

Upset, I decided to just go for a walk and try to calm myself down.

I headed toward the barns, my mind still on the mafia, drugs, shipments, and violence.

Chapter Twenty: Lucas

"We must smoke the rat fuck out and kill him soon."

I leaned back in my padded chair, listening to the other captains bicker and argue about the shipment issue. Arturo had called a meeting of the head of the family to discuss our potential moves.

Which only annoyed me. It was supposedly my operation and my problem, and Arturo had called the meeting anyway. The captains were mainly a bunch of old men, though there were a few sharp and young guys in the mix, men that I respected.

Still, it was my job, and my call. I didn't appreciate hearing idiotic and obvious suggestions from the other captains.

"How though?" asked Ernesto, an older, balding man.

"We can offer money," suggested Alfonse. He was sitting across from me, wearing an expensive suit and idly chewing on a cigar like the biggest cliché in the world.

"Too obvious," I said, bored. "That will only spook him."

Alfonse made a face, but Reginald spoke up. "Luca is correct," he said. "We need subtlety now, especially since we do not know what is going on."

I nodded. I liked Reggie; he was one of the smarter captains.

"What is your plan then, Luca?" my father asked.

"I have an idea," I said, avoiding the question.

"Ideas," Ernesto said, scoffing. "We need more than ideas, Luca."

"Let the boy speak," Nicolas said. "What are your ideas, Luca?"

"I have informants within the police, as we all do."

"Of course, Luca," Gian said, "but aren't you afraid they're also working for the Russians?"

"Maybe," I said, "but you simply don't lose an entire shipment like that and nobody notices."

"That's true," Alfonse said.

"Someone saw, and someone will talk," I said.

"How can you be certain?" Ernesto pushed. "And how can you know the Russians won't hear?"

"I'm not sure it's the Russians," I said.

The others looked at me like I was an idiot.

"Of course it is the Russians!" Ernesto said, laughing. "Those snake fucks robbed us."

"It does seem to be the Russians, Lucas," Nicolas said, frowning.

"Enough," Arturo said, drowning out the commotion. Everyone looked toward him. "We must choose a course of action. Luca, how sure are you of this?"

"I am very sure that I can handle this, father," I said.

There was a murmur of dissent at the table. I noticed most of the captains weren't speaking, though, which was good. They didn't want to get between me and my father.

"Who here believes they should be given control of this task?" Arturo asked.

"I do," Ernesto said.

I laughed at him.

"Quiet," Arturo snapped at me.

"I second Ernesto," Alfonse said.

"Then we vote," Arturo said. "Those for Ernesto?"

Some hands, but not many.

"Lucas?"

The remaining captains raised their hands.

"Lucas takes it."

I nodded to the men, but it was a hollow victory. The fact that there even was a vote spoke volumes.

Arturo didn't trust me. He didn't believe I was capable of fixing this tense situation, and he was looking for an out that didn't put the blame squarely on his shoulders.

Fortunately he wasn't getting that.

The meeting quickly wound down after that. The captains all filtered out of the room, heading into the main banquet room for an extravagant lunch. I stayed behind with Gian and Reggie.

"This whole shit," Gian said, "is just a power play by your father."

I nodded. "I know. But what can be done?"

"You could poison him and assume control," Reggie said softly.

I laughed. "Maybe soon, Reg. Maybe."

"We have your back, brother," Gian said. "We'll back your play."

"Thanks, brothers," I said. We shook hands and they headed off toward the lunch. I stood by the window, looking out over the grounds, my mind clouded with doubt.

The truth was, I did have a difficult road ahead of me. I needed to interrogate and push some buttons to try to track down the shipment, but I had to be subtle. Any overt accusations against the Russians could mean war.

I didn't want a war, but sometimes it felt like the old guard did. They were constantly pushing for blood, while I was only drawing blood where blood was needed. They were wasteful, stupid fools.

As I watched out the window, I caught sight of a small figure heading over toward the barns.

It took me half a second to realize that it was Natalie.

I felt something inside me stir. I remembered the smell of her panties from the night before, and my cock quickly got hard. I gripped the windowsill for a moment, watching her disappear into the horse stable.

And then I decided. I was going to skip the damn lunch. Maybe it was a bad idea since many alliances were made at captain gatherings, but fuck that.

I wanted my stepsister. I wanted my wife. I wanted her dangerous, tight fucking pussy, and I was sick of waiting.

I turned and headed down the stairs, out toward the stables.

Chapter Twenty-One: Natalie

I reached up and he snorted, tossing his head. I laughed, touching his skin.

"What's your name?" I said softly.

He didn't answer.

"I guess you don't speak English. You are a horse, of course, of course."

I laughed at my own joke and softly stroked his snout.

Ever since I was a little girl, I had liked horses. Not in the crazy equestrian way. I never rode them, either, because I couldn't afford them. Or at least that was what my mom had said. In retrospect, we totally could have afforded it. Mom just didn't want me to ride.

But they were beautiful animals. I walked down along the stalls, admiring them.

"Bigger than you expect."

I nearly jumped out of my kin. I turned and saw Lucas standing near the entrance, patting the nearest horse.

"Lucas? You scared me."

"Sorry," he said, grinning.

I looked down at my feet. I hadn't seen him since sending the panties, and I had no clue what he thought about it.

"Want to take one out?" he asked.

"I can't ride."

"You can't ride horses at least." He grinned and laughed. "Another time then."

"Okay."

"Been a busy couple of days," he remarked, walking toward me.

"I guess so."

"I got your present."

He stopped close to me, smirking. I felt my heart skip a beat. "Just returning the favor," I said softly.

"Smell really is the strongest sense for memory," he said.

"So you've been thinking about me."

"Ever since you left my room that night."

"Good," I said, smiling. "How's it feel to want?"

"It feels good," he said softly.

I took a step away and turned. "I'm not in the mood for this, Lucas."

"For what?"

"Your dirty jokes and comments. Just not in the mood today."

"You're never in the mood for it, wife. But that doesn't stop you from liking it."

I felt angry suddenly as my mother's words came back to me. "Don't be such a thug, Lucas."

He laughed, surprised. "A thug?"

"Yeah, a thug. A drug dealer. What do you want from me? Why are we still married?"

I felt my anger rising, and I wanted to push him, to shove him to the ground. But he was too big, too solid, too strong. He could easily pin me to the floor and have his way with me. Half of me wanted him to, and the other half wanted to knee him in the balls.

"Where is this coming from?" he asked, genuinely bemused.

"My mother talked about you people. She said you guys lost some drug shipment lately. What are we wrapped up in, Lucas?"

He stared at me for a beat and then burst out laughing.

"What?" I asked, frustrated. "It's not a joke. Selling drugs isn't a joke."

"She told you that was a drug shipment?"

"Yes," I said, frustrated and annoyed. He was such an asshole. He was still smiling hugely, his face clearly amused. "And I don't want to be involved with drug dealers."

"Natalie, there weren't drugs in that shipment."

I paused. "I don't believe you."

He raised his hands, still smiling. "I swear on my dead mother's soul, there were no drugs."

"So what's the deal with this big shipment that got stolen, then? Why is it so shady?"

"Really want to know?"

"Just tell me, Lucas," I snapped.

"Olive oil."

That stopped me in my tracks. "What?"

"Olive oil. We were selling the Russian mob olive oil."

"That's crazy. Why would mobs be involved in olive oil?"

"Believe it or not, olive oil is the biggest business in Italy. It's a huge, billion-dollar industry, and my family is a big part of that."

"So why were you selling it to the Russians then?"

"Well," he said, laughing slightly, "it's complicated. But basically, most olive oil isn't really pure olive oil. It's cut with something like canola oil, something cheaper. In Italy, that's a huge crime, but my family has been in the fake olive oil business for centuries."

"Fake olive oil," I repeated.

"Yes. We were selling a shipment to the Russians wholesale. They were gong to resell it in their shops, and we were going to make a small profit but a larger business associate."

"So you don't sell drugs?"

He shrugged. "Some captains do. Some of the people that work for me do. I don't personally get involved, but it is lucrative."

I shook my head, annoyed. "Do you or don't you sell drugs?"

"No, Natalie, I don't."

"Okay." I took a deep breath and looked at him. "Olive oil," I said.

He nodded, grinning. "Yep. Olive oil. Lots of fake olive oil."

"I guess that's not as bad as heroin."

"No. I don't think so."

I leaned up against the wall, taking a deep breath. "I feel really stupid right now."

"Don't," he said, coming closer. "You're new to the family, and we haven't exactly been telling you anything."

"Still. I should ask before I start accusing."

He nodded, standing close, speaking softly. "Do you want to see something?"

"See what?"

"My favorite spot out here. It's very close by."

I shrugged. "Okay. Sure."

He started walking toward the other end of the stable, and I hurried to follow him.

I couldn't believe I had gone after him like that. He wasn't a drug dealer after all, although he did sell fake olive oil. Maybe that was immoral, but it wasn't exactly hurting anyone. I knew there were parts of their business that I wouldn't agree with and wouldn't personally get involved with, but I needed Lucas to be honest with me.

And I would believe him. I didn't think he was lying when he said he didn't sell drugs. He had no reason to be fake with me.

I felt better. I felt a little silly, but better.

We went to the far end of the stable, and he shifted a hay bale a few feet to the right. Bolted to the wall was a ladder that disappeared up into the ceiling.

"Up there," he said.

I bit my lip. "That thing looks like it's going to fall apart," I said.

"It won't. I promise."

I stepped up to it. "Okay." I began to climb.

I heard him climbing behind me. I kept going, not looking down, and soon I passed through the ceiling and into a wide, spacious area.

I climbed out onto the floor and he appeared just behind me.

"My favorite spot," he said, gesturing around us.

We were in the attic or the roof of the stable, above the horses. There was hay all over on the floor, covering everything. It was strangely clean tough, and it smelled nice. The one wall was all tinted glass, and we could see out along the grounds.

He led me by the hand over to a hay bale and we sat down, looking out across the yard.

I had to admit that it was beautiful. I'd been so busy feeling stressed out about everything that I hadn't taken the time to just enjoy where I was.

The place the gorgeous. The animals, the building, the architecture, it was all so expensive, clean, and lovely. Despite my discomfort at times, I really was staying in an amazing place.

"So?" he said finally.

"Yeah," I said, looking at him.

He pulled my body against his. "I keep thinking about those panties."

I blushed and looked away. "I was only following your lead."

"I liked it." I looked up at him, and the look on his face sent my heart hammering in my chest.

"What did you like about it?"

"Thinking about you touching that perfect, delicious little pussy of yours. And I know you were thinking about me while you did it."

"I was," I said.

He pulled my chin toward him. "Are you as sick of games as I am?"

"I don't know," I said, breathless.

"I want you, Natalie. I don't know what it is about you, but I need to fuck you. I need to make you come, make you mine."

He pressed his mouth against mine, kissing me hard. Excitement ran in waves down my arms and legs as I pressed myself against him. His arms wrapped around me, pulling me close.

I wanted it. I knew I shouldn't, knew it was wrong, but I wanted it anyway.

I kissed him back hungrily as our bodies pressed together, our mouths working, skin touching, hearts pounding. He kissed my neck and I let out a small gasp as he pulled my hair.

"Were you out by the pool?" he asked.

"Yes," I said.

"Stand up."

I listened, confused, excited.

"Strip," he commanded.

"Lucas," I said, shaking my head.

"I want to see your bikini. Strip."

I did as he asked, pulling off my shirt and shorts and tossing them aside.

"Fuck," he said. "I love your fucking body. Turn around."

I turned, letting him see my ass.

"God you make me so fucking hard," he said.

I blushed, a little embarrassed to be showing off my body, but incredibly excited. I liked his gaze on me. I liked what he was thinking about me. I knew he wanted me, knew he wanted my body, and that made my skin flush with excitement. The embarrassment only heightened that sensation.

"Come here," he said. He grabbed my hips and pulled me into his lap.

He kissed my neck, my lips, my breasts. I couldn't help but let out small gasps and moans as his hands roamed my body slowly, grabbing my breasts, teasing my nipples, before slowly sliding down between my legs.

"Soaked," he whispered. "Soaking wet. You dirty girl."

"I can't help it," I said.

"I know you can't. You're mine."

I felt his fingers slowly part my legs, sliding down my bikini bottoms. He began to rub my clit slowly, softly, sending amazing sensations through me.

"I'm not yours," I said, trying to resist him.

"Pretend all you want, Natalie," he said, working my pussy. I threw my arms around his neck and opened my thighs to give him more room. "But you're my fucking wife. And you're soaking wet every time I come near you."

He reached up and untied the back of my bikini top, letting it drop to the ground. He kissed my chest and teased my nipples with his tongue as he continued to work my pussy, sliding fingers in and out of me, working my clit.

I adjusted myself, straddling his lap. He continued to work me, kissing my lips, rubbing my spot, and I could barely control myself. I'd never been so heightened before, so turned on. I reached down between his legs, grasping his thick cock through his pants. He grunted as I began to work him. I was losing myself in the moment, in his body, in the sensations he was sending through me. He was in complete control of the moment, and I knew it. We both knew it. I'd do whatever he wanted.

He slipped his hand out from my bottoms and I dropped down onto my knees. He was sitting on the hay bale, looking at me as I unbuckled his pants and slid them down off his feet. I tossed his shoes and socks aside, leaving him in only his dress shirt and his tight black boxer briefs.

"I love watching you undress me," he said. "I love that skin, those fucking tits, your lips."

I reached up and slipped the underwear off him, sliding it down his legs and tossing it aside. His cock was thick and stiff, hard as hell.

"See what you do to me?" he said. "My cock is fucking harder than it's ever been."

I reached up and took it in my hand, slowly stroking him. "What do you want me to do?" I asked.

"Suck that cock, Natalie. Take that cock deep into your mouth and suck it hard."

I obeyed, sliding the tip between my lips and sucking him hard. I took him as far as I could, sucking his cock with a frenzy and an excitement that I didn't even realize I had.

He pressed my head down, groaning as I sucked him. I wanted him to feel good. I wanted to suck his cock hard and deep. I pulled back and jerked him off using my spit, and I watched as he slowly unbuttoned his shirt.

"I love the way you look at me," he said. "I can see how badly you want it in your eyes."

I looked away, blushing.

"Don't pretend it's not true," he said, pulling my gaze back.

"I know it's true," I said.

"Good." He finished unbuttoning his shirt, leaving it open. I stared at his chest, his muscular chest, and his ripped abs. I wanted to kiss every inch of that.

"Suck that cock now, Nat. Make me so hard I want to burst."

I went back to work, sucked him slow and hard, looking up at him. He watched me take his cock in my mouth, grunting his pleasure. I kept my hands on either side of him on the hay bale, letting his dick slide in and out from between my lips. He began to thrust himself into my throat, and I took every inch of him, sucking his cock hard and rough.

"Touch yourself while you suck me," he commanded.

I listened, reaching down between my legs. I had never touched myself in front of someone before, but I couldn't help it. I couldn't say no to him, didn't want to say no. I began to rub my own soaked clit as I sucked his cock, and the fact that he was watching me pleasure myself sent excitement roaring through my veins.

"Fuck. I love the way you moan while sucking my cock," he said. "I love having my cock in your mouth, you dirty girl."

I finally pulled back, jerking him hard and fast, moaning as I touched myself.

He stood up suddenly and grabbed his pants, pulling his wallet from his back pocket. H slipped a condom out from inside it and tossed his pants and wallet aside.

"Get up," he said. I listened and stood. "Take off your bottoms."

I stepped out of my bikini bottoms, kicking them away. I felt so exposed up in the loft, but I didn't care. He sat back down on the bale and pulled me close to him.

"Put it on," he said.

I took the condom, ripped it open, and slowly slid it down along his shaft.

When I was done, he took my hips and lifted me up onto him. I straddled him, his cock pressing against my pussy. I wanted to drop down but he held me there, looking into my eyes.

"Tell me how badly you want it."

"I want you to fuck me," I said.

"Tell me you want to feel my cock deep inside you."

"I need it. I need you to fuck me."

He pressed me down, pushing his cock deep between my legs.

The agonizing pleasure flooded through my mind. I tossed my head back, gasping, moaning, as he slowly filled me to the brim.

He kissed me then, leaving his cock inside me. I slowly began to slide back up and down, slowly at first, getting used to his heft, his size.

"Take all the time you need," he whispered, "because I want to fuck that pussy until you scream my name."

"Oh shit, Lucas," I said. "I can't believe how much you fill me."

"Get used to it."

I began to slide over him, and he used his hands to guide my hips. I worked up and down, sliding my pussy up and down his thick, hard cock. I could feel every inch of him inside me, filling me up as he kissed my neck and teased my nipples with his teeth.

"God I fucking love this body," he said, slapping my ass.

I gasped. "Do that again," I said.

He slapped me again, hard. I began to ride him faster.

"You like it a little rough," he said.

"I do."

He slapped my ass again and then thrust his hips up, slamming his cock deep inside me. I gasped, a shiver of pleasure exploding through me.

"Again," I begged.

He slammed himself again, slapping my ass. He took a nipple between his teeth and gently teased me as he slammed himself inside me.

"Oh fuck," I said. "Oh my god, keep doing that."

He continued to fuck me, and I simply let him have his way. I took his thick cock deep into my pussy, letting him press hard and fast, his hands slamming my hips down. I loved the sound of our skin slapping together, the rough sound of his grunts and his hands on me as he fucked me.

I began to take over, riding him, working my hips. He leaned back, putting his hands behind him, and I steadied myself with my hands on his chest.

"Go ahead, girl," he said. "Ride that dick."

I let myself work him, riding hard, fast. I couldn't think or breathe as I rode, moving my hips in circles, working my back. I let out long moans and gasps, loving the sensation.

Suddenly he wrapped his arms around me and lifted me off. We stood for a moment, and then he pressed me down on top of the hay bale, spreading my legs wide for him.

I thought the hay would be scratchy and hard, but it was surprisingly soft. He stood in front of me, his cock at the perfect height. He spread my legs wide and pressed himself deep inside me.

"Shit," he said. "You're so fucking tight."

"And you're so big," I groaned.

"I love slamming my cock inside you." He began to thrust, holding onto my hips, standing in front of me. "I love watching your tits move while I fuck you roughly."

His cock thrust hard and deep inside me, working roughly. His hands roamed by body, gripping my hips and grabbing my breasts. I moaned loudly and openly as he fucked me.

He began to rub my clit, and I knew it was sending me into shivers. I kept my legs spread wide, my hands up above my head, steadying myself on the edge of the bale.

"I want to see you come," he said. "I want to see this pussy come on my cock."

"Keep doing that," I said.

He continued thrusting, one hand on my hips, the other working my clit with soft, agonizing, incredible motions.

"Oh god, keep going," I said, feeling it build.

"Say please," he commanded.

"Please. Please, Lucas, fuck me. Fuck me. Make me come."

He thrust harder, his fingers working my clit faster, and I felt the orgasm come over me.

My whole body tensed, stiffening, twitching slightly from the pleasure as it rolled over my skin and mind. He fucked me deeply, holding my body, rubbing my clit, as I moaned his name over and over.

The orgasm crested and rolled over me, finally ending slowly. He climbed on top of me, pressing me down on the hay bale, sliding his cock in and out.

"Fuck, girl," he said. "That was the sexiest thing I've ever seen."

"Come on," I said, blushing again.

"I mean it. You coming makes my fucking blood boil hotter."

"Then it's your turn," I said, smiling at him.

He moved back off me and I gasped.

"You want me to come?"

"Yes," I said, looking at him.

He grabbed my hips and pulled me off the bale, turning me around. He pushed me over, spreading my legs, bending me down.

"Then I want this ass in the air. You think you can take it?"

"Yes, I can take it," I said.

He grabbed my hips, thrusting himself deep between my legs. I held onto the bale as he began to fuck me from behind.

"God I love this little round ass," he said, smacking me.

"Fuck me, Lucas," I said. "Slap my ass, pull my hair, and fuck me."

He grabbed my hair, whispering into my ear. "I do the commanding," he said, thrusting into me.

"Yes, you do," I said.

"And I want to come in this pussy. I want to fill you up."

"Come in my pussy, Lucas."

He pushed me back down, fucking me roughly. His strong arms gripped my hips, thrusting with such intensity. I could tell he was close based on his grunts, and so I began to work my hips for him, pressing my ass back against him.

He thrust harder, slapping my ass, pulling my hair, taking my body. He completely owned me, his strong arms working me, his cock thrusting inside me, and I wanted him to come more than anything. I wanted him to feel how I felt, wanted his cum inside me. I worked my hips, moaning his name, loving it, loving the pleasure.

He was like an animal in his lust for my pussy, and it made me feel incredible.

I felt him suddenly stiffen as his strokes got longer, harder, rougher. His whole body tensed.

"Fuck, Natalie," he groaned as he came deep inside me.

"Ah shit," he said, slowing his strokes, slowly finishing.

I collapsed onto the hay bale, and he took a step back. I was covered in sweat, and I'd never felt so satisfied before.

"Your pussy is like fucking magic," he said. "My god you're incredible."

He took the condom off, wrapping it up in some hay and setting it aside. He came over and wrapped his arms around me, holding his sweating body against mine.

I felt safe. I felt so safe there in his arms, my head high from the orgasm, floating in a cloud of contented pleasure.

"I want to stay like this for a while," he said.

"I do too."

And so we did. We stayed right there, feeling each other breathe, feeling right.

Chapter Twenty-Two: Lucas

We stayed like that, wrapped in each other, for over two hours.

I'd never done that before. Sure, I'd cuddled women every once in a while, but normally when we were finished, I just moved on. Instead, I actually found myself wanting to talk to Natalie, to get to know her.

She told me about her life, about having a reality TV star mother, and how that had really messed her up when she was younger. She told me about her mom losing the fortune, and how she promised herself that she'd never be like her mother.

And I was fascinated. I wanted to know more, to understand the way she thought about things, to figure her out. It was so strange that although we were just talking, I never got bored.

I found myself telling her things I almost never told people. I talked about growing up in the mob. I talked about the fear, the violence, and about eventually coming into my own as a captain.

My world was a strange, strange place, but I found myself wanting her to understand. Sure, she was my stepsister and living in my home, and so she needed to get it to some degree, but I wanted her to know me. I wanted her to get why I did the things that I did.

And the more she spoke, the more I wanted her to keep talking. Every word she said had me fascinated that a person could have so much inside them.

Time slipped away. The sun slowly sank down below the horizon, and I was well and truly hooked.

"And so she just stumbled back in?" I asked after Natalie had finished a lengthy story about another one of her mother's long benders.

"Yep. Just like nothing had happened."

"And you never skipped school? Didn't throw a wild party?"

"I told you, I was a good girl growing up."

I laughed. "You're not a good girl now."

"I guess not."

We fell into silence, looking out across the property, everything bathed in reds and pinks.

"Okay, I'm officially getting cold," she said.

"I'd offer you my shirt," I joked, "but I'm currently wearing it."

"That's okay." She stood up, stretching. "I should go back inside."

"Sure. Know your way?"

"I'll figure it out."

I followed her over toward the ladder and helped her climb down. Once she was safe, I followed, hopping off.

I felt light, happy. It was strange.

"Well," she said, looking awkward.

I grabbed her hips, pulling her against me. "Well."

"Not sure what now."

I slapped her ass and she giggled. "See you later."

I let her go and she walked away, shaking her head and smiling.

I leaned up against the door to the stable and watched her go. One of the horses behind me made a noise.

"Yeah, I like her too, Rosey," I said to the horse.

"Talking to horses now?"

Vince materialized from the other end of the stable.

"Just Rosey," I said to him, frowning. "Where'd you come from?"

"Came to find you."

"Following me?"

"Relax," he said, smiling. "I have good news."

"Go ahead."

He reached out and strokes Rosey's face. "Well, you asked me to think of a solution it this missing shipment."

"I remember," I said, annoyed.

"We grabbed a guy."

I raised an eyebrow. "You grabbed a cop?"

He laughed. "No way. We grabbed a janitor."

"Still, you grabbed a janitor who works for cops."

"We checked him out. His name is Juan Altered. He's a small-time crook, ex-con, got the job on some work program. Hasn't talked yet, but we haven't pressed very hard."

"Shit," I said. "Good work, Vince."

"Thanks, boss."

"Where's he at?"

"Safe house on 16th."

"Good. Let's go."

I followed Vince out toward the cars, though my mind was still very much on Natalie.

The girl drove me crazy. I wanted her, wanted to fuck her rough, make her come, make her mine. I wanted her to obey my commands and to watch her come hard on my thick cock.

But I also found myself wanting to know her more. It was a strange feeling, something I wasn't accustomed to. Maybe it was weakness crawling its way out of me, or maybe it was just a new kind of strength.

I couldn't be sure, not so soon. Not while my head was still spinning with thoughts of her.

~~~~~~

We wove our way through traffic, heading toward the place on 16th. It was a bit run-down, but it blended in well with all the other houses in the area. We parked a few blocks away and walked around back, pushing in through an old, wooden door.

"Louis," I said, nodding to the guy standing guard.

"Boss."

We moved past and went down some stairs, heading into the basement.

The safe house used to be a normal row home until it was bought by one of the many shell companies my father ran. We used it for interrogations and for people that needed a place to lie low. Not too many people knew about it, mostly just guys in my crew.

Downstairs were two more guys, Joey and Carlo. They were low-level thugs, basically hired muscle, the kind of guys you wanted to have your back if shit hit the fan.

Sitting in a chair, his hands tied together but otherwise fine, was our new pal, Juan.

He was younger than I had expected, maybe in his mid-thirties. Life had been hard to Juan. He had tattoos up his neck, his head was shaved bald, and he had a scowl on his face.

"You the boss?" he asked me.

I nodded. "Good guess."

"Not a guess, man. Look at the way these people stand around you? Like they scared or something."

I smiled and pulled a chair up in front of him. "Do you need anything, Juan?"

"Maybe my fuckin' freedom would be good."

"We'll get there." I leaned back in my chair. "Water? Something to eat?"

"Nah, man. Just get on with it."

"Do you know why you're here?"

"Because I work for the cops and you think I fuckin' know something."

"Exactly."

I smiled. I liked Juan already. He wasn't messing around.

"Well, I don't know shit."

"How about you wait until I ask before you deny?"

He shut his mouth and I sighed.

"Okay, Juan, do you remember the cops bringing in a truck a few nights ago?"

He nodded slowly. "Yeah. I seen that."

"Good. Do you know what was in it?"

"Nah. I didn't look inside."

"Okay. I want to know about that truck, Juan."

"I don't know shit." He looked away.

"Juan, listen to me. Did someone take something out of that truck?"

He didn't answer.

I leaned forward. "I don't want to hurt you. I don't want to get violent. But I have to know this thing, and you can tell me."

"Fuck you."

I sighed and stood up. "Please be civil. We've been kind to you so far."

"You can't do this shit, man."

"Don't be a little bitch," Joey called out.

I gave him a look and he shut up.

"Who stole our shit from the truck?" I asked Juan.

"I don't know."

I stepped forward and kicked him square in the chest. He let out a short cry of surprise and pain as he toppled backward, slamming onto the ground. He groaned, and the boys laughed.

"Pick him up," I said to Joey and Carlo. They each grabbed him and lifted him back up.

"Fuck you," Juan said.

"The truck," I said. "You're not stupid. You know how this works. You talk and you're okay, or you get beat until you talk anyway. Make life easy for yourself."

"I don't know shit."

I reached into my pocket and pulled out a pair of brass knuckles. His eyes went wide.

"Last chance," I said.

"I don't know who they were," he said quickly.

"There we go," I said softly.

"They came in late the night after we took the truck, just loaded all the shit into another big-ass van and drove away. Nobody stopped them or said shit to them."

"What did they look like? Did they speak Russian?"

"Nah, man, no Russian. One guy had a Russian accent, but that was it. They were white dudes, all normal looking."

I glanced at Vince, who just shrugged.

"Okay, Juan. Thanks a lot."

I turned to leave.

"Hey, man, what about me?"

I looked back at him. "Carlo and Joey here are going to rough you up, just so you know that if you speak of this to anyone, we will kill you."

"Hey, man!" he yelled, but Joey had already punched him square in the jaw.

I walked away, Vince at my side while Carlo and Joey beat Juan senseless.

"What do you think?" Vince said when we were upstairs.

"I don't think it's the Russians," I said, "but we still don't have proof."

"You believe that guy?"

"Yeah," I said, nodding, "I do."

Vince shrugged. "Okay, boss. What now?"

"Now we go home and eat some fucking dinner."

He laughed as we headed back out onto the street.

Truth was, I wasn't sure where we needed to go. It was becoming clearer and clearer to me that the Russians weren't the ones behind everything, but that left a huge question mark.

Was is one of our own? Was it one of theirs, working on his own? Or some totally different third party?

I needed more information, but it was so frustratingly scarce. We had our guys keeping tabs on the area's market, looking for any large influx of olive oil, but so far there was nothing.

Unless the guys were unloading their goods in some different state, then they were still holding on to the stuff. And I doubted that they'd move the stuff between states; that'd make it a federal offense.

We climbed into the car and began to roll back toward the compound.

Chapter Twenty-Three: Natalie

I was practically buzzing with excitement as I walked away from the stables.

I couldn't believe Lucas. He always acted like such an asshole, such a confident dick, but he had been tender, almost kind. He was interested in my life, he had asked questions, and he had even told me things that seemed private.

It was almost like he wanted to open up to me.

And yet he still held back. I could sense it, sense that there was something more to him that I couldn't access.

I wanted to figure it out. I wanted to know him, wanted him to give me everything all at once. I knew that was greedy and not fair, but it was the truth. I was falling into him, becoming his, and I hadn't even realized it until those moments in the barn.

Plus, there was the way he made my body feel to consider.

I bit my lip, not thinking at all as I wandered into the house. I was starving, which was mostly why I had left, and my head was completely in the clouds. I wandered around at random, thinking about what had happened.

About his hands on my hips, his cock between my legs, the dirty way he spoke, the strong way he commanded me to show him my ass.

Everything he said and everything he did worked to overwhelm me, to make me dizzy.

Dizzy with a lust and a desire that I hadn't ever felt before.

Almost without thinking, I unlocked a door and pushed it open. It was dark inside, but I heard some strange noises. Confused, I took a step inside.

I instantly regretted it.

Spread out on the ground was a single whit sheet, and on that sheet were two bodies. The room was a storage closet, but I wasn't looking too closely at my surroundings.

It was my mom and the driver, Franklin. He had his face between her legs, and they were both completely naked.

It took half a second to understand the scene. Franklin was furiously eating out my mom right there in the closet.

He tipped her head back, and we made eye contact.

"Oh my god!" she yelled. "Oh my god!"

I stepped back, completely in shock, and slammed the door shut.

Holy fuck.

I backed up and started walking away as fast as I could.

I couldn't have seen that. Camille wouldn't be so stupid, so reckless. She wouldn't cheat on her brand-new mobster husband with one of his staff barely a month after having married him.

But clearly she would, because I saw her doing it.

Oh my god, disgusting!

I wanted to burn that image from my brain, to purge it from my mind. It was so gross, so wrong, so nasty. I practically sprinted down the hall, and it took me a minute before I figured out that I was one floor down, directly below my rooms.

I climbed the stairs and found the right door. I unlocked it and slammed it shut behind me.

I had just seen my mom cheating on her new husband.

I had never, ever seen my mom having sex. At least not that I could remember. And I really, really never wanted to repeat that as long as I lived.

I collapsed onto the bed and grabbed a pillow, shoving my face underneath it. I let out a loud, long scream.

That made me feel a little bit better.

I crawled out from under the pillow and stared blankly at the ceiling. Slowly, my disgust and shock was replaced with anger.

Camille did a lot of dumb shit. She brought around her boyfriends, she got too drunk at parties, she said horrible things to the media, and she even had a sex tape somewhere that I totally refused to ever watch.

But she had never directly endangered me. She had never done anything that could lead to anything that could actually harm me.

She went too far this time. She had fucked up so much in the past, but this was completely different.

There was a knock at my door, and I really didn't want to answer. But I knew I had to speak my mind or else never say it at all.

I pulled the door open.

"Honey," Mom said, "that wasn't what you think it was."

"Get in here."

She walked in and I slammed the door behind her.

"You have to understand," she said. "I'm so lonely here. I have no friends, and Franklin was so nice to me."

"Shut up," I said fiercely to her, surprised by my own anger. "Just shut up, okay?"

She nodded slowly.

"Do you even understand who these people are?" I asked her.

"Of course I do."

"Then you understand what they're capable of."

"Oh please," she said, laughing. "Artie will never find out."

"Stop rationalizing," I said, shaking my head. "This is serious, Mom. If

Arturo ever finds out, we could be dead, or worse."

"You're overreacting," she said.

"No, I'm not. You're fucking everything up for us again by acting like the completely messed-up wreck you really are."

She stared at me, shocked. I had never said anything like that before.

I felt bad. I really did. I had tried as hard as I could to never say things like that to her, to try to support her, even when she was embarrassing and insane.

But enough was enough. She was fucking up. She was fucking up everything, and not just for herself.

"We have a good thing here," I said softly. "We could actually like it here. You could be happy."

"You don't know anything, you silly girl," she said viciously.

I shook my head sadly. "Stop ruining your life. Grow up. Be good to Arturo. Try to find happiness."

"You don't know what you're talking about." She was on the verge of tears. "Arturo can't satisfy me. Sexually, I mean."

"Okay, gross. Enough," I said quickly. "Enough. Just stop."

"Honey," she said, coming toward me.

I held up a hand. "Just leave me alone, okay, Mom? We can pretend like this never happened. I'm sure that's what you want."

She looked at me for a long time. Then silently, she turned and left my room.

I watched her go. I felt devastated and exhausted. I had never come down on my mother before, but I was beginning to truly see her as the immature and messed-up person she was.

I walked over to my bed and climbed in, trying to will away the memories of Franklin's face between her legs.

I wanted to be normal. I wanted to be a family.

But then again, normal people didn't marry their stepbrother.

I groaned to myself, sighing into the pillow.

Chapter Twenty-Four: Lucas

I moved slowly through the halls of the compound, thinking to myself. It felt good to pace the mainly empty space, trying to get a handle on the situation.

Things were beginning to move fast, and yet we didn't have all the information we needed. I felt like I was trying to fight a guy with my hands tied behind my back.

I was stressed out, but some weird part of me thrived on the stress. I liked having a challenge, a puzzle to solve, and the higher the stakes, the more I wanted to step up. My head spun from all the different layers to my situation. There was Natalie, the hijacked shipment, the other bosses on my back, and of course my father.

As I walked, I suddenly found myself standing outside Natalie's room. I checked my watch; it was late, probably too late, but part of me didn't care. I could suddenly taste her skin on my tongue again, her body against mine, the tight squeeze of her pussy wrapped around my cock. I wanted to hear her say my name.

I knocked once and waited. I heard some muffled sounds, and then the door pushed open.

"Lucas?" Natalie asked.

"Can I come in?"

"Sure."

She stepped aside and I walked in, sitting down on her couch. She looked like she had been sleeping, her hair a bit askew, her sweatpants wrinkled, but I absolutely fucking loved it. The girl could be wearing absolutely anything, look like she hadn't slept for weeks, or be covered in mud and I'd still want her. It was absolutely uncanny how she affected me.

"Is everything okay?" Natalie asked nervously.

"Everything is fine." I patted the couch next to me. "Sit."

She shook her head and sat on the arm of a nearby easy chair. "It's been a rough night," she said.

"What happened?" I asked.

She sighed, shaking her head. "Just stuff with my mom."

I grinned wickedly. "Want me to take care of her? I can make her disappear, you know."

Her whole face suddenly drained of color. "No. Oh my god, Lucas, don't say that."

I held up my hands. "I'm just kidding, Nat. What's wrong with you?"

"Nothing," she said again.

I stood up and moved toward her, but she quickly walked away from me.

"What's wrong?" I asked again. "I can help."

"I saw something," she said slowly, "and I'm not sure I can tell you."

"You can trust me," I said, and I knew that I meant it. "We're already so deep in this together, I'm surprised you even question it."

"It's about your father."

"That's okay. You can tell me anything."

"I saw my mom having sex with one of the staff."

I stopped dead in my tracks. "What?"

The story came spilling out of her then. She told me about how she went for a walk and stumbled in on her mom and the driver, Franklin. I knew who she was talking about; he was relatively new to the compound but a pretty reliable worker.

"She said all this stuff about him," she continued, "like how he speaks Russian and a bunch of other languages and how nice he is. I think she's in love with him."

I cocked my head at her. "You really think so?"

"I don't know with her, honestly. She's been in love a million times and it has never once lasted."

I grinned. "So you're saying she's not really in love with Arturo?"

She sighed, exasperated. "I don't know, Lucas. I really don't know."

This was interesting. I had no clue how Arturo would react if he found out about Camille's indiscretions. He'd likely have the driver killed at the very least, probably divorce Camille, maybe even destroy her career.

Obviously I couldn't let that happen. I liked having Natalie around and didn't want to risk any harm coming to her. I knew I should be more loyal to my father, but what did the old fool expect? He had married a notorious reality television star. Did he think she was really going to stay faithful?

Maybe he already knew and didn't care. Maybe they had some sort of arrangement, though that didn't seem likely.

"This could be dangerous," I said.

"I know, Lucas," she agreed. "I'm scared."

"Don't be scared," I said, grabbing her hand and pulling her toward me. "I promise I won't let anything bad happen to you."

She wrapped her arms around me, burying her head in my shoulder. "How can you say that? He's your father."

"He's an old fool," I said softly, "but he isn't stupid. He knew what he was buying into with your mother. And I'm growing fond of you."

"I'm fond of you too," she said.

I laughed. "We shouldn't let your mother acting like a whore cause anything."

I felt her stiffen suddenly and pull herself away. "Excuse me?"

"I'm just saying, your mother being loose shouldn't get between the two of us."

"You called her a whore," Natalie said.

I narrowed my eyes. "Because she's acting like one."

"My mom isn't a whore."

I could tell this was about to spiral out of control. I wanted to pull it back, fix it, but I wasn't about to take what I had said back. Camille was acting like a whore. She was sleeping with another man in her husband's house after less than a month of marriage. If that wasn't loose behavior, I didn't know what was.

"It's the truth," I said. "Your mother is acting like a whore. That doesn't need to affect us, though."

Her face set into a neutral expression. "I think you should go, Lucas."

I laughed again, shaking my head. "Come on, Natalie, I'm on your side."

"And yet you're calling my mother a whore. I think you should go."

I shook my head and turned away from her. "Whatever you say, wife."

"Don't call me that."

"Good night."

I walked away, pulling the door open and heading out into the hall.

I balled my fists and headed back to my own rooms. I didn't understand her, had no clue why she had gotten so upset. She was the first to admit that her mother was a party girl and was an awful mom. And yet if I spoke the truth, suddenly she was going to get angry with me?

I yanked open my room's door and went inside. I headed over to the bar and poured myself a nice, stiff drink.

It made no sense. I wasn't the one acting out and treating her family like an asshole; that was Camille. I didn't get why Natalie would be angry with me, her only real ally and the only person who really gave a shit about her in the whole house. All for speaking the truth?

I slammed back my drink and collapsed onto the couch. I replayed the conversation over in my head, trying to figure out what was really going on.

And then something jumped out at me, something Natalie had said her mother had mentioned about the driver, Franklin.

He spoke Russian.

I stroked my chin, thinking. It was a pretty thin lead, but I was pretty thin on anything else at the moment. And besides, none of our guys spoke Russian, and most of them took pride in that. From what I knew about Franklin, he was just some low-level driver; what was a guy like that doing speaking multiple languages?

I got up and poured myself another drink. I was going to have to investigate this Franklin guy, just in case, which was annoying, since I was already busy as hell with everything else.

And now Natalie was pissed.

Oh well. She'd get over it eventually, or not. I wasn't going to go groveling back to her like some dog.

I slammed back my drink and headed to bed.

Chapter Twenty-Five: Natalie

I woke up late in the morning, feeling almost like I was hungover.

The conversations from the night before came swirling back into my

brain with a vengeance. The image of my mother and Franklin lingered too,

but I tried to keep myself from dwelling on that.

I got up and grabbed the breakfast tray from the hallway and carried it

inside. The coffee was still hot, which was exactly what I needed. I sipped

the strong, black stuff and looked out the window, frowning.

I couldn't believe how willful and reckless my mother was. She was

putting us both at risk. Lucas seemed to think that everything would be

okay, or at least that he would make sure I was protected, but that didn't

make me feel much better. I wanted my mother to be okay as well, not just

me.

Even though she was crazy and selfish and stupid, she was still my mother. And Lucas just couldn't call her a whore, just couldn't disrespect her that way.

Even if she was acting like a whore.

I couldn't let him talk to me that way. He didn't seem to understand, didn't seem to care about anything other than the fact that he was being nice to me and that he was technically right about my mom. He completely missed the point. I wanted him to respect me, and part of that respect meant he couldn't call my mother a whore.

Maybe I had overreacted. I didn't feel as angry about it this morning, but still. I knew I had to draw the line somewhere, or else risk letting him talk to me however he wanted.

I felt at a complete loss. I had pushed away my biggest ally in the house right at the time that I needed him the most. And the feeling of his skin against mine kept ringing in my ears, infusing into everything else. Everything had happened so fast, and right at the moment when I was feeling the best about the sudden change in my life.

I was almost back to square one. It felt like I had finally broken through with Lucas, finally given myself up to him despite the obstacles, and suddenly my mother fucked up and sent it all careening off a cliff.

Frustrated, I dressed quickly and went walking through the halls. The place felt like a museum all of a sudden, and I had nowhere I could go that was even slightly comfortable. I felt like I had to keep my hands to myself and stay as quiet as possible, or else someone would yell at me.

Almost on a whim, I found myself heading toward Louisa's room. I didn't know why, but I felt like she was someone I could talk to. Maybe that was dangerous; maybe she was closer with her father than she let on, and telling her about what my mother was doing could cause some real problems.

But I had a feeling about her, and I couldn't shake it. I stopped outside her door and knocked.

"Go away," I heard her yell from inside.

"Louisa?" I called back. "It's Natalie."

There was a pause. "Hold on."

I waited a second and listened to what sounded like furniture moving around. A minute later, the door slowly pulled open.

"Hey there, sister," she said, smiling.

"Hi, Louisa. Mind if I come in?"

She cocked her head. "You look like shit."

"Thanks." She turned and let me in and I followed her. We sat down on her couches.

Instantly, I couldn't help but notice the influx of computer equipment. It all looked like it was wired into a central mainframe computer, with all her other computers running complicated-looking programs. I could tell it was way above my head, even with my own solid knowledge of the field.

"What's all this?" I asked her.

"Don't worry about that crap," she said, waving her hand. "It's just for my gaming."

"Doesn't look like gaming."

She stared at me. "What did you need, Natalie?"

I sighed, looking down at my hands. "Had a weird night last night."

"What'd my brother do?"

I laughed. "How'd you know?"

"It's always that way in this house. They fuck up and we're left trying to figure out how to put it all back together."

"Not always," I mumbled.

"So what did Prince Lucas say?"

"Well," I said slowly, "it's a bit of a long story."

"Tell me. Now I'm curious."

"It involves my mom and your dad. And it's not very good."

She snorted. "I don't give much of a shit about Arturo, but I'll tell you what. You tell me this story, and I'll tell you one of my own."

I raised an eyebrow. "What do you mean?"

"I'll tell you why I haven't left my room."

"Okay," I said. I didn't know why I trusted her or why I was taking the deal, but something told me I should.

And so I told her. Starting with walking in on my mother and ending with her brother's comments, I told her everything I could remember.

It came out of me in one giant rush. Louisa sat there staring at me, not really reacting one way or the other as I gave her all the details. I actually felt pretty silly when I told her how angry I had been at her brother, but I couldn't really skip that part.

Finally, I finished and felt tired. Better, like I had drained a wound out or something, but so tired.

"None of that surprises me," Louisa finally said when I was finished.

"Really?" I asked. "Not even my mother?"

She shrugged. "I don't know your mother, but she's a person and people make mistakes."

"You're right. And I mean, I get where Lucas is coming from."

"Don't defend him," Louisa said fiercely.

I felt a bit taken aback. "Sorry. I mean, I was just saying."

"Listen, Natalie," she said. "If you're going to stick around, you should know something. The men here, they're stuck in the Old World."

"What do you mean?"

"They want everything to be black and white. And in that mindset, women are just frail creatures that cook and clean. Women are either saints or they're whores. There's no room for a nuance of emotion, for sexual feeling, nothing."

I felt surprised, but it was something that I understood without having ever really said it before. The compound was like the old days in how everything worked, complete with servants.

"I get that," I said. "I know Lucas didn't mean anything by it, and he was probably right. But I want him to know that he has to respect me and my mother, even when she's acting like a whore."

Louisa nodded. "Good. Luca is probably the most progressive of the bunch. He'll figure it out and come around eventually. But don't let him off easy."

"Thanks. That makes me feel better."

"And about your mom," Louisa said. "Don't tell anyone else. My father can be a vengeful, violent man. You're right to feel afraid."

I felt a spike of worry hit my stomach. "What should I do?"

"Nothing," Louisa said. "Lucas will protect you all. He's not so bad, deep down."

I nodded. She had confirmed my worst fears, but she also had strangely made me feel better.

"Okay," I said. "Now it's your turn. Why haven't you left this room?"

She laughed, grinning. "It's funny. It's actually related to what we're talking about."

"What, my mom being a whore?"

"No. The Old-World mentality, the sexism." She paused and adjusted herself and then began talking.

"I was never good at school. I was never interested in it, even though I had always been great with computers. School wasn't hard for me; it was just boring. And plus, I knew what my father and my brother did. I understood what sort of family we were.

"But they kept me from it. They acted like they were protecting me, but I never needed protecting. Finally, I dropped out of school, bitterly disappointing my father. The next day, I demanded that he let me join the family business. I told him that I was a Barone like any one of them and that I deserved to be a part of it.

"He refused. He told me a woman's place was not anywhere near their business. He wanted me to go back to school, to meet a man and get married, to give him grandchildren. Naturally, that pissed me off. In retrospect, I understood he was trying his best to give me a good life, but I didn't want his idea of a good life. I wanted the life that I wanted, and I want to be a part of the Barone family.

"And so I went into my rooms and I've stayed here ever since. It pains my father greatly that I refuse to leave this piece-of-shit room. It's my prison and my statement. I will not leave until my father, or the next leader of the family, allows me my rightful place."

I didn't know what to say. I stared at her, seeing Louisa in an entirely new light.

I had assumed she was a weird, eccentric, crazy person. And she was weird and eccentric, no doubt. But she wasn't crazy.

She was strong. I could see her strength and defiance written in every expression, in every fiber of her being, in every word and gesture. And I was beyond impressed.

"That's incredible," I said softly.

"It's not so amazing. It's just what I have to do." She stood and walked back over toward her computers and began to tinker with them.

"But what happens if your father never gives in?"

"Then I'll die in this room, I guess," she said almost off-handedly.

I could hardly believe her. I shook my head and stood up. "You're amazing, Louisa. I wish I could have half of your determination."

"You do," she said, not looking at me.

"I'm not so sure."

"Stop feeling so bad for yourself. If you want something, take it."

I looked at her for a second and let that sink in. "Okay. Thanks."

"And, Natalie?" she asked. "Your secret is safe with me. I have no love for my father and his little boys' club."

"Thanks," I said, though I wasn't sure which secret she meant. I got the feeling that she meant all of them.

She continued working on her computers, and I got the sense that our conversation was over. I walked over to the door, pulled it open, and left. She didn't even glance in my direction.

The door shut behind me and I suddenly felt so much better. I felt lighter. Louisa was an inspiration, and her strength made me feel stronger just for having spoken with her.

I didn't know what I was going to do about Lucas, but like Louisa had said, I should take what I wanted.

There was no shame in it.

I headed back toward my room, my head abuzz with questions and plans.

Chapter Twenty-Six: Lucas

I stood with Vince on a small bridge overlooking a steam. We were well back in the woods in the back of the compound, well away from anyone that could possibly overhear.

"Well?" he asked. "Why'd you drag me out into the goddamn forest?"

"I got a lead," I said.

"Must be serious."

"Might be, but it might not be." I paused, throwing a stone into the water. "You know that young driver, Franklin?"

"Nice guy," Vince said. "What's the deal?"

"I got some information about him. Apparently he speaks multiple languages, and Russian is one of them."

Vince paused, thinking. "What's a driver doing speaking a bunch of languages?"

"My question exactly. Knowing Russian isn't all that suspicious, but if he's so smart, why's he just driving us around?"

"Maybe he's trying to work his way up?"

I shook my head. "I spoke with Roger. He said Franklin never mentioned any languages when he got hired. Said that Franklin just seemed like another city goon looking to get into the crew."

"Seems odd," Vince said, "leaving that bit off your resume. How'd you find this out?"

"Can't say."

Vince raised an eyebrow. "That's new. What, you don't trust me?"

"I do," I said, "but I'm choosing to hold this one back."

"Okay, boss. Your call."

We stood looking out over the water together in silence. I wondered how many times we'd come back to this spot to talk about confidential shit over the years. I'd known Vince most of my life; we were around the same age, and he had joined the crew around the same time that my father had allowed me to start getting my feet wet in it.

But as loyal as he was, Camille's indiscretions were too dangerous to share. I didn't know who Vince spoke to or who he trusted, or what he joked about when he was drunk. If it ever slipped out, even by mistake, I couldn't live with myself. I wasn't about to be the reason Natalie got thrown out with her trashy mother.

"So what's the plan?" Vince asked finally.

"Research him," I said. "And have one of the boys keep an eye on him."

"Got it. Anything else?"

"Keep it low, if you can."

"Will do. Only trusted guys."

"Good."

We began walking back toward the compound.

"I gotta ask you boss," Vince said, "about your sister."

"Louisa?"

"Natalie."

"She's my stepsister."

He shrugged. "Whatever. She's your wife, too."

"Where's this going?"

"I just want to know what you're doing with her. That's all."

I eyed him. "Seems like it isn't your business."

"It is and it isn't, boss. If you're actually into this girl, fine, great. But if you're just messing around, maybe it's not the best time to be putting your dick into something dangerous?"

I had to take a deep breath to steady myself.

I knew that Vince had my best interests in mind. I knew that he didn't mean anything by the way he was speaking. We always talked about women that way. It was all bravado and fun. But for some reason, I despised it when he talked about Natalie that way.

She was different. I knew it from the moment I saw her in the club and decided to make her my wife. I knew it when she moved in, and in every moment I was around her.

"Don't ask me about this again," I said to him.

He shrugged. "Okay. Your call."

We walked back toward the house in silence. Vince waved and peeled off toward the west wing, probably to get started on researching Franklin, and I walked back toward the house alone.

My mind was abuzz with Natalie. Just the mention of her name set my veins on fire. I wanted her again, needed her. The thought of her drove me wild with desire.

But she was pissed. I hadn't heard from her since the night before when she threw me out of her room for talking shit about her mother. In the cold light of day, I understood that I had crossed a line in calling her mother a whore, even if she was acting like one. I wouldn't accept that sort of talk about my family, and I couldn't expect any less of Natalie.

But I wasn't about to apologize. That just wasn't my style. I wasn't going to go groveling at her feet like a pathetic loser, especially not after she had kicked me out.

Still, I wanted to make it right. I wanted to taste her again, and that wasn't happening unless I owned up to my errors.

I grumbled to myself as I walked into the house, trying to figure out how I could win her back over without actually saying sorry.

Because I wasn't really sorry. Her dumbass whore of a mother was threatening to fuck everything up already. I had known it was only a matter of time before Camille blew up, but I had hoped that was at least a few months away. Back when I didn't know Camille or Natalie, I almost was rooting for her to fuck up, if only to rub my father's stupid mistake in his face.

But suddenly I found myself caring. Natalie did that to me.

And so I had an idea. Simple, but hopefully effective. I headed toward the kitchen to make it happen.

Chapter Twenty-Seven: Natalie

I was ready to call it a night. I'd spent the day wandering around the grounds, and I was prepared to simply admit to myself that I was going to be doing absolutely nothing all day.

I had my hand on my room's door when I got the text. I pulled my phone out of my pocket and saw Lucas's name and his short message. *Come to room 34-C. I have something for you.* That was it, no context.

I bit my lip, unsure. I was still annoyed with him, but in the long run it really wasn't something worth hating him over forever. And besides, I still felt so drawn to him, even through the danger.

Louisa's words rang through my ears as well. I needed to take what I wanted.

Making up my mind, I turned and headed back down the hall.

It took me longer than I'd like to admit to actually find the room. It was a small door tucked into a back corner of a random hallway on the third floor. It looked totally normal, pretty much like everything else in the house, and I wondered why Lucas was calling me there.

Maybe his father would be waiting on the other side. He'd force me to tell Arturo the truth about my mother, and then they'd both throw us out.

Or maybe he just wanted to be an asshole some more and figured a neutral place was the best way to go about it.

I didn't know why my brain instantly went to worst-case scenarios. I'd been out of it all day, and my paranoia wasn't helping.

Taking a deep breath, I unlocked the door with my card and pushed it open.

What I saw took my breath away.

The room had paintings on every inch of the walls. Beautiful paintings, gorgeous, expensive art. It was a lot like the stuff hung in the halls, but I recognized some of them for once, stuff by Picasso and Renoir. Expensive, serious art.

But that wasn't what caught my attention. The room was lit by hundreds of white candles, each set on every single surface of the room. Then, in the very center was a small table set as if it were some expensive, fancy restaurant.

"What do you think?"

I looked over to my right and saw Lucas standing there with a drink in his hand.

"Did you do this?" I asked.

"I had help."

I took a step inside. "Is this an apology?" I asked.

"It's something like that."

I frowned. "Lucas."

"Wait," he said, holding up a hand. "Before you tell me off, listen. I won't apologize for what I said, but I understand your reaction. You want me to respect your family as I want you to respect mine."

I nodded. "Exactly."

He walked toward me. "I want you to know that I respect you, Natalie. I respect you very much."

"Then apologize."

"No." He stopped near me, and I could feel my heart pounding.

"Don't be stubborn," I said.

"I can't apologize for speaking the truth," he answered. "But I'm hoping you can understand that."

I took a deep breath. Did I really need to hear the words from him? I looked around the room and knew that I didn't.

Lucas wasn't the type of man to do this sort of grand gesture for someone. That much was obvious. He was gruff and intense, and it didn't seem like romance was something he ever even considered.

And yet he had put all this together for me simply because I had felt disrespected. He understood why I was angry and was taking steps to try to fix it.

"Fine" I said, smiling. "Okay. I get it."

"Good." He pulled me against him and kissed me hard.

I felt a rush of blood to my head as he held me and kissed me.

I knew I needed to take what I wanted.

And in that moment, I wanted him. I was so full of stress, so pent up and frustrated, that I needed him.

Without thinking, I reached down and felt his cock with my hand. He grunted his surprise, but I could feel that he was hard already.

"Hard from one kiss," I whispered.

"You have that effect on me," he admitted.

I began to stroke him. "I want you to fuck me, Lucas."

He took my hair and pulled me close. "Say please," he whispered in my ear.

"Please fuck me, Lucas," I said, stroking his hard cock. "Please fuck my pussy hard. Make me come again."

He grabbed me by the hips and steered me away from the candles. There was another door in the back wall. He quickly pushed it open and led me into another room filled with paintings, though this one didn't have any open flames. Dimly I realized that this whole wing was probably one long gallery.

He pressed me against a wall, banging against a painting. He wasted no time in pulling my shirt over my head and kissing my neck. I continued to stroke him, working his cock, wanting him so badly, needing him.

I quickly unbuttoned his pants, yanking his zipper down. I dropped to my knees, pulling his pants down around his ankles. I reached up and pulled down his boxer briefs, taking his thick, hard cock in my hand.

"I like this new aggressive Natalie," he grunted as I pressed his cock between my lips.

I began to work him, sucking his tip in and out of my mouth, tasting his salty skin, loving the way he grunted.

"Suck that cock, Natalie," he said. "Fuck yes. You really are a dirty girl for me, aren't you?"

I kept working him, and he pressed his hands to the back of my head, moving his cock deep between my lips, deep into my throat. He groaned loudly as I sucked him, jerking him off, working his cock.

I was starving for him, in a frenzy. I needed it, needed him ready. I could feel my pussy dripping wet, ruining my panties, but it didn't matter. All I needed was him inside me.

"Suck me dry," he groaned. "Work that cock."

I kept moving, my head bobbing, taking his cock in my mouth. I looked up at him as I sucked him, loving the expression of pure hunger on his face.

After another minute, he moved his hips back and reached down to lift me to my feet.

He quickly tore off what was left of my clothes. He unhooked my bra, yanked off my jeans, and spun me around. I put my hand up on the wall as he kicked my legs apart.

"You want this, don't you?" he said.

"Fuck, please," I said. The thrill was pounding through my veins. I was afraid I was going to come the second he entered me.

He reached forward and began to tease my soaked pussy with his fingers. His other hand slapped my ass.

"I love this body," he said. "Your pussy is like fucking fire, you know that?"

"God I need to feel you inside me," I said, writhing against his hands, pleasure flooding my mind.

He moved back and grabbed something from his pants. I looked back and watched him tear open a condom wrapper and slowly slide the condom down along his thick cock.

He grabbed my hips, pushing himself against me. I felt his breath hot on my neck. I could barely think as I ground my body against him, begging for his cock, needing his cock more than anything.

"You're mine, Natalie," he whispered in my ear. "You're my wife.

Your body is mine to do with as I please."

"Yes. Please. I'm yours."

And then he pressed his cock deep between my legs.

I threw my head back, releasing a long, low moan.

It was exactly what I wanted and needed. Pleasure exploded through my mind as he began to fuck me in slow and amazing thrusts, deep in and deep out.

"Oh my god," I moaned. "Oh fuck, Lucas. Keep fucking me."

"I love the feel of this tight cunt," he whispered in my ear.

"Fuck me rough," I begged. "Make me come."

I felt his thrusts get deeper, more insistent. He slapped my ass, hard, and it only made my hips rock back against him, working his cock inside me. I kept my hands pressed on the wall as he fucked me, slamming his cock deep inside me.

His hands were strong on my hips. He reached up, feeling my breasts, my clit, pulling my hair. He ravaged me, fucked me rough, hard, deep. It was what I needed, what I'd been thinking about all day long.

"Lucas," I said, over and over. "Fuck me, Lucas."

"Every inch of this cunt is mine," he said. "I want to feel you come on this cock. I want you to scream my name while you come."

He kept working my pussy, fucking me deep, and his hand moved around to rub my clit.

It was too much. I was on the edge before, and his savage, powerful thrusts mixed with his fingers on my clit shoved me over the edge.

"Lucas," I said loudly. "Oh fuck. Oh, Lucas." I came loudly, saying his name again and again as he fucked me, my body sweating, my skin his, everything his.

He continued to work me insistently, and although my orgasm had passed, I could tell he was working himself up. He was close as he slammed into me, but I wanted one last thing.

I moved forward, slipping him out of me, and then dropped to my knees. He looked surprised as I pulled off his condom and began to suck his cock like I'd never done it before. I sucked him hard and fast, his big dick filling my mouth, and I knew that the surprise of it was what pushed him over.

He came in my mouth hard. I swallow every single drop of his cum, savoring it, loving that I could surprise him and get him off like that.

"Oh fuck, Natalie," he groaned as the orgasm slowly faded. "Holy shit, girl."

I licked him clean and smiled up at him. "Did you like that?"

He growled and lifted me up, wrapping his arms around me and kissing me savagely.

Slowly the kiss ended, and I smiled at him, my head spinning, our naked, sweating bodies pressed together. "I'll take that as a yes," I said to him.

"You drive me insane," he whispered.

He held me like that for a while, kissing me softly, whispering in my ear.

Eventually, we got dressed.

"Might as well enjoy this meal," he said.

"I forgot about that," I said, laughing.

"Right. There's a room full of candles in there. Figured I couldn't do this to you there or else I'd burn down the building."

"A very smart call."

We laughed together and went back into the other room.

It felt right as we sat down. Lucas sent a text, and a few minutes later, a staff member arrived with our meal.

We ate, talked, laughed and laughed. It felt good, right, to sit there and eat with him. My whole brain was on fire from the orgasm still, and I felt incredible.

He was incredible. He was driving me wild. Even after that intense and vigorous sex, I still found myself wanting more, and I realized I might never get my fill of him.

He was all the surprise I needed.

Chapter Twenty-Eight: Lucas

It was late by the time we finished dinner.

I'd never done something like that for a woman before. Normally I never took it past a single night, but with Natalie it was different. She made my blood boil, made me crazy, made me want to do things I'd never done before. Except apologize, of course. Maybe that was just my pride, though.

We walked out of the gallery room. I trusted that the staff would extinguish all those candles before they set a few million dollars worth of art on fire.

"Still mad?" I asked her as we headed back together to my room.

"A little bit," she said, smiling.

"Good. Take it out on me in a few minutes."

She pressed herself against me and kissed me. "I can handle that."

"I'm not sure you can," I said. "You're trying, but I don't think you can handle how much I want to make you come."

"You're all talk," she said, kissing me again. "But I want to see you back it up."

I smacked her ass as she walked away from me, grinning to myself. My cock was hard already, and I couldn't wait to show her exactly what I meant.

The whole night had been exciting, starting with the rough, incredible sex surrounded by priceless art and finishing with a long, comfortable dinner. I could feel myself slipping. I was falling into something I couldn't quite explain, something I had never experienced before. Watching her look back over her shoulder and smile at me made my stomach do flips. I wanted to take her right there in the hallway and make her feel things she had never imagined before.

"Sir?"

I glanced over to my left and Natalie stopped walking. A staff member was looking at me.

"Yes?"

"Sir, your father requests your presence in his study."

I sighed. "What the hell does he want at this hour?"

"I'm sorry, sir, he didn't say. But he seemed very agitated."

I paused and glanced at Natalie. I could see what she was thinking clearly on her face: Arturo knew about the two of us.

And I was thinking the same thing. He was bound to find out eventually. Our marriage record was public and we weren't doing a good job hiding what we were up to. I had hoped we had more time to figure out what we were doing before Arturo got involved, but maybe that time was up.

"Okay," I said to the man. "I'll be there soon."

He nodded and walked off.

Natalie came over to me, frowning. "What does he want so late?"

"It's probably nothing," I said, smiling at her, covering up my worry. "Probably a business thing."

She nodded uncertainly. "I'm sure you guys do this sort of thing late at night all the time in your line of work."

"Crime is a twenty-four hour business."

She laughed softly. "Come to my room when you're done."

"Okay. I will."

She kissed me quickly and I watched as she walked off back down the hall.

Damn Arturo. I had been going to be cock deep in Natalie's pussy, and now I was going to have to sit around in my father's study and listen to him complain about some inane bullshit.

I headed off, walking through the familiar old hallways. I eventually stopped outside his study and took a deep breath.

I wasn't sure I was prepared for what was gong to happen inside. I had

no clue how Arturo was going to react to finding out that I had married my

stepsister. I expected him to be angry, but how angry was the real question.

Maybe I was going to have to get violent, possibly wrestle control of the

mob out from under him. Or he was going to order me to divorce her, and

that would be that.

I knocked hard.

"Come in," I heard him yell.

I pushed inside. "You summoned me?" I said.

"Sit."

He had a half-empty bottle of scotch sitting on his desk, which he

promptly poured into an unused glass for me. He topped himself off and

took a healthy swig.

"What's this about, Father?" I asked, sipping my own scotch.

It was the cheap stuff. That was a bad sign.

"I found something out an hour ago," he said, sounding sad.

"Something that angers me and saddens me."

I frowned, sipping my drink again. I savored the burn of the liquid as

it rushed down into my stomach.

"What's happening?" I asked.

"Security tape showed me the truth." He looked over toward his window, out at the ink-black yard. "I saw everything, Luca. Everything. Do you know how betrayed I feel?"

I opened my mouth and then shut it. I simply shook my head, remaining silent. I didn't know where he was going with this, and frankly I felt nervous. He seemed more sad than angry, though that was probably because of the alcohol.

"I am a fool, you know? A fool for trusting those around me. I am always betrayed in the worst ways."

So it was true. He had found out. My heart was racing.

"I can explain," I said slowly.

He looked at me sharply. "You knew about this?"

I was taken aback. "About what?" I asked.

"About my whore wife," he spat angrily. "She's been cheating on me, Luca, fucking some lowly driver."

I stared at him, open-mouthed.

He didn't know about me and Natalie. He had found out about Camille and Franklin.

Which, in some ways, was much, much worse.

"I can't believe it," I said.

"Nobody can," he said mournfully, drinking his scotch. Clearly he had already forgotten my slipup. "I was in love, Luca. Love blinds us to the faults of other. I never saw this, never imagined this, but I could have." He slammed his glass down, sloshing the liquid over his desk.

"What is going to be done?" I asked.

He glared at me. "That's why you're here. I want you to find this driver and shoot him in the skull."

I nodded. "What about Camille?"

"I will send people for her when I am ready. Her and her daughter will be held until I can decide what to do with them."

My heart skipped a beat. "Her daughter too?"

"Both of the fucking harlots will pay for this," he said violently.

"Natalie is innocent, completely unlike her mother. Let the girl go. I will take care of Camille."

He stared at me. "Have you grown fond of your whore stepsister?"

"I'm just not in the business of punishing the innocent," I said.

"Too fucking bad." He finished off what was left of his scotch. "Kill the driver. I will take care of the women."

I stood, my head spinning. "Very well," I said.

"Go." He turned back to his bottle, forgetting about me.

I finished my drink and then left his office quickly, walking fast. I had to think at top speed, had to decide how things were going to happen.

Because they were going to happen, and very, very fast.

Fortunately, Arturo seemed too drunk to do anything anytime soon. If I knew him, he'd likely finish that bottle off before he decided to send some men after the women, which meant I likely had a half hour head start before his goons came.

Finally, I reached her door and knocked loudly. "Open up," I called out.

I waited a pulse-pounding thirty seconds, my mind spinning over the possibilities. Finally, the door pulled open.

"Good evening, brother," Louisa said. "What's happening?"

"Arturo found out about Natalie's mom," I said, "and is going to snatch them. We need to get them both out."

I had no clue how she would respond. Lou hadn't been a part of family politics in a long time. Though we were still close, she refused to entertain any conversations about the business until she was allowed to be officially a part of it.

"Come in," she said.

I walked in and she shut the door. "You'll help?"

"Of course, dear brother," she said, grinning. "I was bored tonight. I could use a little action."

I let out a relieved breath. "Thanks, Lou," I said.

She sat down at her computer and began typing. "You get them out. I'll handle the rest."

"I'll owe you one."

She looked back at me. "I'm not dong this for you, Luca."

"Why, then?"

"I like having a sister."

I smiled as she turned back to the computer. Once I was sure she wasn't saying anything else, I quickly left her rooms and headed toward Natalie, my pulse pounding, my excitement rising.

Chapter Twenty-Nine: Natalie

I lounged on the couch in only a pair of panties and a black bra. It was the lingerie set that Lucas had bought for me as a joke, but now it didn't seem so funny.

It seemed exciting.

I felt drunk on the thought of him, beyond excited for him to come back to me. I hoped whatever business he was dealing with would be over soon, because I was so impatient for him.

Dinner had been amazing. Sure, he was too proud to actually say the words, but I could tell that he was sorry. Lucas wasn't the kind of man to grovel, let alone to make some sort of big romance gesture. And yet there he was, making the gesture for me anyway, and I could barely explain how exciting and important that was.

He made me feel something I could barely describe. Not just the sex, though that was incredible. No, it was in the moments afterward, when we spoke about our lives, flirted, laughed, and teased each other. It was in those moments that I knew I had something, something important.

It was something that I hoped would last. For the first time, I really felt good about being in the compound. Not just about being a part of Lucas's life, but actually being a part of the family.

Sure, the mob thing still made me feel a little uncomfortable, but at least it was exciting and powerful and made my life feel like something more than it was. If someone like Louisa could be strong, then so could I.

My heart practically skipped a beat when I heard the knock at my door. "Just a second!" I called out. I wrapped a light silk robe around my body and padded over to the door.

"It's me," I heard Lucas call out. "Hurry up, Nat."

"Don't be so impatient," I said, smiling as I opened the door.

The look on his face completely wiped the smile off mine.

"Lucas?" I asked as he moved into the room, shutting the door. "What's wrong?"

"Has anyone been here?" he asked.

"No, nobody."

"Do you know where your mother is?"

"No. What's wrong?"

He took me by the shoulders. "Listen to me carefully, Nat. Things are going to happen very fast from here, and you need to trust me. Can you

trust me?"

I felt dizzy. "Of course I can. Just tell me what's happening."

"Arturo knows about your mom, about her cheating with the Franklin

kid."

I felt like I was falling through the floor. A spike of fear ran down my

spine. "What are we going to do?" I asked.

"I'm taking care of it," he said. "First, we need to get your mom here.

Can you call her?"

"Okay." I walked over to the phone numbly and dialed her room

number. It rang and rang, but nobody answered. "She's not in her room," I

said.

"Fuck. Try her cell."

I nodded, dialing. It rang twice, and then she answered. "Hi, sweetie,"

she said.

"Mom? Where are you?"

"Oh just taking a little late-night dip. Did you know there's an indoor

pool here?"

"Mom, can you come to my room right now?"

She sighed. "What's wrong, honey?"

"Listen. It's really, really important that you get here right now."

"Can it wait? I was just about to finish my laps."

"Please," I said. "Please. You need to get here right away."

I didn't know if it was because I pushed or if it was because of the fear that she heard, but for whatever reason she listened.

"Okay," she said. "Be there in a minute."

I hung up the phone and looked at Lucas. "She's coming."

"Good," he said. "Pack a bag. And one for your mother too, if you can."

I nodded, moving quickly. I grabbed a suitcase from the closet and began to throw things into it. Meanwhile, Lucas paced nervously, constantly glancing at his watch.

I filled the suitcase with enough clothes for me and my mom. We weren't exactly the same size, but I figured it wouldn't matter. We could get more clothes down the line.

Five minutes passed, though every second felt like an eternity. Lucas was on edge, pacing back and forth like a caged animal. His intensity made me feel both comforted and terrified. I believed that if anyone could get us to safety, it was him, but he was still so strong and terrifying.

"What's the plan, Lucas?" I asked him.

"I know a place you and your mom can stay until this all blows over."

I wanted to press him, but suddenly there was a knock at my door.

Lucas looked at me, holding a hand up for me to be quiet. I watched as he pulled a gun from his pants. He slowly opened the door.

"What's wrong, Nat? I was just—" Mom started to say, but Lucas quickly pulled her inside. "Lucas! Oh, what are you doing?"

"Mom," I said to her, "Arturo knows about you and Franklin."

She gaped at me for a second. "You silly, dumb bitch," she said icily. "You shouldn't have told."

I was so completely taken aback that I barely even noticed when Lucas stepped between the two of us. "Natalie," he said. "Natalie, calm down."

I realized that I was trembling and barely in control of myself. I took a deep breath.

"It wasn't her, Camille," Lucas said. "Arturo saw you on security footage."

Her face dropped. "Oh. Oh dear. I'm so sorry, Natalie," she said.

"Listen to me, Mother," I replied. "We're going to do exactly what Lucas says tonight. Once this is all over, and we're both safe, I want you out of my life."

"But, sweetie," she said, "it was just a mistake. I'm so sorry."

"I'm tired of your mistakes." I turned away. "We're done after tonight. If you care about me at all, you'll at least listen to Lucas."

"Okay," she said softly. "Okay, sweetie. I'm so sorry."

But I wasn't listening. I quickly threw on a sweatshirt and some sweatpants and tossed another pair to Camille. She pulled the clothes on over her still-damp bathing suit.

"Okay, listen up," Lucas said. "The plan is simple. We're heading down to the garage where we'll grab a car. From there, we'll go to safe house where you two will stay until this all blows over."

"Sounds easy," Camille said.

"What about the cameras? And the gates? And the guards?"

"I'll worry about all that," he said. He walked over and put his hands on my shoulders. "You can do this."

I nodded. "I know."

He kissed me softly. I kissed him back, wrapping my arms around him.

Camille cleared her throat. We broke apart.

"What about Franklin?" Camille asked.

"Don't worry about him. Just follow me," Lucas said.

"But he's in danger, isn't he?"

I glared at Camille. "Stop. Just listen to Lucas."

She nodded, frowning.

"Okay. We're heading out now. Stay close to me. Don't run. Got it?"

"Got it," I said.

"Come on."

I grabbed the suitcase and followed him, Camille right on my heels.

We moved out into the hall and started heading in what I assumed was the direction of the garage. I was instantly lost after only a few turns.

We didn't see anyone, or at least we didn't see an unusual number of people. The whole place was quiet, which wasn't a surprise since it was so late at night. But it felt eerie, strange, and unnerving. We were running for our lives through an enormous mansion, but that mansion was empty. The only sounds were our footsteps and the wheels of the suitcase rolling behind me.

We went down a series of short halls that finally opened up into the kitchen. Lucas stopped and turned toward us.

"Garage is coming up," he said. "Things might get hairy up there. Just stay behind me, okay?"

"Got it," I said.

We began walking again, but I could tell that Camille wasn't following. I stopped and turned toward her.

"Come on," I said. "We have to move."

She frowned at me. "Sorry, kiddo," she said, "but I have to help Franklin."

"Camille," Lucas growled, "it's too late for him. We have to go."

"Wait for me," she said before turning and running back down the hall.

"Wait!" I said, but before I could go after her, Lucas grabbed me.

"Stop," he growled. "Stop struggling."

"Let me go. I have to get her!"

"Natalie, listen to me," he said fiercely. "She made her choice, over and over again. She doesn't care about you. Why do you care about her?"

"She's my mom. She's all I have left."

"I know," he said. "I'm sorry. But she chose this. You have to let her go."

I knew he was right. I knew I couldn't keep paying for her mistakes, couldn't keep letting her bad choices affect me.

So I relaxed. Lucas let me go. "Ready?" he asked.

"Ready."

We began walking again through the kitchen. The staff ignored us entirely and obviously didn't care. Lucas even nodded to a few people, and they smiled back.

Soon we turned a corner and moved out into the garage. It was packed with cars, rows and rows of cars. Lucas led me toward the back, closest to the doors.

Standing there were two armed guards. Lucas held his hand up and stopped me. They were looking in our direction, probably because they had heard my suitcase, but hadn't seen us yet.

"I'll take care of them," he said.

I nodded, terrified, as he stepped out into the light.

"Evening, guys," he said.

"Boss," the one guy answered.

"I need a car tonight."

He nodded. "Where you going? Arturo said we're to monitor all cars that leave here."

"I got a package to deliver."

"Where to?"

He narrowed his eyes. "Not your business. Now get me the keys."

"Sorry, Lucas," the other guy said. "Did your father approve this?"

"I approved this," Lucas growled.

"Sorry," the guy said again. "Orders are orders."

Lucas moved so fast I barely followed. His fist shot out, catching the first guy in his throat. He doubled over. The second man stepped back, reaching for his gun. Lucas quickly grabbed the gun, forcing the guy back. He kicked the guy in the groin and smashed him in the face with his forehead. He toppled down.

The first guy came at Lucas. They tumbled down, but Lucas quickly twisted his body, landing on top. He smashed his fists into the guard's face until the man stopped moving.

Lucas quickly got up and checked the other man, disarming him.

"Natalie," he called out, "come on."

I moved out toward him, fear lancing through me.

"It's okay," he said. "Come on."

Lucas grabbed a pair of keys from the second guard's pockets and hit the unlock button. The big SUV two cars over blinked; it was the same

SUV Franklin usually drove.

"Probably here to make sure he didn't run," Lucas said.

"Are they okay?" I asked him.

He shrugged. "They'll live. Get in."

He threw my bag in the back as I climbed into the passenger seat. He got into the driver's side and the engine roared to life.

"Come on," he mumbled. A second later, the garage door started to open. He grinned hugely. "Hold on."

We flew out the open door, out onto the road heading toward the front gate.

As we drove, something caught my eye. "Lucas, stop!" I yelled.

He slammed on the brakes. "What's wrong?" he asked.

"It's my mom!"

We looked across the lawn and saw Camille sprinting toward us, followed by four men. I climbed into the backseat and threw open the door. "Camille!" I yelled.

She veered toward us, sprinting fast, her hair flopping in the wind. The men were yelling at her to stop, and I could tell Lucas was pissed, but I didn't care. It was my mother, after all. I couldn't just leave her.

Camille slammed into the car, practically diving inside. Lucas hit the gas and we lurched forward just before the men got to us. They were yelling, but we couldn't hear them as I yanked the door shut and we flew forward.

"I told you to wait," Camille said.

I glared at her. She didn't say anything else.

Up ahead, the gate was still shut. "Lucas," I said.

"It'll open."

"How?"

"Louisa. She's in control of the compound right now." I saw him grin in the rearview mirror. "The computers aren't just for games. She shut down the security cameras too, let us move around."

I nodded, and suddenly something welled up inside me. It was hope, and gratitude.

Louisa didn't have to help. Lucas didn't, either, but they both wanted to get me to safety. My mother too, I guessed. But I was willing to bet that they were both going to get into deep shit for this.

For all the insanity, for all the awful shit, I was happy that I was in their lives. I was happy they were in mine.

Ahead, the gate swung open. The guards in the booth were yelling, standing in the road.

Lucas pressed the gas down, the engine roaring.

The guys dove out of the way as the car shot out onto the main road. Lucas swung the car around, pointing it toward Chicago. The gate closed silently behind us, blocking the cars that were already starting to chase us.

Chapter Thirty: Lucas

I watched as the city flashed by, the lights blending into nothing. I was headed toward my own personal safe house, one of several that I kept scattered across the city. It wasn't exactly luxurious, but the girls would be safe there at least.

And I knew Louisa would be safe, too. No matter what she did, my father would never bring himself to punish her. She could play him like a fiddle, although she couldn't get him to allow her to join the business.

No, I was more worried about my ability to solve this problem. My father was not going to allow Camille and Natalie to simple go free; he'd scour the city if he had to. And if I knew my father, he wouldn't stop until someone gave them up.

Which meant that I had to lie low. I didn't know how I was going to convince him to pardon the girls, especially after I had taken out two of his guards pretty violently.

Worries within worries swirled in my mind as we drove silently toward the safe house. Even though I knew I was in a shitty situation, I felt incredibly alive. I glanced at Natalie and caught her looking at me. She smiled, and I smiled back.

I thrived under pressure, and this was the most pressure I had ever been under.

It took was twenty minutes to get to the house. I drove carefully, doubling back twice just to make sure that nobody was following. I pulled up outside the place and cut the engine.

The house was a row home in a sketchy neighborhood. Camille made a face. "We're staying here?" she asked.

Natalie glared at her and then looked at me. "Are you staying with us?"

"We'll talk inside," I said softly.

She nodded and went to climb out. She fumbled with something, and I watched her phone clatter down between her seat and the console.

"Shit," she said and began to dig it out.

I got out of the car and helped Camille climb out. I grabbed their bag from the trunk and put it on the sidewalk. Nat shoved something into her sweatshirt and climbed out of the car.

"Ready to see your home?" I asked.

Natalie nodded.

I walked up to the front door and unlocked it. We all walked inside together.

I watched their reactions carefully.

Natalie just smiled at me. Camille, though, looked like I was asking her to sleep inside of a dead, rotten corpse.

"It's not much," I said, "but it's safe. Nobody knows where this is."

"It's gross," Camille said.

We walked into the living room and I put their bag in the corner.

The place was pretty dingy, I had to admit. I hadn't exactly put a lot of effort into cleaning and furnishing over the years. We pulled the covers off the couch and the other furniture, revealing the mostly second-hand stuff. Nothing hung on the walls, and the kitchen was mostly bare, but there was enough in there for them to live. I knew the linen upstairs needed to be changed, but the clean stuff was in the closet, ready to be deployed.

It definitely wasn't the lavish rooms of the mob compound, but it wasn't so bad. Utilitarian and sparse, but not dirty.

"Where are you staying?" Natalie asked me as Camille climbed the stairs, saying something about finding her room.

"I can't stay here," I said, frowning.

"Why not?"

"Because my father is going to be looking for me. I can't risk leading him to you guys."

"Lucas," she said.

I grabbed her and pulled her close against me.

I wasn't going to let her down.

I wanted to stay with them. I wanted to sleep with Natalie, to hold her, to make her feel safe. But I also knew that I needed to be able to move around the city, and I couldn't risk getting followed if someone spotted me.

"I have another place," I said. "Vince will meet me there."

"Does he know about us?"

"Not yet. He doesn't know about this place, either."

"Okay."

"We can trust him, though."

She kissed me. "I believe you."

Camille came stomping back down the stairs. "How long are we here for?"

"That's what I wanted to talk to you about," I said. "I don't really know."

"Of course not," Camille said, sitting on the couch.

"But we need a few rules. First off, I need you both to give me your phones."

"No," Camille said flat out.

"Camille," I said slowly, "you can give it to me or I can take it. Your call."

Natalie handed me her phone. Camille got up and reluctantly placed hers on top of Natalie's.

"Okay," I said. "I'll get you new phones. Just be careful what you do online. Don't use your social media accounts. Don't post anything."

"Seriously?" Camille complained.

"Mom," Natalie snapped, "we're in hiding from the mobsters you pissed off, remember?"

Camille sighed but said nothing.

"You both also need to stay inside. You can't risk getting spotted."

"You're telling me," Camille said slowly, "that we're stuck in here without real internet for an amount of time you can't specify? Maybe forever?"

"Not forever," I said. "I'll fix this. But for now, you have to sit tight until it all blows over."

"No," Camille said, standing. "No, thanks. I'll go to the police. I'll hire bodyguards if I have to."

"Camille," Natalie said.

"No. I'm not doing this."

Natalie rounded on her. "Sit your ass down, you self-centered asshole," she said. "You're going to stay here and you're going to shut your fucking mouth the whole time or I'm going to beg Lucas here to duct tape you to a chair in the basement."

Camille stared at Natalie. "Don't speak to your mother that way."

"You're not my mother. You're just a problem," Natalie said.

Camille's expression was absolutely delightful.

"As fun as this is," I said, "I have to get going."

"Stay a little longer," Natalie said, pressing herself against me. "Please."

"Sorry, wife," I said to her. "Got to go."

We kissed, long and hard. Neither of us cared when Camille cleared her throat.

Eventually we pulled apart. "Come back soon," she said.

"First thing in the morning. You two need to rest."

She nodded. Reluctantly, I pulled away from her and left.

I quickly got into the car and began to drive. I needed to ditch it, so I parked it in a handicap spot out front of a government building and walked away. I caught a bus going south and got off two blocks from the safe house that I shared with Vince.

He was already there when I walked inside.

"Big night," he said, grinning.

I had my hand on my gun. "We good?"

"Still on your side, boss."

I relaxed. "I got the girls out."

"Yeah? I thought they'd be here."

"Sorry, Vince, but I got them in a spot only I know about."

"Good," he said. "Safer that way."

I sat down in a chair. Vince got up and handed me a glass of whisky.

"The fuck were you thinking?" he asked.

"I wasn't, honestly."

"Arturo is having a fucking fit. I barely got out of the compound with my head on."

"Sorry about that. I'll give you a warning the next time I have to escape with my stepsister and her slutty mom."

"Okay. Good."

We drank in silence then for a few minutes. It was close to four in the morning and I was absolutely exhausted. I knew the car would be towed or found soon; I wasn't sure which, and I didn't much care.

All I knew was that I had to come up with a plan, and fast.

"They find the kid?" I asked Vince.

"Apparently not," he said. "Someone must have warned him."

I laughed, shaking my head. "Camille. She disappeared during our escape. Must have warned him."

"Crazy bitch."

"She came tearing across the west lawn like a fucking psycho. I almost didn't stop."

We laughed together. I felt like I was beginning to relax, loosen up.

"How dumb can they be?" Vince asked.

"I'm more surprised at the kid. He at least knows my father."

"Yeah," Vince said. "He's lucky Camille is bat shit insane."

We fell into another silence.

"So," he asked me finally, "how the fuck do we get out of this one?"

"Not sure yet. Did you contact the other captains?"

"The loyal ones, yeah."

"And?"

"Same answers. They'll back your play."

I nodded. That was the last resort. If I couldn't reason or bargain with Arturo, I was going to have to go through with my plans for a coup.

And that wasn't going to be clean. If I tried to take the mob by force, there were going to be bodies in the streets, and lots of them. I didn't want to kill my own people, but I was willing to do what I had to do to survive this.

Arturo had a choice. He could pardon the girls, maybe in exchange for something useful, or I was going to cut him down at the knees. I was going to take the mob from him and slit his throat if I had to.

My own fucking father. I didn't want to bring ruin down on him, but I would and I could. He'd been underestimating me for years, and now that may be about to bite him in the ass.

Louisa would back me too; I knew that. She had a lot more power than most people realized.

But this was all hypothetical. I didn't want any of that to happen. One day I'd take over the mob, but I'd let the old man retire first. I didn't want to murder my own father to make that happen.

I shot back the rest of my whisky and stood up. "Time to sleep," I said.

"Night, boss," Vince replied.

"Thanks for being here," I said to him. "We'll fix this shit."

He grinned. "You know me, always down for a little action."

I laughed and left, heading upstairs.

Plans were forming, dissolving, reforming, breaking, forming again. I was abuzz with possibility, timing, logistics. Vince was a huge asset, and I was a lucky man that I had a loyal number two like him.

Because I was going to need all the help that I could get in the coming days of violence.

Chapter Thirty-One: Natalie

I stared up at the unfamiliar ceiling, and for a moment I thought I might roll over and find Lucas in bed with me.

Instead, my bed was empty, and so was the room. It was totally sparse, with just one night stand and the bed filling the space.

I slowly got out of bed and stumbled into the bathroom. Camille's door was still closed, but that was fine. I wasn't really interested in any mother-daughter bonding, especially now that I felt like I was finished with her. I'd help her if I could, but I wasn't letting her drag me down anymore.

I brushed my teeth and rinsed off my face, spending a long moment staring at my face in the mirror. I looked haggard, and for good reason. I had to remind myself that we were on the run from the mob and that scary, violent men wanted us dead.

It wasn't exactly a reality that I was used to.

"Hello?" I heard a voice call from downstairs.

"Lucas?"

"Hey," he said, walking up the steps. "Good morning."

He looked tired, too, but at least he had changed his clothes. I was still wearing the same sweats from the night before.

"I'm really happy to see you," I said. He made it up the steps and I threw my arms around him, hugging him close.

"Same to you, Nat," he said. "I can't stay long, though."

"Why not?"

"I have to do some stuff. But I came with your phones."

I nodded and he kissed me softly. I followed him back downstairs and we sat down at the kitchen table, the phones between us.

"Now," he said, "don't use this for anything stupid. Don't access social media or banking or something like that. Don't message friends."

"Maybe you shouldn't give my mom one," I said, frowning.

He paused. "You're probably right." He slipped Camille's phone into his pocket.

I sighed. "Are you sure you can't stay?"

"Sorry. I need to get to work. Somebody has to solve this problem."

"How pissed is your dad?"

"Pretty mad." He grinned. "But that's okay. He's a big teddy bear."

"Somehow I don't think that's true."

"No, it's not."

We sat in silence for another minute before he stood up.

"Come back later?" I asked.

"I will as soon as I can."

He walked around the table and hugged me again, kissing me softly.

"It's going to be okay, right?" I asked him.

"It's going to be okay."

And I believed him. I had no real reason to expect anything good was going to come of our situation, but I didn't think Lucas would lie to me. I trusted him.

"See you later," he said as he walked out the door.

I stared for a few minutes before getting up and locking the dead bolt after him.

〜〜〜〜〜〜〜〜〜〜〜〜〜〜〜〜〜〜〜〜〜〜〜〜〜〜〜〜〜〜〜〜〜〜〜〜〜〜〜

Life in a safe house was boring.

Camille got up an hour later, sat on the couch, and refused to talk to me. She watched trashy soap operas all day, which worked fine for me. I much preferred not talking to her; at the moment, I wasn't sure I could remain civil, let alone be nice.

I retreated up to my room with the burner phone and idly looked around news sites. I wasn't sure what I was looking for, but I needed

something to occupy my mind.

And then I remembered the weird notebook.

The night before, when my phone had fallen down between the seats,

I had found something jammed in there. At the time I hadn't thought much

of it since everything was moving so fast, but I decided to take a look while

I had a free second.

I fished the thing from my bag. It was small, the sort of small

notebook that a reporter would carry. It was clearly well-used, though, as

the pages were smudged and the cover was old and stained.

I opened it up and began to leaf through. At first I had no clue what I

was looking at. Most things were numbers, with some English words and

what looked like Russian mixed in. I recognized the Russian because it used

that weird script; I think it was called Cyrillic. At any rate, I couldn't read

the vast majority of it, and the numbers just made no sense.

Still, a few words jumped out at me. Toward the back, the word "oil"

was followed by some numbers, and the word "meet" was followed by

what looked like a time and a date.

That instantly struck me as strange.

I pulled out my phone and turned to a page of Russian script. I took a

picture and then did a Google search for a forum for Russian speakers.

Once I found one that I could actually read, I made an anonymous post asking for someone to translate the page, or at least to give me an idea of what it said.

The notebook was clearly important. I wasn't sure who's it was or what it meant. I wanted to get in contact with Lucas, but I didn't want to seem like a needy alarmist. I wanted to confirm that the notebook was important before I started to bug him with it.

An hour went by before someone finally made a comment on my post. Apparently, the page was a list of people's names and addresses. That didn't tell me much, so I posted another page and asked the same question.

The response came back much faster.

Looks like he was taking notes on a meeting, NaNaKlashnikov said. *There's something about Russians (?) and about a third group of people. This is actually really shady. Where did you find this thing?*

I felt chills run down my spine.

That confirmed it for me. I was holding something important, though what exactly it said was beyond me.

I opened up the contacts list and found only one: Lucas. I tapped his name and let it dial.

Maybe this was the break we needed.

Chapter Thirty-Two: Lucas

"Where did you get this?" I asked her.

She looked down at the floor. "I'm sorry if I'm wasting your time."

"Hey." I grabbed her chin and tilted it up. "This is important."

"Remember when I dropped my phone last night getting out of the car?"

"Not really."

"Well I did, and I found this wedged down between the seats right next to it."

I shook my head, absolutely amazed.

"Do you know what this is?"

"Not really, no."

I paged through it, laughing to myself. Most of it was in some damn Russian writing, but there were a few names and numbers that I recognized.

There was the amount of olive oil in the stolen shipment, plus the time and date of the exchange. There were also a few other names of guys in the mob, plus at least one Russian name I recognized.

"Remember Franklin?" I asked.

"How could I forget?" she mumbled.

"This is his notebook. I'm sure of it."

"Okay. Well, how?"

"That was his car we grabbed on the way out."

"So this is important?"

I grabbed her face and kissed her hard. "Very," I said when I was done.

She smiled. "Good. I'm glad."

"I think this is the proof that I need. I think Franklin was a part of a group inside both us and the Russians."

"And they stole the shipment?"

"At least, yeah." I laughed, paging through the book. "But there are numbers and dates in here that I vaguely recognize. They could have been stealing from us for a while without anyone noticing."

"This doesn't change the fact that Camille cheated on your dad."

"No," I said, "it doesn't. But Camille can tell me where Franklin is. Then maybe I can convince Arturo that you two are worth keeping alive."

"Gee, thanks."

"At the very least he'll be distracted and I'll be able to get you two out of the city."

"What happens then?"

"I don't know," I said honestly. "But no matter what, I won't leave you."

She nodded. "Okay."

I stood up, pocketing the notebook. "Now, let's go talk to your mother."

Natalie followed me downstairs. With every new step I took, the plan in my mind slowly began to come together.

Somehow Franklin was at the center of this. I had been right to be suspicious, but he clearly had been careful. We hadn't followed him to any secret stash of treasure or anything like that. From what Vince and his people could tell, Franklin was a model employee.

That was, until he started fucking Camille.

Truth was, Franklin may have gotten away with everything had he not stuck his dick in Camille. If we had never gotten in that car that night, and Natalie hadn't found his notebook, we would probably have moved on eventually.

Instead, fucking a married woman was coming back to really bite him in the ass.

We found Camille sitting on the couch, looking miserable. She glanced up at us.

"Came to yell at me some more?" she asked me.

"Not if you decide to be helpful," I said.

She crossed her arms. "What do you want, Lucas?"

"Where is Franklin?"

She raised an eyebrow. "I don't know."

"You saw him last night. You warned him."

"So? He didn't say where he was going."

I sighed, sitting down on the coffee table in front of her. "I don't

believe you."

"I don't care," she snapped. "I don't answer to you."

"Actually, Camille, you do. See, I'm keeping you safe. If my father's

people found out where you were hiding, they'd probably cut your throat

and dump your body in an alley."

I watched the color drain from her face.

"They would never. Artie would never."

I laughed. "Artie? My father is a violent businessman. He'd cut your

body to pieces without a second thought. You're nothing to him now."

She looked away. "You won't let that happen. You care too much

about my daughter."

I looked over at Natalie. "Would you mind if your mother

disappeared?"

"No," she said. "I'm finished trying to protect you, Camille. You can deal with the consequences yourself from now on."

She gaped at Natalie. "You wouldn't let these men kill me?"

"I wouldn't do anything," Natalie said. "This is your choice."

Camille looked back at me. "This is insane."

"This is what happens when you treat being married to a mobster like it's some fucking game," I said to her.

"I don't know what you want from me."

"Where is Franklin?"

"I said I don't know."

"Listen to me carefully, Camille," I said softly, leaning in closer to her. "In a minute I'm going to ask Natalie to go upstairs, close her door, and put her head under a pillow."

"You don't scare me," Camille said.

"After that," I continued, "I'm going to take this knife"—I lifted up my shirt to show her my blade—"and I'm going to start hurting you until you tell me what I want to know."

I could see the fear in Camille's eyes. "You wouldn't do that, not with my daughter around."

I turned and looked at Natalie. Her face was passive, almost neutral. "Go upstairs, Nat."

She nodded and left.

"Natalie!" Camille called out. "Wait. What are you doing?"

Natalie ignored her. I heard the door shut upstairs. I pulled the blade from the sheath at my hip and leaned in toward Camille.

"Just me and you now," I said.

"I don't know anything."

"Why are you protecting him?" I asked.

"I love him," she answered softly.

I laughed loudly. "Love? You don't know anything about love."

"And what do you think you know? You're just some violent psychopath."

I reached out and grabbed Camille by the hair. She shouted and tried to fight me, but I simply held her harder.

"I know what love is," I said into her ear. "I'm willing to risk everything to save someone that I love. Unfortunately, you're now standing in my way, and I will do what I have to do to make you talk."

I held the knife up against her face.

"Okay," she said quickly. "Okay."

"Where is Franklin?"

"He said he has a place on Sawyer in Little Village."

I tightened my grip. "What else?"

"I have his number. You can call him."

"And?"

"I swear that's it."

I could hear the fear in her voice, and I believed her. I let her hair go and she quickly scrambled away from me. I slipped the knife back into my sheath.

"Thank you, Camille," I said.

"You're a monster," she spat. "You're a sick monster. You don't love my daughter."

"No, Camille," I said, "you don't."

I walked away from her and headed upstairs. I opened the door to Natalie's room and she looked up.

"Did you hurt her?" she asked.

"No," I said. "Just scared her."

"And?"

"She talked."

Natalie looked relieved. "Good. I'm glad."

"I have to get going."

She got up and walked over to me, throwing her arms around me and hugging me tightly.

"I love you," I said to her. "You know that?"

"Yeah," she said, "I know."

And I kissed her hard, kicking the door to her room shut.

Chapter Thirty-Three: Natalie

I heard the door shut, but almost from a distance. He kissed me hard, pressing himself against my body. He pulled off my sweatshirt, pulled off my sweatpants, and pushed me down onto the bed.

He loved me. He said he loved me, and I hadn't said it back.

But I didn't need to, not with his lips on my skin, kissing my neck, his fingers slipped down my panties. He could feel how I felt about him. He could feel the way my body responded to him. I was soaking wet as he began to slowly rub my clit, sending spirals of pleasure through my body.

He didn't say a word as I stripped his shirt off. He quickly resumed teasing my pussy and kissing me with a frenzy I hadn't seen from him yet.

My whole body was flooded with intense desire. I needed a release, but more than that, I needed him. I pushed him back, rolling over and on top of him, and began to work his pants off.

"Easy there," he said, grinning. "Grab the condom from my wallet before you toss them aside."

I did as he asked, fishing the condom out and then tossing his pants aside.

He took the condom from me and I began to slowly work his shaft through his boxer briefs.

"You see what you do to me?" he whispered, gently pulling my hair. "You make me so fucking hard I can barely breathe."

I slipped his underwear off and tossed them over with his shirt and his pants. I took his thick, hard cock in my hand and began to slowly jerk him off while looking in his eyes.

His handsome, beautiful eyes. He was full of desire for me, looking at my body, my breasts and lips.

"I could watch you do that forever," he said. "You have such perfect fucking lips."

I smiled and slowly moved down toward his cock. He grunted as I slipped his tip between my lips and began to suck him.

"Fuck," he grunted. "God you're fucking good at that. Suck that cock like you can't stop yourself."

The truth was, I couldn't stop myself. I began to suck him, sliding his cock in and out of my mouth, getting him nice and wet and hard. I wanted to slide my soaked pussy down along his shaft, but I wanted him to need it first.

I worked him that way, sucking him, jerking him, all the while looking up at his beautiful face. He looked back, watching me intensely, letting me do all the work. I continued sucking his cock, working him.

Finally, he reached down and pulled me up. I straddled him, and he ripped open the condom. I watched impatiently as he slowly rolled it down over his hard cock.

Biting my lip, I shifted myself forward. This time he didn't make me beg. I couldn't wait even if he did. I simply pressed myself down and felt his cock push deep inside me.

I let out a gasp and threw my around him. He grabbed my hips and pressed me down harder, filling me to the brim.

"That's what I wanted," he whispered, "this tight fucking cunt wrapped around my cock."

"Lucas," I whispered. "Oh my god, Lucas." He began to move my hips, sliding me up and down. I fell into his rhythm, working my hips, using my legs to ride him.

He stayed sitting upright, our bodies pressed together. I rode his thick cock, sliding my body up and down, feeling his chest, his muscles, his hair. He slapped my ass and thrust hard into me. I let out soft, low moans as he began to fuck me like that.

"I want you to say my name while you come," he whispered. "I want you to say it loud."

I wrapped my arms around him and looked in his eyes as I rocked up and down. His hips thrust up, his hands guiding me down, and I slammed up and down along his hard shaft.

It was exactly what I needed. All my pent-up frustration and anger and his words kept ringing in my ears. He loved me. He fucking loved me, and I wanted his cock so badly I could barely stand it.

Pleasure washed through my body as we kept working like that. Our faces were inches apart, and I could feel his breath against my lips. His cock filled me up as I rode him, rocking up and down, grinding our bodies together, pushing harder, deeper.

"Lucas," I whispered. "Oh fuck, Lucas. I'm so close."

He pressed harder, slamming my hips down. His eyes never left mine, and I could tell what he wanted. He wanted me to come on his heavy cock, and I knew I was seconds away.

"Oh my god," I whispered. "I love you. I really love you."

"Come for me, Natalie," he said. "Come on my fucking cock."

The orgasm rolled through me faster than I could have imagined. It burst through my mind, exposing everything and cleansing everything. In that moment there was nothing but Lucas, our bodies moving together, moving in hard thrusts. He fucked me roughly as I rode him, and my whole body tensed, the orgasm taking me over.

"Lucas," I said, over and over.

It happened so easily, so fast and perfectly. I knew I couldn't hold it back even if I tried. I had been teetering on the edge of frustration all night, and now it was finally bursting out.

The orgasm slowly ended. As it did, he took me and rolled me onto my back, getting on top. I opened my legs wide as he kissed my body, my neck, my breasts and continued to grind himself deep inside my pussy.

"Oh yes," I said. "Oh shit, Lucas. Are you going to come inside me?"

"I'm going to fill this pussy up until you can't take any more."

He began to fuck me again, hard. I pushed my hands up against the headboard, pushing myself back against him as he fucked me. I writhed my hips, watching him look at my breasts, my pussy.

He knelt in front of me, fucking me hard, my legs spread wide. His cock slammed into me, and sweat dripped down his body. I could tell what he wanted—the same thing I wanted. He needed to come for me, to come inside me, inside my pussy. And I wanted to take every single ounce he had for me.

I kept moving my hips. "Come on, Lucas, fill my pussy up," I said. "Fill my tight pussy up."

"You dirty girl," he said. "You dirty girl. I'm going to come deep in this cunt."

"Come for me, Lucas."

I pressed my arms on either side of my chest, pressing my tits together. I could see the hunger in his eyes eclipsing all other thought as he fucked me roughly and savagely, ravaging my body.

And finally he dipped forward, his muscles stiffening. His thrusts got deep, insistent, as he came deep inside me.

"Oh fuck, Natalie," he said, grunting through his orgasm.

I worked my hips, helping him come.

Finally, his thrusts slowed and then stopped.

We lay there together, wrapped in each other, covered in sweat and breathing deeply. I kissed him softly. "I really do love you," I said.

"I know."

I kissed him again and we just lay there, feeling each other's bodies. I knew he had to leave soon, but I wanted to feel him go soft inside me. I wanted to feel him for a little bit longer.

Because I didn't know what the future held. Everything was so damn dangerous, and there were still so many secrets.

But in that moment, his cock still inside me but spent and satisfied, I knew the truth. I knew I'd follow him anywhere.

I knew he'd take me anywhere.

Chapter Thirty-Four: Lucas

I looked at Vince sitting in the seat next to me. "Fucker should be here somewhere," I said to him.

Vince nodded. "Assuming the bitch didn't lie."

"She didn't."

We were sitting parked on the street in the area Camille had said Franklin was hiding out. I had two other squads at either end of the street, keeping a lookout for the bastard in case he wasn't in his little rat hole.

An hour before, my mind had been completely on Natalie. We had just stayed in bed together, talking quietly as our sweat slowly dried on our bodies. Eventually, though, the real world came crashing back down, and I had to get up out of bed. I didn't want to leave her, hated that she was unsure of what was happening, but I had some rat fuck to possibly murder, and I couldn't wait any longer.

So I picked up Vince, briefed him and the boys, and started our little stakeout.

But it wasn't moving fast enough. The sun had set not too long ago, and we still hadn't seen any sign of Franklin. I was starting to think we needed to smoke him out.

"I got an idea," I said to Vince.

He just looked at me, amused. I took out my phone and dialed the number Camille had given me for Franklin.

The asshole had the gall to answer on the second ring.

"Hello?"

"Franklin, don't hang up," I said quickly.

Silence on the other end.

"You know who this is. Listen to me, Franklin. We have you."

"What are you talking about?"

"Sawyer Street in Little Village."

Another long silence. I let him stew on this one.

"How did you know that?" he asked.

"Tracked your phone. Well, I did. I haven't told my father yet."

"What do you want?"

"Stay where you are. Stay there and talk to me. I'm coming in fifteen minutes."

I saw Vince grin at me.

"And if I stay?"

"I'll protect you. I'm going to overthrow my father tonight, Franklin. And if you can speak to the other bosses, show them that my old man is a pathetic cuckold, well, maybe they'll follow me."

Another short pause. "I need guarantees."

"Isn't the fact that you're still alive enough?"

"Fine," he said, a little too fast. "I'll be here. Building 1734, apartment 3C."

"See you soon, Franklin."

I hung up the phone and looked at Vince.

"We go in now?"

"Nah," I said. "He gave me a bogus address." I shook my head. There wasn't a 1734 on the block. "But I think we might have scared him."

Not five minutes later, Vince's phone rang.   "Yeah?" he said. "Grab him." He hung up and looked at me. "You lucky bastard."

"He make a run for it?"

"He made a run for it."

I laughed. "Dumb bastard. Who's got him?"

"Joey and Carlos."

"Let's go."

I started the engine and pulled out into traffic. I headed down the block and spotted Joey and Carlos standing with another man next to their car. We pulled up behind them.

Sure enough, it was Franklin. He didn't look roughed up at all, which was good. I climbed out of my car and walked over to him.

"Lucas," he said. "Man, I'm sorry."

"Idiot." I punched him in the gut, hard. "You should have stayed in your little hole."

He coughed and struggled for breath. "I can help you," he said finally.

"Yeah, you can." I nodded to Carlos and Joey, and the boys tossed him into the back of their car. "You're going to disappear for a while, and when you return, you're going to tell me where the fuck you hid the shipment."

He stared at me, but I was already walking away. Joey and Carlos pulled out into traffic, heading back toward the safe house.

Poor Franklin had no clue what he was in for.

Vince stood next to me. "One problem down."

"Yeah," I said, "but shit doesn't get any easier from here."

"One thing at a time."

"Sure."

We walked back to my car and pulled out into traffic.

~~~~~~

Vince and I got some dinner before heading over. We had to kill some time to give Joey and Carlos the opportunity to work Franklin over.

By the time we got there, Carlos was sitting in the kitchen drinking a glass of wine.

"What's up?" I said to him.

"Joey's down there," he responded.

"Our guest?"

"Ready to sing like a fucking bird." Carlos grinned wickedly.

I looked at Vince, who rolled his eyes. We headed down into the basement, down the familiar steps, and saw Franklin chained to a chair. Joey was standing off to the side, trimming his nails.

"Boss," Joey said. Franklin looked up.

"Don't stand," I said to Franklin. "You look like shit."

He spit blood onto the ground. Joey and Carlos had worked him over all right; really, they'd beaten the ever-living fucking shit out of him. I was surprise Franklin was even still conscious.

I pulled a chair over and sat across from him. "Ready to talk?" I asked him.

"Why bother?" he said slowly. "You'll just kill me afterward."

"Maybe," I said. "But we'll kill you much more slowly if you don't help us out."

"I have nothing to say."

I glanced at Joey and he just shrugged. I reached into my jacket and pulled out the notebook. "Do you recognize this?"

I could tell from his initial reaction that he did. "Never seen it before," he said.

"Liar." I pulled out my knife. "Lie again, and I cut you."

"It's not mine."

I sighed and ran the blade along his thigh. He screamed.

"You're not doing yourself any favors, Franklin."

"Okay, fuck, okay," he said. "Okay, it's mine."

"There we go. Good." I flipped to a page. "What does this say?"

"It's a list of names. Guys with the Russians."

"Why are they listed here, Franklin?"

"I was watching them."

"That seems strange, considering you're just a driver."

"I wasn't watching them for you guys, you fucking cunt."

I frowned and cut his thigh again. He cried out in pain.

"That was just for being annoying," I said.

"Fuck you, Lucas."

"I know it was you. I know you stole the oil. I know you're working with some Russians. What I don't know is where it's all hidden."

"Why would I tell you?"

"Because maybe you can save your worthless life."

That gave him pause. "You want me to roll on my crew, and you let me live?"

"Franklin, listen. I already have your crew." I waved the notebook in front of him. "I just need the location of the oil. Then I'll let you live."

That was when I saw it. It was barely there, barely visible in his bloodied, swollen eyes.

But it was there.

It was hope.

"Come on, Franklin," I said. "Save everyone some fucking trouble and tell me where the shit is."

"Give me your word."

I stood up, sliding my chair away. "You have it."

"I'll talk," he said.

I smiled at him. "Good choice. Tell Joey what you know. I have some calls to make."

I turned and headed back up the steps, followed by Vince.

"Easy enough," Vince said. "But now how are you going to play it?"

"Call Arturo. Set a meeting for tonight."

Vince raised an eyebrow. "Seriously?"

"Do it."

He walked off and I sat down with Carlos, pouring myself a hefty glass of wine. He grinned at me and I smiled back.

The night was almost fucking over.

~~~~~~

We pulled up into the empty construction site in our cars. We were early, which was how I liked it. I nodded to Joey and Carlos, who both moved out with high-powered rifles to cover us from a distance and to make sure there wasn't an ambush.

I shoved Franklin down to his knees. He was duct taped and tied up, so he wasn't saying much. Vince looked around.

"Ominous," he said. "I hate these places."

"They're fine during the day."

"Noisy during the day."

I laughed and we waited. Ten more minutes we waited, until finally we saw lights come up the road.

"Ready?" I said to Franklin, kicking him.

He grunted in response.

"You sure about this?" Vince said to me.

"Not at all."

The cars pulled up and guys poured out of them. They were all in battle gear, holding rifles and wearing Kevlar vests. Finally, my father emerged from the center car and walked toward us.

We were outnumbered ten to one at least.

"This is a surprise," Arturo called out.

"I brought you something," I said, kicking Franklin again.

"Is that the traitor fuck?"

"It's him."

Arturo frowned. "What the fuck do I want with that?"

"We know where the oil is."

He looked surprised. "Do you now?"

"And we know who the traitors are."

Arturo looked at me and then gestured. Vince and I walked forward, Franklin in tow. We stopped just in front of him. Alfonse and Ernesto were standing on either side of him, and none of the other men could hear what we were saying.

"Okay, son," Arturo said. "Talk."

"Franklin here is working with some guys in our organization, along with some Russian guys, to steal from both the mobs."

Arturo raised an eyebrow. "Ambitious."

"It's been working, too," I said. "Until they got a little too cocky."

"How did you find this out?"

I held up the notebook. "Natalie found this in Franklin's car. She translated it, basically solved the whole damn thing."

"Show me."

I tossed him the notebook and he paged through it. He passed it to Alfonse, who just frowned at it before passing it to Ernest.

"It's in fucking Russian," Ernest said.

Arturo silenced him with a finger. "Can you take us to the shipment?"

"I can," I said.

"So what's the deal then?"

"It's this: I'll give you everything if you pardon the girls."

Arturo laughed. "I don't fucking care about them. They're pardoned."

I nodded. "And you'll bless my marriage to Natalie."

That surprised everyone.

"The fuck you doing, boss?" Vince whispered.

"Married?" Arturo asked.

"Before I knew who she was, we got married in Vegas. And I plan on staying married."

Arturo shook his head. "I won't have a traitorous bitch in my crew."

I pulled out my pistol faster than anyone could react. By the time Ernest and Alfonse were aiming at me, I had already pressed my gun to Franklin's skull.

I pulled the trigger.

Franklin's face bloomed red. He collapsed to the ground, dead.

"Hold your fire!" Arturo yelled.

There was a tense moment, and then Arturo began to laugh.

I smiled at him.

"This is the traitor," I said, "dead at your feet. Natalie is innocent, and she's mine."

"Very well," Arturo said. "You can have her."

"One more thing," I said to him. "You're not going to like this, but, please, I insist that you wait until I've explained."

He frowned. "Very well."

I held my hand up and then lowered it quickly.

Shots rang out in the night.

Four men standing by the cars fell dead with bullets in their skulls.

"Hold!" Arturo yelled. Ernest and Alfonse were on the verge of freaking out.

"Before you all start shooting," I yelled, "those men were traitors. I have the proof."

"He's telling the truth," Arturo yelled.

The men shuffled, but nobody opened fire. I could tell we were on the brink of war. Arturo wheeled on me.

"Killing anyone else tonight?"

"That's it. For tonight."

"You will never disobey me like this again. Do you understand me?" Arturo said.

"Yes, Father."

"Ernest, Alfonse, go see to your men."

They simply turned and walked away. I could see the fear in their eyes.

"Maybe I misunderstood you, son," Arturo said to me. "Or maybe I was right. A wife really had made a man out of you."

"Vince will show you where the stolen oil is," I said to him.

I smirked, turned, and walked away. I heard Arturo's footsteps recede back toward the trucks, Vince in tow.

I got into my car, my heart racing.

But it was over. Arturo would keep his word, although I had broken mine. Franklin was a traitor, and a man's word meant nothing when it was given to a traitor.

I started the car and began to drive back toward Camille and Natalie.

They were safe now. Camille would have to leave the city, but Natalie was going to stay with me.

Because she was mine. Our secret was out, and although I was sure Arturo was unhappy about it, at least she wouldn't be my stepsister for much longer.

She was going to be my wife instead.

Chapter Thirty-Five: Natalie

Two Months Later

I moved through the hallway confidently, nodding to staff members and other mob guys.

It felt so strange knowing my way around the compound. I could remember my first few days here, barely knowing anything, wandering around like an idiot. Now, though, things were different.

Very different.

I knocked on the door and waited. "Louisa?" I yelled. "Open up."

No response.

"I'm coming in," I called.

I pushed the door open and stepped inside. It was filthy, as usual, since Rosita was refusing to clean her rooms again. I spotted Lou sitting at her computer with huge headphones on. She was engrossed in her game, so

I simply walked inside, sat behind her, and watched.

I could still vividly remember the night Lucas came home and asked me to be his wife.

True, we were already married, but this time he was doing it right. I had opened the door to the safe house, terrified that we were about to be killed or worse. Lucas had walked in and ordered Camille out of the living room, which she complied with after only minimal complaint.

Finally, we sat down on the couch.

"You guys are safe," Lucas said. "I found Franklin and traded his information for your safety."

I threw my arms around him, hugging him close. He gently moved me back.

"There's one more thing."

He dropped to one knee and pulled out the box. Inside was a ring, a ridiculously huge diamond ring.

"What are you doing?" I asked him.

"I told my father about us. I told him that you're mine."

I have no clue what to say. My head was spinning. It was crazy, so crazy, so fast and so intense.

"Natalie, be my wife. By my bride for real."

"Yes. Okay."

He slipped the ring over my finger and kissed me hard.

I couldn't imagine ever feeling that happy again. Tears had moved down my cheeks as he'd kissed me, and every time I thought about it I choked up a little bit.

We didn't need to have a ceremony, but we had a short one anyway. All the mobsters were there, and it was just so *Godfather* that it was absurd. They gave me gifts of cash just like in that movie. We danced, drank too much, and Lucas fucked me until I couldn't walk anymore.

"You're here," Lou said, yanking me from my memory.

"Hey," I said.

"How long have you been staring at me?"

"Sorry. I wasn't really paying attention."

She turned around and crossed her legs. "I've been meaning to ask. How's it feel to be queen of the mob?"

I laughed. "Hardly."

"It's the truth. All the men adore you."

I blushed. "Stop, Lou. You know you're still the most important woman in this house."

"So long as you know it," she muttered.

"Listen," I said. "Come to dinner tonight."

"Same answer as every day. No, thanks." She turned back toward her computer.

"Okay," I said. "I guess I'll be back tomorrow."

"See ya, sister."

I patted her back as she returned to her game. I stood up and left her room, smiling to myself. Every day I went to Lou's rooms and invited her to dinner. Sometimes we talked, sometimes we didn't. She was pretty hard to predict, but I was quickly thinking of her as my closet friend in the compound.

Aside from Lucas, of course.

I moved down the hall and made my way back toward our rooms. When I had moved in, Lucas had claimed a larger part of the house for us to live in. It was so silly, since either one of our original rooms were more than big enough, but he had insisted.

I opened the door to our apartment. It was essentially the entire eastern wing.

The living room stretched out in front of me, too big and too richly furnished.

Things had moved so fast up until the wedding. Then, after that, it was like nothing had ever happened. Lucas and I lived in the compound, he continued his work, and I finished my school work by doing online classes.

Pacey wasn't happy with that, of course. But how could I explain to her that I never wanted to leave the compound? It was strange; I went from hating it to absolutely loving it.

All become of him.

Lucas stepped into the living room from the bathroom. He had just showered, and his whole body was damp.

"Wife," he said.

"Husband." I stood up and went to him. I wrapped my arms around him and kissed him deeply.

I couldn't go anywhere. I had nowhere to go, really. I didn't want to be anywhere near Camille, and anywhere else would have paled in comparison to being with Lucas.

Sure, I still didn't love his job, but I was beginning to get used to it, maybe even enjoy it. He kept me from the worst of it, and I was thankful of that.

And the nights with him were incredible. It was like he never got enough of me, and I definitely never got enough of him.

"How was my sister?" he asked.

"Stubborn as always."

"She'll never break, you know."

"We'll see."

He smirked. "Barones don't break."

"Don't you?" I reached down and grabbed his cock, surprised that it was already half-hard. "I think I could break you."

He growled. "Please, girl. I'll snap you like a twig." He grabbed my hips and spun me around.

"I doubt it," I said, but my pants were already around my ankles, and his face was between my legs, his thick tongue curling out toward my soaked pussy, eating me, lapping me up.

That was what my life had become.

Lucas all night, the compound all day. I didn't want for anything, had a staff at my beck and call. I didn't see much of his father, but I preferred it that way. The other mobsters had taken to me, though, and were all really nice to me.

And Lucas was the nicest of all. As my back arched and he got me off again and again, I kept thinking about how thankful I was that I had married my stepbrother.

My brutal, violence, cocky stepbrother. His amazing tongue between my legs, his body against mine.

I loved him and I was his. I always was, from that first moment onward.

It only took me a little while to figure it out.

I wasn't going anywhere. It was Lucas and I forever. I was his bride, and he was my husband.

Nothing would ever change that.

About the Author

B. B. Hamel lives in the Philadelphia area with her husband and her two dogs. She has been a lover of romance from a very young age, and can't wait to share more hunky stories with you.

Sign up for her mailing list! Go to www.bbhamel.com to get a free, exclusive book, plus the opportunity to receive advance copies and more! Keep reading for the first eight chapters of BB's exciting novel *Smash*!

PREVIEW

Smash: A Stepbrother MMA Romance

Chapter One: Alexa

It all started with a mistake.

A big, stupid mistake, but I couldn't help myself. Not when he grabbed me by the hips and steered me through the doorway, whispering, *Come on, be my fake bride. I want to consummate this trip until you can't stop screaming my name.* I was powerless when it came to him, and he knew it. We barely knew each other, but I'd learned enough over the last few days to know that he got what he wanted. I didn't even bother saying no anymore, because I knew that saying yes would feel so much better. He had deep blue eyes, a perpetual five o'clock shadow, tattoos all over his body, and muscles that just didn't quit.

Frankly, he was the most attractive man I'd ever seen, let alone touched, and he definitely knew it. Cole was cocky, too cocky, but he had the swagger to back it up.

Come here, girl, he whispered in my ear. *You're going to be my bride of paradise. I'm going to sink my cock deep into that pretty little pussy of yours, right after we say these words.*

We didn't understand what was really happening. The staff didn't either, but what did they care? They didn't know what we really were to each other. We were just some stupid tourists, a little drunk on wine, a little drunk on each other. When we asked for the deluxe ceremony, they figured we understood what we were really getting.

They figured we really wanted to be married. Legally married, not just as some stupid joke.

We stood there in front of the priest as he spoke in Thai, a language neither of us knew. The air was thick and humid, even at night, and Cole held my hand the whole time, his eyes drilling holes in mine. We were in paradise, one of the best vacations of my life, even if my best friend had ditched me on the second day for some lawyer she'd just met. I wasn't going to let it ruin my good time.

It was all fun and games until I met Cole. Then it was much, much more.

Later, much later, his strong body pressed up against mine in the cool white expanse of my bed, our bodies sweating, pleasure rushing through my skull. *Is that how you like it, little wife?* he whispered into my ear.

Yes. Please.

His fingers moved down between my thighs and did things I'd never felt before.

~~~~~~

"Are you kidding me?" Lacey said, exasperated. "Your dad got married *again?*"

"Yeah, and this time he didn't even bother telling me about it."

I stood with Lacey in line at Starbucks, my backpack heavy from my last day of class. Finals were over and done with, which meant I was headed back home for the summer.

Junior year was finished. I was pretty sure I already had senioritis.

"Typical Frank. Always thinking with his dick."

"Gross," I said, laughing. "He's still my dad, you know."

"Sorry, but it's the truth. Your dad is the biggest horndog I've ever met."

"Okay, that's enough."

"I know it's hard to hear, Alex, but it's the truth. Your father is a grade-A player."

I sighed, shaking my head. Nobody likes hearing about their parent's sex life, but unfortunately, in this instance, everything she was saying was the truth. My dad, Frank Miller, was on his third marriage, plus however many girlfriends he'd had over the years. He seemed to constantly go from one "true love" to the next with no real regard for anyone else around him. He insisted that it was different this time, that things were going to last for a long time, but he almost always said that.

I was pretty used to it, though. These new women appeared in my life like a hurricane, trying to be my friend, sometimes trying to be my mom, but they never lasted long. Frank didn't have "commitment" or "monogamy" anywhere in his vocab, no matter how hard he tried otherwise.

"Yeah, well, I haven't even met this one yet," I said.

"Seriously? He got married again and didn't even invite you to the wedding?"

"Supposedly it was a low-key thing. She's this high-powered CEO of the company that just bought him out."

We got to the front of the line and ordered our coffee. As we moved over to wait for the drinks, Lacey gave me a look.

"Her company bought his, and now they're married? Seems pretty weird."

I sighed, nodding. "Yeah. It's some big scandal in the business community or something."

"Classic Frank."

"What I don't understand is why this woman would want to go

through all this for him. Don't get me wrong," I said quickly, "I love my dad. But who's worth that much trouble?"

"What a cynic."

"Like father, like daughter, I guess."

Lacey laughed as our names were called. We gathered up our caffeine-and-sugar beverages and headed out into the warm afternoon.

I really wasn't looking forward to going home for the first time in a long time. In years past, going back to my dad's house in San Francisco was usually pretty great, but for some reason I was dreading meeting his new wife.

I'd heard bad things about her. They were both CEOs of up-and-coming tech firms, and Cindy was supposedly something of a hard ass. Everything I knew about her was either from the mouth of a PR firm or from some gossip rag online, but so far nothing seemed to really paint her in a flattering light.

And yet when Dad called me to tell me about the nuptials, he sounded really happy. For the last few years, his life had been all about work and more work, with the occasional girlfriend of course. But that never seemed to make him happy, just more and more stressed. He needed something in his life to brighten up his days, and if Cindy was doing that for him, well, then I couldn't get in the way of it.

Still, I didn't have to be excited to meet another woman that was going to want to be my replacement mother. Or maybe this one was going to

want to be my best friend instead. You could never tell until you met them

which direction they'd take.

"You'll be home this summer, right?" I asked her.

"Of course. What else would I do, pay rent?"

I laughed. "Solid point."

"Between prostituting myself for cash and living with my parents for a

few months, I choose parents."

"Not an easy choice, though."

"Not at all." She paused, looking thoughtful. "You get to make your

own hours as a hoe. On the flip side, free food is a big bonus."

We both laughed, and I shook my head at her. I was pretty sure she

was genuinely considering becoming a prostitute to avoid going home.

Lacey and I had been best friends all through high school. I moved

around a lot when I was younger, because my dad got jobs all over the

country. Eventually, though, he wound up at his company Blingo, and we

stayed put in San Francisco. I met Lacey my second day of school, and we

had been inseparable ever since.

"Well, you know where to find me if you ever need to escape the

oppression," I said.

"Please. You'll come crawling to me first I bet."

"How long before I'm knocking on your door? A day?"

"Four hours. Tops."

The University of California at Berkeley's campus was more or less empty by the end of the school year, and we didn't have any trouble finding a prime spot to sit down and watch what few students were left walk by.

"You know," Lacey said after a few minutes of relaxing silence, "you haven't mentioned your little problem recently."

I frowned, sipping my coffee. I hadn't mentioned it because I was sick of thinking about *him*. Even though I hadn't seen him since we'd gotten back from vacation, he hadn't been too far from my mind at pretty much at all times. Cole the fighter, the cocky asshole, the gorgeous stranger.

And my husband, of course.

Technically, at least.

"Wish I had an update for you," I said. "Just counting the days until I can legally pronounce him dead."

"Seriously?"

"No. I wish. I can just push the divorce through without his consent at that point."

"How long?"

"End of the summer."

"Have you told your dad yet?"

I snorted. "Yeah, right. And disappoint him? No, thanks."

"Still, he could probably help you. I bet he has contacts and stuff like that."

"Maybe, but at this point, why bother? It's almost over."

Lacey nudged me, grinning. "You sure you want to divorce him? I mean, I remember what he looked like."

I thought for a second. Flashes of Cole's body as he walked from the ocean, dripping salt water, his eyes looking at me both playfully and intensely.

"Yeah, I'm sure," I said, not sure at all.

"What a shame. Waste of prime real estate, if you ask me."

"Who knows if it's a waste? He's gone and I'll never see him again."

Which was exactly how it was supposed to be. But one stupid night, half drunk on wine and half drunk on each other, we had stumbled into this Vegas-style marriage chapel. Normally, the marriages were just for fun, a kind of fake ceremony to make couples feel good about themselves.

But we ordered the "deluxe" package. Cole said that if we were getting married, then we were doing it right, and how could I argue with him?

What we didn't know, of course, was that the Deluxe Package meant we were marrying legally. The staff probably did try to explain that at one point, but we were either too giddy to listen or just too stupid.

And so when I got home and tried to register to vote, I got a nice little surprise. In the field for "Marital Status" in the official records website I was browsing, I saw a nice big fat "M." After a bunch of phone calls, and at least two total meltdowns, I found out that I had been legally married in Thailand to one Mister Cole Redson.

Of course, once I figured it out, I tried to track him down. I tried everything, but Cole Redson basically didn't exist. I knew he was an MMA fighter, but there were no records of him fighting under that name. I found an old address, but he had moved away from that place a long time ago. I decided not to do too much research about him, because I could tell I was already starting to obsess. I decided I needed to just get the divorce pushed through, with or without him.

Cole Redson had just disappeared. He'd swept into my life during a stupid spring break to Thailand and then had disappeared again, leaving me a married woman and a wreck.

Fortunately, though, all I needed to do was prove that I had tried everything to find him, wait the required amount of time, publish a notice in the newspaper, and then I'd be rid of him. No more husband, no more problems.

"I still can't believe you actually married him," Lacey said, probably for the millionth time.

I gave her a look and she grinned at me. "What? I'm just saying."

"I know. You've been saying it for almost a year now," I grumbled.

She cackled again and I sighed, dipping my head. I knew I deserved the jokes. Frankly, I felt like a total idiot. I mean, how did you end up married without even realizing it? And to a total stranger, apparently one that didn't even exist?

How stupid did I have to be?

"Anyway," Lacey said, sipping her drink. "This summer won't be a total bust, you know? I am making it my mission to get you back on the whores."

I looked at her. "It's 'horse,' not 'whores.'"

"No. In this instance it's definitely 'whores.' You need to get laid, and soon."

I smiled and shook my head. Lacey could think like a guy sometimes.

"I don't *need* to get laid, Lace. I'm just in a dry spell."

"Yeah, a year-long dry spell. Come on, it's time to make moves. Your husband isn't really your husband."

She was right and I knew it. Still, the last year had been busy. I'd switched majors the year before, and so I spent both my semesters overloading my schedule to make up the required credits.

Plus, I felt strange putting myself out there again. The last time I went for a stranger, I ended up married to a guy that may or may not exist. The frat boy douches and college hipsters just didn't do anything for me, or at least not enough to make me want to step outside my shell.

But my divorce was coming up soon. By the end of the summer I was going to be single again, at least legally speaking.

Cole wasn't my husband. He never was. How could he be my husband if I didn't even know where he lived?

"We'll see," I mumbled.

"We will see. All those guys you're going to bang."

I rolled my eyes as she laughed at her own joke.

I wasn't looking forward to going home, but maybe it would be good for me. U.C. Berkeley was nice and all, but it wasn't home.

Maybe I just needed a relaxing summer to get back to myself.

~~~~~~

A few days later, my cab pulled up outside my house. Dad wasn't home, of course, because he was working late. But he promised he'd be back soon, and with my new stepmother.

I unpacked and lay around my bedroom, glad to be home. As much as I was dreading it, as soon as I walked into the familiar foyer, I felt instantly better. There was just something about home that could make things a bit better.

As much as I wanted to deny it, Lacey was right. I was in a rut, but I was also still hung up on *him*. I probably could have found a faster way to get divorced, but I just didn't feel all that motivated. Sure, I went out and met people all semester, but nobody felt right, not since Cole.

I just couldn't stop thinking about the first time I met him.

It was night at the resort, and Lacey had already disappeared with her lawyer guy, or maybe he was a movie producer. Either way, I decided to walk down the beach.

The moon was bright and full, which should have helped with my visibility. Instead, I was too busy looking up at the beautiful view to notice the huge rock down at my feet.

As I hit the sand face-first, he appeared.

Cole. Tall, covered in tattoos, grinning this knowing smile like he could tell what I was thinking about him. He appeared at my side, his strong hands on my arm.

"Are you okay?" he grunted in my ear.

"What? Oh, yeah, totally fine," I stuttered as I got to my feet.

I was so fucking embarrassed. When was the last time I had actually tripped on something? It was like out of some horrible romance novel where the girl was just a dumb, empty klutz and was obsessed with her shiny boyfriend. It took me a second before I really got a good look at him, but when I did, he took my breath away.

"Careful out here," he said softly. "Those rocks are vicious."

"Uh, yeah. Sorry." Why was I apologizing?

Probably because he made me feel like I couldn't speak in complete sentences. His cut jaw and laughing blue eyes were enough to send me into spasms, but his tall, muscular frame and tattoos just made him all the more delicious.

It was completely unreal.

"What are you doing out here alone?" he asked.

"Friend ditched me, so I'm going for a walk."

"Mind if I join you?"

"Yes."

He raised an eyebrow. "Okay then."

"I mean," I said quickly, "yes, please join me."

He laughed and offered me his arm. "For protection from large rocks."

I smiled and slipped my hand around his ripped bicep. Holy shit, is it the ocean or am I already soaked? *I thought.*

"I'm Cole," he said as we started to walk.

"Alexa."

"Do you make it a habit to walk alone on strange beaches?"

"Ah, it's not a strange beach. We're in a resort."

"True. Still, you managed to land face-first."

I could feel myself blushing. "I'm really not a klutz."

"I bet."

"It's just this place," I said quickly. "It's really beautiful."

I could feel his eyes staring into me. "Yes. It really is."

I couldn't remember anymore what we talked about after that, but we did talk for a while. Eventually we ended up in this little outcropping of trees on a hammock, our bodies shoved together.

I didn't think I'd ever felt more tension in my body before or since. And of course it was right around the moment when I was about to throw myself at him that Lacey found us and dragged me off.

But after that first night, I kept seeing him around. It seemed like everyone was his friend, everyone knew Cole.

And then after everything that had happened between us, he disappeared into thin air. My husband, the stranger.

I sighed, stretching, when suddenly I heard the front door open.

"Great. Show time," I muttered to myself."

"Honey?" Dad's voice called out. "Are you home?"

I opened my door and headed downstairs. "Hey, Dad!" I called out.

"Alexa." He smiled hugely and hugged me as soon as I found him in the kitchen. "Glad you're home."

"Me, too, Dad."

Once he let me go, I saw her standing over by the table, smiling. I recognized her from the pictures, but she was even more stunning in person. Cindy had long blond hair, bright blue eyes, and was dressed expensively but conservatively.

She didn't look like Dad's usual type. She was age appropriate, for one, and she wasn't showing more skin than she was covering. Instead, she exuded grace and poise, even from the very first second we met.

"Alexa," Dad said, "this is Cindy."

"My new stepmom," I said.

Cindy laughed. "Just Cindy, please. It's really good to meet you. I've heard lots of good things."

We shook hands and I instantly forgot about all the negative things I had read about her in the press. Maybe she was the Ice Queen, the dominating woman warrior, but I didn't care. In my kitchen, she seemed like just a regular person.

"I'm so happy you two could finally meet," Dad said.

"Me too," she added, nodding.

"Well, it's about time I meet my dad's new wife."

She laughed, a little embarrassed. "We are sorry about that, Alexa. We could have invited you."

"I know," I said. "I'm just giving Dad here a hard time."

He frowned. "We really are sorry, honey. It's just, after Cindy's company bought mine, things happened fast. And the press hasn't exactly been kind to our relationship."

I caught a dark look cross Cindy's face, but it quickly vanished. I knew what Dad was talking about, though. I'd read some rumors about the two of them, rumors that he was kept around only because he was Cindy's new "boy toy" or something like that. Apparently, them getting married was a pretty huge deal and had the potential to screw the whole merger up.

Fortunately, so far things had worked out. But I could tell that Dad was stressed, even from seeing him for just a few minutes. Not as stressed as he usually was, but still. There were lines around his eyes, and he looked like he hadn't been sleeping enough.

"We've gotten a lot of bad press," Cindy added. "But it's been worth it."

I smiled as she kissed my father.

"Okay, enough of that," I said, laughing.

Dad beamed, his new bride on his arm.

Things seemed like they were going to be okay. I had been so nervous for this meeting, so torn up about it, but Cindy seemed perfectly lovely.

"You know," she said, "my son should be here soon." She checked her watch. "But he's late, as usual."

"Honey, you were in Thailand, right?"

"Dad, you know I was. You paid for the whole thing."

"Well, that's where her son's been for the last year. You two can bond over that."

I shrugged. "I was only in that resort. I barely saw the country."

Cindy waved her hand. "He's been in the jungle or something equally crazy, so I doubt he knows much more than you do."

I raised an eyebrow. "What was he doing there?"

"Training, I think. He's a mixed martial arts fighter."

"Wow, that's pretty amazing," I said.

"I suppose."

As if on cue, the sound of a loud motorcycle roaring down the street filtered in through the open windows.

"Speak of the devil," Cindy said. "I bet that's him."

Just as the noise of the engine peaked, it suddenly cut off. I followed Cindy and Dad over to the front door. We stepped outside onto the front stoop.

I'd never had a brother or a sister before. I had to admit, I was looking forward to meeting him. I hadn't realized that Cindy had kids since nobody mentioned him in the press, but it wasn't surprising. I knew Dad wasn't her first marriage.

I watched as a tall, muscular man stepped off a black-and-chrome bike. He reached up and pulled the dark helmet off.

My eyes widened and I took a step back.

That night almost a year ago came rushing back. The moonlight through his hair, the cocky grin as he walked down the beach with me.

"Alexa," Cindy was saying, "this is Cole, my son."

I couldn't speak. I couldn't even move.

It was him. It was my stranger, my husband.

My stepbrother.

I was horrified. I couldn't move.

"Alexa," he said, grinning hugely and walking up the stoop toward me. "Good to meet you."

There was something playful in his eyes, something knowing. He definitely recognized me, there was no doubt about it, but he was pretending for our parents' sake.

"Uh, sure," I said, shaking his hand. I hadn't gotten myself together enough for more.

Everything about him was so familiar. All those moments came rushing back to me. The ache of my body, our limbs stretched out together, the warm sand under my feet as he laughed and threw seashells into the waves.

My husband was back.

I was so damn close. *I was so damn close* to getting away from him.

"I look forward to getting to know you better, stepsister," he whispered.

I could only stare at him, wide-eyed in terror.

Chapter Two: Cole

It was humid as hell the first night I saw her. I was sweating in my button-down shirt and shorts as I made my way down to the beach, bored of the drunk tourists.

Thailand wasn't a vacation for me, even though I was staying at a resort. It was my last hurrah before the next year, a final week to blow off steam before I went into hardcore training mode.

My two main goals were pussy and alcohol, not necessarily in that order. I knew I was going to have to abstain from everything when the real work began, but I was going to indulge as much as I could all week first.

It wouldn't be easy for me to go a while year without pussy, but it was the sort of sacrifice I knew I needed to make to take my career to the next level.

As I made my way toward the water, there she was. More specifically, I watched as she tripped and landed face-first in the sand.

My initial instinct was to laugh. Yeah, I admit it, I was an asshole. But you'd want to laugh, too, if you saw someone trip on a seemingly perfectly flat beach.

Instead, I walked over to her and made sure she was okay.

Sometimes, I wished I hadn't done that. In the next few weeks, in the dead of night when I was being eaten alive by fucking bugs and I couldn't get her body out of my mind, I'd almost regret it.

But I'm not the type to have regrets, not really. I wanted to fight hard and fuck harder. That's all I cared about in life.

Except there she was, this sexy as fuck girl slowly getting to her feet.

I knew I needed her. I knew I needed to posses her, fuck her, make her come on my big cock until she couldn't think of anything other than my dick and my body against hers. I was completely sucked into her, and I knew I'd do whatever to have her.

And at first, it was exactly like that. Her pussy was like fire for my mouth as I tongued her little clit in the middle of the afternoon, making her back arch. It was incredible, my fingers exploring every inch of her, and yet still she held back. I wanted more, always more, but she wasn't ready to let me have it all.

I couldn't get that last night out of my head. We'd just done on this stupid fake marriage ceremony, for some dumb reason. It was funny and lame, but for some reason I felt like it almost meant something. Later, back in my room, I slipped her panties down her smooth, tanned skin and pressed my mouth up against her pussy.

"Who are you?" she gasped as I began to tongue her clit.

"Just someone who loves to taste you," I said in between mouthfuls of her sweet cunt.

"Shit," she gasped, grabbing my hair. "Seriously. Where did you learn all this?"

"You pick things up when you live as hard as I do."

I slipped a finger deep inside her and watched her eyes close in ecstasy.

"I fight for a living, babe. I put my body on the line for fun. I've figured out what I like and how to get it."

"But why me?" she gasped as I began to kiss her neck, pistoning my fingers deep inside her the way I knew she loved.

It was a good question. Why her? I could have been fucking a new girl every night. It wasn't like it was hard, especially in fucking paradise.

But for some insane reason, the second I got a taste of her, I needed more. I couldn't stop myself from getting her off again and again and again. I loved the way sweat rolled down her chest as I worked her body hard and rough, my mouth and fingers all over her, not caring how loud she was.

"Because that's what I want, and I get what I want," I whispered to her, pressing my tongue harder against her spot.

Weeks later, in the dead of night, I'd remember the gasp she made as I nibbled her slightly and slipped another finger deep inside her.

Alexa. I'd remember that name when things got rough. It was torture sometimes, remembering that sweet pussy, knowing I'd never see it again. I knew that I just needed to get back to civilization to forget about her, move on to some new stranger.

But despite that, I kept thinking, wondering, where my fake wife was. And if I'd ever get to taste that pussy again.

Still, I was in Thailand for a reason. After the vacation was over, I took a bus out into the countryside, out into the fucking jungle, to meet with one of the greatest Muay Thai fighters in the whole country.

It was the opportunity of a lifetime. Skad was legendary in the fighting community, and he took only three students every year for an intensive training course. Every one of his students had gone on to do special things, and so I knew that I could catapult my career into stardom if I could get his training.

I was lucky. He must have watched the tape I sent him, because I was invited out only a few weeks after I sent it. I wasn't sure what he saw in me, but I figured I was about to find out.

And it was unlike anything I'd ever experienced. The word "intensive" didn't do it justice. We lived, breathed, ate, fucked, and shit fighting. Learning Skad's techniques, training under his tutelage, was the air we breathed and the food we ate. There were no cellphones, no Internet, no television, nothing.

There was only violence and hard work.

And I fucking thrived on it.

I was a hard man before I met Skad. I grew up in the octagon, training from a young age. I used to get in street fights just to test my skills. I was undefeated and had a reputation for violent aggression, a reputation I loved and built lovingly for myself.

But I was nothing compared to the man Skad made me. Before I was all untapped potential. I had so much more inside me but couldn't get to it. Skad refined my edges, made me faster and more dangerous. Skad changed me from a talented fighter to a deadly killer.

All it cost me was a single year of my life.

~~~~~~

I thought I was ready to come back to civilization. Compared to the deep silence of the jungle, though, the airport was like a chaotic mess of sights and sounds and noises.

There were people everywhere. I hadn't seen more than a handful of people my entire time out in the jungle, and suddenly I was shoved into a crowd of total strangers.

But it was my time, and I knew it. As soon as Skad said I was ready, I got back on that bus and got my ass to civilization.

There was only so much time I could spend in the jungle before I completely lost my fucking mind.

Still, the crowds of cow-eyed people annoyed the shit out of me as I made my way across the terminal and toward baggage claim. I was meeting my mother, or at least my mother's driver, out front. I was running a little late already, which was of course going to be blamed on me and not on the airline.

My mother was a hard ass. We got along if you considered not talking often as getting along. When we did talk, it was mainly about her work since she basically ignored my fighting career.

Fine by me. I didn't need or particularly want my mother's approval.

Once I found the driver, I gave him directions to my storage unit just outside the city. He gave me a look like it was the last thing he wanted to do, but I slipped him a twenty and hopped into the back.

Apparently, that was enough. We were on the road, heading toward my destination.

The plan was simple. I had a bunch of shit kept at the storage unit, the most important of which was my motorcycle. I'd drop my bag off there and take the bike over to my mother's new husband's place, pay my respects, and then be done with that.

The sooner I got it over with, the sooner I could find a cheap room and get back in the fighting game.

We made it to the unit with no problem, and I had the driver drop me off. He clearly had instructions to drag me to Cindy himself, but I wasn't some kid he could just order around. I gave him a nod and walked into the storage facility, leaving him stuck outside.

The unit was right where I left it. I unlocked the door and found everything exactly as I wanted it to be.

I smiled to myself and took a deep breath. It was finally feeling like home.

I didn't have much time to waste, though. I got changed and looked over my bike, satisfied that it was in pretty good condition despite having sat around for the better part of a year.

I hopped on and kicked it started, moving slowly out toward the exit. The bike made a deep hum as I rode it through traffic. I was running a little late, but that couldn't be helped. I passed a few slow cars in the right lane and wove my way over to the left, dodging in and out, loving the feeling of the speed and the power between my legs. The only things better were fighting and fucking.

Finally, I pulled up outside an expensive-looking brownstone, the sort of thing only millionaires could afford in San Francisco. That made sense, since I couldn't imagine Cindy marrying anyone with less than a few million in the bank. She wasn't a gold digger, not at all. She had her own money.

Rather, she was attracted to power, and money brought power, at least

according to people like her.

I knew better than that. Real power came from training your body,

pushing it to its limits. Real power was mastering yourself and your

opponents.

As I cut the bike's engine and climbed off, three people emerged out

onto the stoop. Instantly I recognized my mother and her stern expression.

She was clearly pissed off that I was late and had ditched the car. My new

stepfather looked pretty typical, like your classic old and white business

CEO, not too fit but not flabby either. He had a warm smile on his face.

And finally, my gaze fell on her.

I had a brief moment of full-on shock as my eyes ran up and down her

body.

It was her, my paradise bride. Alexa, the girl I hadn't stopped

dreaming about ever since I went to train in the jungle.

How was that fucking possible?

Everyone was looking at me, and so I had to get my shit together

pretty fast. I took a deep breath and pulled off my helmet, ignoring the girl

for the time being.

But she clearly recognized me, because she looked like she had seen a

ghost as soon as my face was visible to her.

She remembered me, then. Not a surprise considering how hard I had made her body come over and over, but still. It had been a long time, and I did look different. I was harder, darker, and stronger than the last time I had seen her.

When I shook her hand, I knew she was on the verge of passing out. Cindy quickly ushered everyone inside to have lunch, and as we moved toward the kitchen, Alex hung back.

I stared at her body, at the familiar curves, but most of all at her angry expression.

The girl was fucking pissed, and I had no clue why.

Sure, I fucked her and left, but that wasn't my fault. I didn't tell her about the training because what was the point? It was a vacation fling, and we both knew it. It was an absolutely batshit crazy coincidence that our parents had gotten married, but that sort of shit happened all the time. It wasn't like I knew anything about it.

Except she looked like she was about to have a fucking heart attack.

"You know," she said loudly, "I've always wanted to see a motorcycle up close."

The group stopped walking. "Honey, can't that wait?" her dad said.

"Why don't you two get everything ready while Cole here shows me his bike?"

I grinned at her. What a fucking flimsy excuse. "Sure thing. It'd be my pleasure," I said, overly formal.

My mother scowled. "Okay," she said. "Make it quick."

I followed Alex back out the front door. As soon as it shut, she whirled on me like a demon, spitting rage and fire from her eyes.

"Where the *fuck* have you been?"

I stared at her, completely taken aback by her fury. I'd had plenty of chicks get pissed when I didn't call them back the next day, but this was something different.

"Good to see you too, princess," I said.

"Don't give me that shit, you asshole."

I laughed. Her anger was comical in its intensity. "Look, I'm sorry I didn't call. You know how things are."

"No, you idiot, you jerk, you, you—"

"Asshole?" I finished.

"Yes, asshole!"

I laughed, shaking my head at her. "I know being with me is an experience, but you seem a little too angry."

"It's not that, you idiot! Don't you know?"

I cocked my head at her, confused. "Know what? I've been in the damn jungle for the last year."

She took a deep breath. "The jungle?"

"Training. I'm a fighter, remember? I haven't had Internet, email, phone calls, or pussy since I last saw you."

She looked at me silently for a second, still clearly fuming but getting herself slowly under control. "So you don't know?" she asked.

"Did you have my baby or something?"

She rolled her eyes. "God, no. Thankfully."

"Please. You'd be honored to have my kids."

"Listen to me," she said seriously. "Remember that wedding ceremony?"

"Sure," I said, getting nearer to her. She reacted the way I remembered, like being close to me was a fucking drug. And honestly, it felt the same damn way to me. All the memories were rushing back all over again, but there she was, right in front of me, still as fucking sexy as I remembered. "But I'm more interested in what happened after."

"No, listen. That ceremony was real."

I laughed. Was she actually crazy or something? "No, it wasn't. It was some stupid tourist thing."

"Normally, yeah. But when I got home and tried to register to vote, I found out that I was legally married to some asshole I barely knew."

She couldn't be serious. She wanted me to believe that she and I were actually married, for real?

"There's no way," I said. "It was in Thailand. How would it be official here?"

"You dickhead," she said, exasperated. "I've been dealing with this ever since I got back. Believe me, we're really married."

I stared at her for a long second and finally burst out laughing. It was the most hilarious and insane thing a girl had ever done to me, and I just couldn't believe she was trying to pull it off. I had to admit that she was pretty impressive, but there was just no way I was married. Let alone to my new stepsister.

"Nice try," I said, turning away. "Come on, let's eat. I haven't had a real meal in a fucking year."

"Cole," she said, still angry. "We chose the deluxe package. Remember that?"

I paused at the doorknob. "Sure, I remember."

"But we didn't get anything extra. Right?"

I nodded slowly. "Right."

"Deluxe meant that it was real, not that it was anything special."

I frowned at her for a second. Thinking back to it, I did find it strange that their special marriage package hadn't come with any extras. But no, how could we even have known that? Maybe the deluxe package just meant the priest didn't pass out drunk at the end.

"Good try," I said again. "But if you wanted me to finally fuck you, all you had to do was ask nicely."

She gaped at me as I opened the door and walked back inside.

My stepsister was fucking gorgeous. She was sexy and wild and passionate, and possibly fucking insane. Hardly the girl I remembered from paradise.

So why did I have a nagging feeling in the back of my mind?

Chapter Three: Alexa

How could he not believe me?

I'd been waiting nearly a year for that moment. I'd been thinking about it, dreaming about it, hoping for it. In my head, I would tell him about the marriage, and he would instantly apologize and beg to make things right. He would be so hurt that he let me suffer through this sham marriage for so long that he'd swoop me up into his arms and carry me off into the sunset to make sweet, tender love to me.

Well, maybe not that last bit. But I did expect some sort of apology, maybe even a little surprise.

Instead, he didn't believe me. He thought I was lying!

I couldn't believe I hadn't realized his mother was Cindy. They had the same last name, after all. But there were no pictures of him and her together, and she never mentioned having a son in the press. I could never have imagined that they were mother and son, not in a thousand years.

As I stood there alone on the stoop, staring at the door, I felt angrier than I ever had in my life up to that point. How arrogant did he have to be to think a woman would lie about being married to him? What possible reason could I have for that? I was fuming, ready to storm inside and beat the living crap out of him.

He was so damn cocky, so damn full of himself. That asshole was probably thinking about how much of a psycho I was being or something. I was so mad I could scream.

And yet. seeing him again had dredged up a bunch of feelings, stuff I had thought was long-buried. As soon as his helmet was off and I got a look at his chiseled face, his muscular body, and his piercing blue eyes, I knew that I was happy he was back. I wanted him to take me up into my bedroom and make me feel the way he had back in paradise.

And then reality came crashing back when I realized that he was my stepbrother. And also my husband.

I took a deep, calming breath. That asshole really did think he was so amazing that somebody would lie about being married to him, but the joke was on him. All I needed to do was show him the marriage certificate, which I could easily print off my laptop.

Lunch came first. I had to get through the next hour or so, and then I could prove the marriage to Cole. And I couldn't let Cindy and Dad find out about anything. For one, I had kept it from Dad for a long time already, but more importantly, they were dealing with enough scandal already. They didn't need their irresponsible daughter married to her equally crazy stepbrother.

Except I wasn't crazy. I was just married to my asshole stepbrother.

As I pushed open the front door, I could still barely believe that was true.

"Lots of hard work," Cole was saying as I walking into the kitchen

Cindy turned to me. "Cole was just telling us about his time in Thailand."

"He was training with a master fighter out in the jungle," Dad said a little too reverently.

"I'm sure it was hard," I replied, uninterested.

"I've had harder," he said, grinning at me.

I rolled my eyes at him and Dad gave me a look.

"Anyway," Cindy said, "let's go into the dining room."

We filed in and took our seats at the table. In the kitchen, I heard some staff bustling around, getting the meal ready. I felt a little weird about having staff suddenly, but apparently Cindy had insisted on it. Dad and I had gotten along just fine without having servants, but I wasn't about to say anything.

"Looks great," Dad said as the food was served.

"My first real meal in a long time," Cole said.

"Really? What did you eat out there, bugs?" I asked him.

"Sometimes, sure. Mostly vegetables, though."

"No talking about eating bugs at the table," Cindy said. "Plus, you didn't really eat bugs. Did you?"

Cole grinned and just began to dig into his food without answering. Cindy sighed, taking small bites of her salad. Dad gave me another look, and I knew exactly what he was thinking. It was probably pretty obvious that I was annoyed with Cole, but how could I explain it to him? Better to let him wonder.

"So, Alexa," Cindy said, "how's school?"

"It's good," I answered. "Can't complain."

"Berkeley, right?"

"Yep."

"Smart girl," Cole said. "Must be nice. Makes your father here proud, I bet."

"Very proud," Dad said.

"Where did you go to school?" I asked Cole, knowing the answer.

"Nowhere," Cindy muttered.

"Nowhere is right," he said loudly, ignoring her. "I skipped the bullshit and went right into training."

"Must be rough. Being an uneducated person, I mean," I said acidly. I knew I was being a jerk, but I was just too annoyed with him to care.

Dad and Cindy both stared at me.

"Oh, it's not so bad," Cole said simply, as if I hadn't just insulted him. "It's easier since I'm married, you know?"

Dad looked at him. "I didn't know you were married."

I cringed. Dad was taking the bait. I gave Cole a look but he ignored me.

"Oh yeah, Frank, I sure am. Married to fighting, I mean. She's a crazy mistress, but I love her."

He was looking at me the whole time he was speaking, and I wanted to throw my fork right in his eye.

"Ah, that's good," Dad said. "It's good to love what you do."

"Even something so violent and dangerous," Cindy said.

"Maybe dangerous, and definitely violent, but people do crazy things all the time." Cole looked at me. "Right, Alex?"

"I wouldn't know," I spat back. "I'm too busy, you know, being a normal person."

Not marrying a stranger and then traipsing off into the jungle, I wanted to add, but I didn't.

Dad looked between the two of us. "I don't think fighting is crazy or abnormal," he said, oblivious.

"I do," Cindy said.

Cole glared at her, and I couldn't help but wonder what her deal was. Did she seriously care so much about what Cole did that she was going to make passive snipes about it at lunch?

But no, I didn't care about that. I didn't feel bad for Cole. I didn't care if his smiling blue eyes were piercing into me, making me want to cross my legs. I didn't care if I kept imagining the way his fingers had made my back arch all that time ago.

I didn't care that he was the last guy I had kissed. Or that he was my stepbrother.

I just wanted a damn divorce.

We started eating then and the conversation drifted toward more normal topics, like Dad and Cindy's jobs. Apparently, things weren't all they were cracked up to be in the company, and life was pretty stressful. But they seemed to genuinely enjoy each other's company, or at least for as long as lunch lasted.

"So, Alexa," Cole said suddenly during a lull. "Any men in your life?"

"Cole," Cindy said.

"What? I just want to inquire after my new stepsister's virtue."

"My virtue is none if your business," I said.

"Can we stop saying 'virtue'?" Dad asked sheepishly.

"Don't be so uptight, sis," Cole said, learning forward. "I just want to get to know you better."

"That's a wonderful idea!" Cindy said suddenly. "You two should get to know each other better."

"Oh, I'm sure you want to learn all about me. Right, sis?"

I nearly gagged. "That's okay."

"Alexa," Dad said sternly. "Don't be rude. We're family now."

"That's right, Alex. We're going to be very close," Cole added.

That smug bastard. He'd been flirting with me all afternoon, hinting at our past right in front of our parents. It was all I could do not to explode. He was such a jerk. I wanted to wipe that cocky smile off his face.

"I have an idea. Why don't the two of you go to dinner, on me?" Cindy said.

"Perfect," Cole said quickly. "Tomorrow?"

"I don't know," I stumbled, trying to think up an excuse.

"She's free," Dad cut in. "Right, honey?"

Everyone was staring at me, and I knew I couldn't refuse. It would look way too suspicious, even more suspicious than I already did.

"Okay," I said softly.

"Great. It's settled. I'll pick the place. We'll hammer out the details later," Cindy said, clapping her hands.

Great. Not only did he think I was a psycho stalker, but now I was going to have to go on a date with him? I couldn't take any more. I stood up abruptly.

"Excuse me. I'm not feeling well," I said.

Dad looked concerned. "Was it the food? I'll talk to the staff."

"No. I'm just exhausted. Excuse me."

I turned and left the dining room, not bothering to look back.

I knew I probably looked even crazier to him storming off. I could only imagine what our parents were thinking. But if I had to sit for one more second at that table with that smug, self-centered, gorgeous asshole, I was going to scream.

I went upstairs as quickly as I could and closed my bedroom door, flopping down on the bed. I closed my eyes and breathed, slowly getting myself under control.

Cole was back. My mistake husband, my secret shame, my stepbrother. The guy that made my body feel things I never thought I could feel. He had been so charming back in paradise, but now he seemed only cocky and brash.

Part of me had wanted him to come back, not so that I could divorce him, but so that I could get to know him. Yeah, it was crazy. We only knew each other for a few days, but still. Something felt right when I was with him, like it would be easy to be myself.

Plus, he was absolutely stunning. Even his smell drove me insane, which was totally unlike me. I didn't usually get really into a guy's looks, but he was something else, something I couldn't explain. And I felt it right between my legs every time he grinned at me, even when he was being an ass.

But I couldn't let him keep thinking that I was just some crazy stalker. I grabbed my laptop and navigated to the official marriage registrar, dealing with the agonizingly slow website until finally I found it.

Our marriage license. I hadn't looked at it in a long time, and it felt like it wasn't real. But I knew it was since it was from a government website and was on official government letterhead with all the seals and whatever.

As I went to hit print, there was a soft knock at my door.

"Yeah?" I called out.

"It's me." Cole's voice.

"No, thanks."

The door opened and he came inside, shutting it behind him.

"You can't just barge in here," I said, annoyed.

"Your dad sent me to check on you."

I sat up, frowning. "Well, I'm fine."

"You sure? Looked like you weren't fine at lunch."

"Yeah, well, you're an asshole, and I'm looking forward to when you're out of my life."

He laughed, coming closer. I took a sharp breath of air into my lungs as he looked around my room, clearly judging the décor. I hadn't updated it since I was in high school, so it was embarrassingly late-2000s, but whatever.

"Cool posters," he said.

"Thanks."

He picked up a Nirvana CD from my dresser. "You a fan?"

"Yes. Don't touch my stuff."

He put it back. "Me too. *Nevermind* is my favorite album."

"Mine too," I said grudgingly.

"See, sis, we have so much in common." He sat down on the edge of my bed.

"Stop calling me sis."

"What should I call you then? Wife?"

"That'd be more appropriate," I mumbled.

"Come on, Alex. You think I really believe that shit? I know you're just trying to get back at me for fucking you and then disappearing."

"I don't care about that," I snapped back. "And I'm not lying."

"Okay, okay," he said, holding his hands up. "That's fine, whatever. We can at least be civil."

I sighed. "I can prove it to you."

"Go ahead."

I turned the laptop toward him. "See? That's an official marriage license. Take a look."

He pulled the computer toward him and looked closely at the screen.

His face clouded over for a moment as he considered it, but I couldn't read his expression.

Finally, he looked up. "This is impressive," he said.

"You believe me now?"

"I mean, it's impressive that you'd go to so much trouble. It's a really good fake."

I gaped at him, uncomprehending. "You think I forged this?"

He shrugged. "Sure. Wouldn't be impossible. Doesn't look all that real to me."

I wanted to scream. I couldn't believe what I was hearing. "But it's from a government website!"

"Is it?" He shrugged, standing up.

"Cole," I said through my teeth, "you have to understand. We are really married."

"Look, sis," he said, "I had a good time with you. Frankly, I still get hard thinking about that tight pussy."

I blushed and looked away. "Stop," I said.

"You don't want to hear about it? In the jungle I used to think about your body. I dreamed about making you sweat. I wanted to track you down and get you off one more time, and look what happened."

"You're not getting anything off. You were just an attractive stranger."

"Glad you still think I'm attractive."

I sighed, completely exasperated. "That's not what I said."

"It is, actually." He crossed his arms, smirking at me. "Look, you can keep up this whole marriage joke if you want, but I'm not interested."

"It's. Not. A. Joke." I practically spit the words at him.

"Fine, whatever you say. But we might as well get along."

"Look, if you think this is all a joke, will you sign some papers for me?" I got out of bed and dug into my bag. "I have them in here somewhere."

"Really? You carry around fake divorce papers?"

"Not fake," I said, ignoring him. "Ah ha! Here we go." I pulled them out and showed them to him.

He glanced at them and handed them back. "No, thanks."

I felt like falling over. "Come on. Please?"

"Begging now?" He smirked and grabbed my waist, pulling me against him. I stumbled right into his chest, my heart beginning to hammer. "Sounds familiar."

"Cole," I mumbled. I breathed in his smell and it all came rushing back again, the way he made me feel, the way my back arched under his strong hands. He was the same man I knew back then, except he was being an asshole for some reason. "Don't be a dick."

He laughed, whispering in my ear. "We both know this is what you want."

"I just want a divorce." I pushed myself away and he laughed again.

"Whatever you say, sis."

I made a face. This day was just too insane, too intense. I needed to be done with all this. Maybe tomorrow he would be more willing to listen.

"When are you leaving?"

He cocked his head as he opened my bedroom door. "Leaving?"

"Yeah, like, leaving my house, going home."

"You don't know."

I looked at him. "What?"

"Oh, this is getting better and better."

"What are you talking about?"

"My mom is moving in with your dad." He was halfway out of my room. I felt a bolt of lighting run through my core.

He turned back, smiled, and spoke slowly.

"And I'm staying here for the summer."

Chapter Four: Cole

After months in the Thai jungle working my ass off, training harder than I

had ever trained before, I came back home and suddenly had a wife.

I'd thought she was fucking with me. I really did. I hadn't been able to

tell if she was just a psycho trying to trap me into a relationship or some

shit, or if she just wanted to bust my balls for not calling her after the

vacation was over. But as soon as she showed me that marriage certificate, I

knew it was real.

That wasn't any reason to stop messing with her, though. The way she

looked when she got so angry it was hard for her to speak drove me

absolutely wild. I'd never before wanted to throw a woman down on the

floor and fuck her raw right where we were standing, but Alex made me

feel that way. Maybe I hadn't gotten that far before, but I wanted it now.

I fucking needed her again, that was for sure. My time back home was supposed to be all about debauchery and catching up on lost time, but as soon as I had laid eyes on Alex again, I'd known that shit was done. I knew what I really wanted.

It was her lips, wrapped around my cock. I wanted to hear her pant my name, to feel her body stiffen as she came, over and over.

Except she was my wife and my fucking stepsister.

How could so much change? I go away into the jungle for one year and suddenly my shit is all blown up.

I wasn't the marriage type. I wasn't interested in having babies with her, moving out to a house with a white picket fence, none of that bullshit. But I was interested in fucking her sweet pussy rough and deep. Finally having her completely.

And plus, what else was I going to do? I had no other plans or prospects, not yet at least. When my new stepfather suggested that I move in with them, well, it just seemed too good an opportunity to pass up. So why the fuck not? I hadn't lived with Cindy in years, but that was fine. Frank's house was fucking enormous, so I doubted I'd even run into her.

Best of all, though, Alexa's room was right next door. I could practically hear her panting my name already through the thin walls.

Alexa didn't emerge from her room for the rest of the night, and that was fine with me. I was too busy unpacking my shit to really care what she was up to. I had plenty of time to tease my new stepsister, or maybe I should think of her as my new wife? Either way, I would get what I wanted

soon enough.

First, I needed a workout.

~~~~~~

I dipped down and grunted, finishing up my set. My body was

covered in sweat as I caught my breath, changing the song on my phone.

The music blared through the buds in my ears.

Frank had a decent gym down in his basement. It wasn't exactly

professional quality by any means, but he did have a nice set of machines

and free weights. There was enough to get my lifting routine in and then

some. It made sense that he had a gym, considering how fit the man was for

his age.

As I began to cool down, something caught my eye over near the

stairs. I looked up and saw Alexa waving at me.

I pulled the buds from my ears. "What's up, sis?" I said.

"Don't call me that," she grumbled as she came downstairs.

She was wearing a thin pair of short cotton shorts and a sweatshirt.

Her hair was all disheveled, and she looked like she had just woken up from

a nap. And all I could think about was fucking her up against the mirror,

making her watch as I fucked her tight pussy deep.

"What can I do for you?" I asked her. "Come down to sweat with me?"

"No, thanks. I wanted to talk to you about something."

"If this is about marriage, I'm not interested."

She made a face, and I had to bit my tongue to keep from laughing at her. "This isn't about the fact that we're married. Well, it is, but not exactly."

I leaned up against the wall and crossed my arms. "Spill it."

"Did your mom talk about our parents and their jobs with you at all?"

"Not really. Can't say I'm interested."

"Well, try to be. Apparently their marriage is some huge scandal or whatever."

"Because Cindy's company bought Frank's?"

"Yeah."

"Get to the part where I should give a shit, sis." I loved the look on her face, pure annoyance.

"You should care because she's your mother."

I rolled my eyes at that. "You don't know Cindy very well yet, but she's not exactly the nurturing type."

She was silent for a second. "Yeah, maybe I can see that."

"Cindy and me aren't on the best terms."

"So why are you even staying here, then?"

"Because I need a place to stay while I get my fighting career going again."

"Don't you have savings?"

I laughed, shaking my head. How naïve was this girl?

"Savings are for people that know they're going to be around in a year, sis. I put my body on the line for a living. Planning for the future is tough when you're not sure you have one."

She frowned at that. "Seems pretty crazy to me."

"Maybe," I said, moving toward her, "but you've never felt what it's like in the ring."

"I've seen it on TV. Looks like it hurts."

"Hurts like hell," I said, stopping right near her. I could tell her breath started coming quicker. "But I feel more alive in there than I do any other time. I don't care about the past or the future; in the ring, it's just my opponent and me. It's pure, fast, and dangerous."

"Not my kind of thing," she said.

I wanted to tip her chin back and bite her lip. Maybe I'd teach her to make it her sort of thing. In fact, I could see it being something she enjoyed, maybe even loved.

"Yeah, well, that's fine."

She shook her head, stepping away. "Whatever. The reason I'm here is to tell you not to tell anyone about what happened between us."

"Why? Embarrassed?"

"Our parents don't need another scandal. It could ruin them."

"Can't say I care all that much, honestly. No offense. Your dad seems like a nice enough guy, but my mom has never given me a reason to give a shit."

"Do it for me, then," she said, exasperated.

"What's in it for me?" I asked, smirking at her.

"I won't tell anyone what a big fucking asshole you are," she snapped.

"That's no secret, sis."

"Just don't talk about it, okay?"

I shrugged, turning away from her. "Sure. Whatever you say." It didn't matter to me one way or the other; I just loved giving her a hard time.

"Okay. Thank you."

I stripped off my shirt and began to towel off. I caught her staring at me out of the corner of my eye but didn't say anything. I wanted her to enjoy the show. It was obvious how much she wanted me, too, by the way she reacted every time I so much as came near her.

She may have acted like I was the biggest dick in the world, but she wanted my big dick, and I knew it.

"Still on for tomorrow night?" I asked her.

She nodded, biting her lip. "Yeah."

"See you then." I gathered up my stuff.

"Where are you going?"

"Taking a shower. Care to join me?"

She blushed, looking away. "No, thanks."

"You sure? I'd love to tongue your lovely little pussy while the warm water runs down your body."

She bit her lip again and then turned and left the basement without another word.

I watched her go, grinning hugely.

~~~~~~

The next day, I was too busy calling up my contacts in the fighting world to bother with Alexa. I found a nice spot up on the roof deck in the sun, set up my laptop and phone, and began to make my calls.

Back before I left for Thailand, I had a pretty decent career. Promoters were calling me up all the time, begging me to fight random guys all the time. I was lucky enough to get to be a little selective with who I fought and when. Now, though, I needed to take whatever fights I could get, prove that I was still worth watching.

That was something I liked about fighting. Nobody gave a shit who you were or what you looked like. If you could fuck some guy up with your bare hands, then you were good to go. Skill was the only thing that people looked for, and I had plenty of it.

Unfortunately, I had to prove that still. Even though I had just gotten back from training with Skad, which was a huge boost to my profile, I couldn't just jump into the ring with some big-name fighter.

After maybe an hour or two, I finally had a match set up for the next week. Normally fighters wanted more time to study tape and shit like that, but I wanted to get into the ring as soon as possible. My manager wasn't too happy about that decision, but he could go fuck himself. The fight was with some young guy who probably considered himself lucky to get into the ring with someone a little more established, like me.

But that made it a dangerous match. I didn't know the kid and he didn't know me, so we were going into this blind.

As I sat there Googling his name, Frank slowly came up the steps.

"There you are," he said. I looked up from my laptop.

"Frank." I nodded to him.

He stood near the railing, looking out over the city. "Nice view, isn't it?"

"It is," I said.

"I wanted to talk to you about something," Frank said, sitting down at the table with me.

"Go for it." I leaned back in my chair, crossing my arms.

"Cole, I'm glad you're staying here with us. The house is usually very empty for Alex since I work so much."

"I'm happy to help."

"It's just, I want to make this work, with your mother. But things are difficult. We have a lot of outside stress."

I nodded, frowning. "Alex mentioned some of that."

"Yes. Well. Your mother wanted me to say . . ." He looked away, clearly uncomfortable. "She wanted me to say that we hope you'll try and help out, while you're around."

"Frank, did Cindy send you up here to try and tell me to behave?"

He sighed, shaking his head. "It's not like that."

I held up a hand. "Yes, it is. And it's fine. I don't blame you one bit."

"I do mean it when I say I'm glad you're staying. I hope you'll at least try and be friends with Alex."

"I'm sure me and your daughter will be very close."

"And try to get along with your mom, too."

"That I can't promise."

He nodded. "Good enough." He stood up to leave. "Sorry to have bothered you. Consider this matter closed."

He turned to leave. "Frank?" I said. He looked back at me. "Don't be my mother's errand boy. She doesn't respect that."

He opened his mouth as if he was going to respond but decided against it. Instead he just smiled and left.

I watched him go, curious. Most men would have gotten pissed off at a comment like that, but he seemed to genuinely take it to heart. Or at least he did on the outside.

Frank was an interesting person. Maybe he wasn't a total douchebag. Then again, he was married to my mother, so who could say?

I checked the time on my laptop and cursed. It was much later than I had expected. I shut the lid and went back into the house.

I had a date with my stepsister soon.

~~~~~~

I was leaning up against a tree when Alex came walking down the stoop.

For a second, I felt my heart almost skip a beat. She was wearing this short, tight dress that clung to her hips and heels that made her ass look like fire. She wasn't showing much skin, but the dress was tight enough to show off her perfect fucking tits and body. Frankly, she looked incredible, and I had the urge to take her right there on the street.

"Sis," I said. "You look nice."

She frowned at me. "You could at least dress up."

I looked down at myself. I was wearing a pair of jeans, boots, a black T-shirt, and an old denim jacket. "What's wrong with this?"

"You look like a greaser or something."

I grinned. "Maybe I am."

"Whatever." She looked around. "Where's the car? Your mom said it was waiting out front for us."

"About that," I said. "We're not taking the car."

"I am not walking in these heels."

"Don't worry, princess. We're taking my bike."

She gaped at me for a second and then shook her head. "No. No way. I'm not getting on the back of that thing."

I walked over to it and tossed her a helmet. She caught it, but barely. "Come on. I thought you liked motorcycles?"

She walked over. "That was just for show," she hissed. "Don't be a jerk."

"Better get on," I whispered. "Your father is watching us from the window."

She moved to look but stopped herself. She took a deep breath and let it out. "Fine," she said, and she slipped the helmet on without another word.

I climbed onto the bike and she got on the back.

"Hold on tight," I said as I kicked the bike to life. "Now wave to daddy," I said.

We waved to her father as I slowly pulled the bike out into traffic.

She gripped my body like steel. I could tell she had never been on the back of a bike before in her life, which only made it that much better. Unfortunately, the restaurant wasn't too far away, and so I couldn't really open it up and get some speed at any point.

Still, I was surprised that she had gotten on without too much of a fight. Sure, she didn't instantly jump on the back, but who would in her situation? I was just impressed that she didn't throw a fit. I had her pegged as a rich little daddy's girl, but maybe there was more lurking under that exterior.

That fucking too damn sexy exterior.

I parked the bike and we walked a half block to the restaurant. It was an expensive place, clearly new, and was some kind of Italian fusion place. I didn't much care since anything was better than the shit I had eaten in Thailand. We were seated pretty fast and had drinks in front of us almost faster.

"Not bad," I said, looking around. "Cindy knows how to pick them." I sipped my whisky.

"I can't believe we even got into this place. It just opened last week, and the wait list is months out."

I snorted, shaking my head. "What a waste."

"What do you mean?"

"My mom could probably make anything happen, but she wastes that shit on good reservations."

"This is really nice of her, you know."

"It is, but don't get used to it."

"What's that supposed to mean?"

I considered telling her the whole truth about Cindy. I considered telling her that Cindy had been a controlling psycho my entire childhood, barely letting me out of the house. I was homeschooled and didn't have any friends my own age for a very long time. She had been oppressive and insane ever since my dad had died of cancer when I was two, probably because she was afraid of losing me, at least on some level.

I didn't know if she was insanely controlling because of his death or if she had always been that way. I suspected it had always been there and was just aggravated by his death. That controlling drive served her very well in her business positions, but it made her a monster at home.

But Alexa didn't need to know any of that. It was just some shitty, sad story from my past. I got out of that house when I turned eighteen, and I never bothered looking back.

"Cindy can be tough," I said simply.

"She's the CEO of a huge company. Of course she can."

I just shrugged and sipped my whisky, not bothering to argue.

"Anyway," I said, "here's to you and me. Husband and wife, finally back together."

She made a face and sighed, clinking her glass to mine. "I actually have a surprise for you," she said.

"Great. Is it your panties?"

"What? No, it's not my panties."

"That's a shame. If it were, I'd take you back into that fancy bathroom and fuck you until we got kicked out or you came, whichever happened first."

She ignored me, digging into her bag. She slowly pulled out a thick, crinkled-looking piece of paper.

"Here it is," she said triumphantly.

"What's that?"

"Proof." She held it out.

I took it and unfolded it. I looked at it for half a second before bursting out laughing. It was an official marriage license, signed by the two of us plus the priest from Thailand.

"What's funny?" she said, annoyed.

"Alex," I said, handing her back the paper, "I know we're married."

She stared at me for a second. "What?"

"I believed you as soon as you showed this to me on your laptop."

"You asshole!"

She was furious, but I couldn't help but grin at her. I couldn't tell if she was going to storm out of the restaurant and get a cab back home, throw her drink in my face, or both. I took a deep sip of my whisky, savoring the delicious taste since I suspected it was going to be my last drink before I got tossed out.

Instead, she didn't make a scene. She took another deep breath and put the paper back into her bag.

"What now?" she asked.

I blinked, surprised. If I were her, I would have been cursing me out, maybe throwing a punch or two. Instead, she was rolling with it.

This was the second time she'd impressed me tonight.

Before I could answer, the waiter returned and took our orders. When he was gone, she looked at me expectantly.

"I'm not sure what you want," I said.

"A divorce, obviously. Let's fix this stupid mistake."

"Mistake?" I grunted. "You're lucky to be married to me."

She held back a smile. "Yeah, right. You're just an arrogant jerk."

"An arrogant jerk that can get you off with his pinky finger."

"Arrogant and cocky."

"Cocky for good reason." I leaned forward, grinning at her. "Remember our wedding night?"

She blushed. "I remember."

"You know what I can make your body feel, sis."

She shook her head, smiling. "Cut it out, Cole. I'm not interested."

"Your loss then."

"Are you always like this? Or did the jungle mess your brain up?"

I laughed. "The jungle just made me hard. Though not as hard as you make me."

She rolled her eyes, groaning. "Good one."

"Thank you."

The waiter returned and refreshed our drinks. I was feeling looser, lighter, and I could tell she was too.

"Back to that divorce."

"Divorce?" I ask innocently. "What divorce?"

"Cole."

"I'm just saying, Alex. You haven't even given this pairing a chance."

"There's no *pairing* here. This whole thing was just one stupid, drunk mistake. It was a misunderstanding. It was . . ."

"The best orgasm you've ever gotten?" I offered while she searched for the word.

"Yes. I mean, no. It was regrettable."

I smirked at her. "So the orgasm was great. You're finally admitting it."

"That's not what I'm saying. There's no orgasms here, Cole. Just a divorce."

"I don't know," I said slowly. "That dress screams sex to me."

She blushed. "What about this dress?"

"Come on. You wore that dress just to tease me. Don't pretend otherwise."

"I didn't. It's a nice place. I wanted to dress up."

"Sure, you can tell yourself that. Truth is, you want me to take you back home and peel that thing off you slowly, make your toes curl with my mouth."

"God, you're frustrating," she said, taking a deep sip of her wine.

"Only because I'm right."

"You're definitely not right." She looked around the place and leaned in. "You're an arrogant dick. Now, please, will you sign the divorce papers?"

I gave her a long look, leaning back in my chair. I sipped my drink and pretended to think about it. She looked at me apprehensively, clearly on the edge of her seat.

I knew what the right answer was. I should just divorce her and be done with it. I was not interested in having a wife, much less a wife that was also my fucking stepsister. Plus all the drama with our parents. I didn't need any of that shit.

But the look on her face was just too damn much for me. She was all sex, pure fire and sin, and I couldn't help myself when I was around her. It was too much damn fun stringing her along, playing this little game, and I didn't want to give it up just yet. I wanted to get her to the point where she was begging me for it before I finally gave it to her.

It was a challenge. I wanted to make her mine, finally and fully mine, while denying her the thing she truly wanted. In the end, she'd get what she wanted, both the divorce and my cock. But for the time being, I wanted to see how it all played out.

"No," I said finally. "No. I think we'll stay married." I smiled broadly at her. "Wife."

The look on her face was more than worth it.

I knew it was the wrong thing. Part of me wanted to just be done with it all.

But sometimes the wrong thing was too much damn fun. And I was the type of guy to give in to the wrong thing more often than not.

Maybe I could teach her a little more about living like the future wasn't coming. Either way, I knew it was going to be a fun summer.

Chapter Five: Alexa

I was speechless. After Cole told me that he wasn't going to give me a divorce, that he believed me but just didn't care, I was absolutely speechless.

I wasn't even angry, at first. It just seemed like a nightmare, some kind of bad joke, and it didn't register. We finished up our meal and went home without much more happening. I even barely noticed the motorcycle ride.

Back alone in my room, it began to sink in.

The asshole believed me. He had just been messing with me the whole time.

Worse, he wasn't going to sign the papers. He wasn't going to make this easy for me, after all the stress and worry I had gone through, after everything.

My chance to divorce him and be done with the whole embarrassing episode was right there, but he refused to help me.

Asshole. Arrogant, self-center, unbelievable dickhead.

What made him think he could say no? We weren't married, not really.
Sure, okay, legally we were married, but what did that even mean? It wasn't
like we were in love or had any sort of connection. The man had
disappeared into the jungle as soon as the vacation was over, rendering any
sort of relationship impossible.

Yet somehow he felt that he could call me "wife" and move into my
house and boss me around. Who the hell was this guy?

Aside from my husband and my stepbrother, of course.

I was practically fuming as I sat at my desk, scrolling through Twitter.

some people need to understand BOUNDARIES I tweeted. I was so
annoyed that I had succumbed to random acts of vague social media
complaining. I hated when people said really generic things that were
obviously aimed at specific people, but I couldn't help myself.

sometimes what you want isn't as important as you think it is I tweeted next. It
made me feel a little bit better, even if nobody understood what I was
talking about. Actually, that was part of it. I liked that I could complain
about my secret in public without anyone knowing anything.

quit being so arrogant. You're not that cool and motorcycles are stupid.
#mmaisforlosers. I grinned at that one before finally hitting send.

It didn't change anything. I was still in the same situation as I was before, except now I had just sent out some passive-aggressive and vaguely

bratty messages to a bunch of strangers. Still, it made me feel a little better

to vent. Maybe I needed to give Lacey a call. She knew all about my

situation and definitely loved a good bitch-session. If anyone was going to

appreciate me being mean about Cole, she definitely would. Plus, I was

looking forward to hearing her surprise at my insanely impossible situation.

A few minutes later, I checked my feed again and stared at what I saw.

Somebody had liked my last tweet, but it wasn't someone I recognized.

His username was FighterColeMMA.

I clenched my fists. There was no way it was him. He couldn't be

stalking me online, too, could he?

I stood up, deciding not to waste any time. I pushed open my

bedroom door and then banged on his door. "Cole!" I said.

"Come in."

The door pushed open and I was ready to shout at him, to tell him

what an asshole he was being, how he couldn't just refuse to divorce me,

but it all just died on my lips. I stared in at him as he continued to do his

sit-ups.

He was shirtless and had a thin sheen of sweat. I remembered that

body very, very well from all those months ago. Tattoos snaked up his skin,

and his muscles were ripped and tough. I wanted to tell him what a dick he

was being, except it was hard when I also wanted to lick every inch of his exposed torso.

He finished his set and looked over at me. "What can I do for you, wife? Come to spend some time in our marriage bed?"

That snapped me out of it. "Are you stalking me?"

He gave me an innocent look. "What do you mean?"

"Twitter. I know you saw my tweets."

"Not my fault your profile is public."

My jaw dropped. It really was him. I couldn't believe he had the gall to like a tweet that was so clearly making fun of him.

"How did you find me?"

"You used your real name."

I let out a thin breath. Of course. All he needed to do was search for my name.

"So you refuse to let me divorce you and now you're cyber stalking me."

"Not exactly. You're the one insulting me publically."

"I wouldn't have to do that if you would just divorce me."

He stood up and stretched, grinning. "Why would I do that? I want to try and make our marriage work."

"We don't have a marriage."

"Call me old fashioned, but I think the state would disagree with you."

"Legally, fine. But, Cole, we're not married and you know it."

"I don't know. Maybe we could give it a try."

He moved across the room, and I could practically feel my pussy go from normal to dripping in six seconds. He was ripped and smooth and slightly sweaty in an incredible way. It wasn't fair at all. How was I supposed to win this argument when he looked like that?

How was I supposed to divorce him when he made me feel that way?

"Why are you doing this?" I whispered.

"Because I can." He grabbed my waist suddenly and pulled me against him.

I didn't fight.

"Because I want to," he continued, talking into my ear. I felt a shiver run down my spine. "Because I want to take you again, Alex, make you feel things you thought you forgot about. I want to take it further."

"And I just want to move on with my life, maybe not be married to my stepbrother."

He paused and then laughed and moved away from me. I took a sharp breath, wishing he'd come back.

"Yeah, that is inconvenient."

"Seriously, we can't do this. If somebody found out, our parents would be screwed."

He walked over to the bed and pulled his shirt back over his chest. I wished he hadn't done that, but it did make it easier to talk to him.

"Maybe I don't much care about Cindy's career anymore."

I rolled my eyes. "Typical. Rebelling against mommy."

"That's not what this is about."

"Isn't it? You're staying married to me to get back at your mom."

"You don't know anything about me."

"Exactly. That's why we shouldn't be married."

He laughed, shaking his head. "You're a clever one, Alex, but you're my wife."

"What am I going to have to do to get a divorce?" I said, desperate and angry.

He looked at me for a second. "How about this. For starters, you have to come see an MMA fight with me."

I raised my eyebrow. "Are you joking? I have no interest in that."

"Take it or leave it."

"Fine," I said quickly. "Fine. But I'm bringing a friend."

He shrugged. "Do whatever you want."

"If this is your way of trying to prove that MMA isn't lame, you're going to be disappointed."

He gave me a wicked grin and turned away. "I doubt that."

The next night, we stood outside of the venue and I did not want to go in at all.

It was crowded, way more crowded than I would have guessed was possible for an MMA fight. I knew it was popular with some people, but figured it was still pretty small.

But the place looked packed. Like, hundreds of people packed. I had expected a lot of old fat men and bros, but it was a strange mix of people. There were even a few young kids in the crowd, which freaked me out. Who would bring a kid to a violent fight?

"This is crazy," Lacey whispered in my ear. "So many people!"

"I know, right?"

"And I half expected to get murdered."

"Surprisingly, I feel a lot safer than I expected."

"Like, I thought this was some sort of street fighting?"

"But it's legit," I said, mystified.

"I know! And so many hot guys."

I looked around, frowning. "Really?"

"Get your head out of your ass, Alex. This place is crawling with testosterone-laden beefcakes. It's like a buffet of muscular men."

I laughed, shaking my head. "I guess. I didn't really notice."

"What are you two whispering about?"

I looked up as Cole returned, holding our tickets.

"Cole, you didn't tell us these things were full of hot guys," Lacey said.

"They're not really my type," he said.

"You have a type of guy?" I asked.

"Nope. They're not my type because they're guys."

Lacey and I laughed as he handed out our tickets. He walked confidently through the crowd, and I had to admit that I was pretty impressed so far. The venue was large and clean, even though it was completely packed inside. Our sets weren't far from the ring, only a few rows back.

"How'd you get these?" I asked Cole.

"I know a guy."

We sat down and he looked around the place.

"See anyone you know?" I asked him.

"Plenty," he grunted.

"Any friends?"

"Nope."

I turned back toward Lacey to make a joke, but she was too busy ogling a group of men in business suits that looked like they would have been comfortable in an economic summit.

The lights were bright and the crowd was crawling. It was full of noise, nervous excitement, and prefight jitters. People were buying drinks and food and generally wandering around the place. Most of the seats were full already, and people were slowly filtering in. Music blared through the loudspeaker, but it wasn't anything I recognized.

"Look at those hunky nerds," Lacey said, staring blatantly.

I shook my head, smiling. "You're unreal."

"What? They're like sexy accountants. I'd let every one of them bang me if they'd do my taxes, too."

"Prostituting yourself for tax help?"

"What can I say, I hate doing my taxes."

Suddenly, Cole stood up. "I'll be right back," he said.

"Okay."

He stalked off into the crowd. I watched, curious about what he was doing, but he quickly disappeared into the mass of people.

"Where's your husband going?"

I shot her a look. "We agreed. No jokes about that tonight."

"Oh come on. Just one."

"Whatever. I'm not sure where he's going."

I looked around and spotted him across the way. I watched as he approached a group of men and began talking to them. They looked like they all knew each other, shaking hands and laughing. I watched as Cole took over their conversation, dominating whatever they were talking about. He seemed completely at ease and in control, totally calm and collected. In the middle of the sea of wild people, Cole was like an oasis of cool and collected confidence.

Meanwhile, Lacey was still scouting out the crowd. I was afraid that if I turned my back on her for too long that she'd end up going home with the first mildly attractive guy that spoke to her.

Cole came back a few minutes later and sat back down. "What was that?" I asked him.

"What do you care?"

"Curious, I guess."

He leaned in toward me. "Curious about me?"

"Yeah, I am."

"I knew you would be, wife. Can't help yourself."

"I'm just trying to be nice."

He smirked. "Sure you are. Well, that was just business."

"Just business?"

He leaned back in his seat. "Sure. Business."

"You're so mysterious," I said sarcastically.

Whatever comeback he had prepared fell short as the crowd began to cheer, drowning him out. I looked over toward the ring as men began to climb inside.

They were muscular and mostly naked, though not as large as Cole was. I looked at him and he nodded at the ring, a little smile on his face. The excitement of the crowd began to build, the electric shiver of excitement running through our bodies.

It was the buzz before something happened. It was the buildup to the fight. I glanced at Lacey, and I knew she felt it, too. The rush of excitement, anticipation, and even a little bit of fear.

It was exhilarating. I loved how in tune with the crowd I felt as the bell rang and the two men attacked each other savagely.

I didn't think I liked violence. Well, I knew that I didn't. That wasn't what I liked about the fight, honestly. I could have gone without watching the thing entirely. But the feeling of being there with the crowd as we cheered the men on, the two of them pitting their bodies against each other, well, it was incredible.

They were at the pinnacle of their physical skills, and we were watching them work as hard as they possibly could to destroy their opponent. MMA was different from boxing; there was a wider variety of moves allowed, not just punching. The two men kicked and wrestled and punched each other, and the fight went for a few rounds, seemingly close.

And I was on the edge of my seat the entire time. I could feel Cole next to me, and he felt it too, that same adrenaline boost. When the taller man landed a rough punch on the smaller one, knocking him down, the crowd went absolutely insane. The taller man pounced on the smaller one, pummeling him, and then the fight was over.

It happened so fast. One second they looked evenly matched, though both of them pretty were beat up, and the next second the one man was standing in the middle of the ring, victorious.

The crowd was on its feet, cheering wildly. Cole was clapping, a huge, vicious smile on his face. I couldn't stop myself from cheering along.

It was such a rush. I'd never experienced anything like it before. Although the fight still wasn't really my thing, I was beginning to understand why Cole loved it and why so many people wanted to get involved with it.

"Come on," Cole said over the roar of the crowd.

He shifted his way through the seats, and I had to struggle to keep up. Lacey was right behind me. I gave her a look, but neither of us knew where Cole was going. We went back up the ramp and toward the front. Cole pushed open an unmarked door and led us through a back hallway and into another room.

The sounds of the crowd receded, and I glanced at Lacey again. She gave me a confused smile but didn't say anything.

This was smaller, more intimate. There were still a good amount of people in there, but it was quieter. There was a bar in the back with a TV showing replays of the fight just above it. Men and women all sat around talking, drinking, and watching each other.

"What's this?" I asked Cole.

"Bar for the fighters," he grunted.

"Oh hell yeah," Lacey whispered. "Showtime."

She disappeared toward a table of young men before I could say anything. I couldn't believe how forward she was being, but then again, you never knew with Lacey.

"Come on," Cole grunted.

We made our way to the bar. Several people in the room gave Cole a nod of recognition, and he nodded back, though nobody came up to him. We sat down on stools and ordered drinks.

"How many people in here do you know?" I asked him.

"Most of them."

"These are your people, then, I guess."

"Used to be."

We got our drinks and I looked at him, interested. There seemed to be something bugging him, though he wasn't saying what.

"What do you mean by that?"

"Since I was gone for so long, it's like they all forgot about me."

"You were gone a long time. You'll get back into it."

He nodded. "I know. It's okay."

"When do you fight again?"

I didn't know why I asked, because I shouldn't have cared. I just wanted my divorce and that was that. But being there, in that crowd, I suddenly had a new respect for what Cole did.

"Soon," he said. "Very soon."

I sighed, sipping my drink. He didn't seem very talkative, and I didn't feel like drawing him out all night. If this was his way of convincing me to stay married to him, he wasn't doing a good job.

As I sat there looking around the room at all the interesting people, at the trophies lining the walls and the women in too-short dresses, I couldn't help but wonder why he even wanted me around. The fight seemed so exciting, almost glamorous, and I was just a regular, boring girl. There didn't seem to be any reason for him to want to mess with me so much. It wasn't like he actually wanted to be my husband; I couldn't imagine that was the case, at least.

"Are you sure it's a good idea to leave your friend over there alone?" Cole grunted at me, breaking the silence.

"She's a big girl. Plus, she does this a lot."

He raised an eyebrow. "Yeah?"

"She doesn't mean anything by it. If I really cared, I'd tell her."

"Bet she doesn't do it in a fighter bar much."

"What's that mean?"

"Means these aren't your usual guys, sweetheart. She should be careful."

I looked over and watched Lacey take a shot, laughing loudly with the group of guys. They seemed harmless enough, or at least they weren't the scariest guys in the place. She was going to be fine.

"Since when do you care?" I asked, frustrated. "And what am I doing here, anyway?"

"Having a drink."

"What's your game?" I was about ready to get up and leave. I was suddenly frustrated again as the memories of the last year came back to me. It had all been pushed to the background because of the excitement of the fight, but I couldn't hold it all back forever.

He gave me a long, penetrating look. I felt a shiver run down my spine. "See that guy over there?" Cole asked, nodding across the room.

I risked a glance in that direction and saw a man sitting at a table with an older woman.

"Sure," I said.

"He's a pimp and a drug dealer. And he's one of the better trainers in the business."

"Seriously?"

"And that guy," Cole went on, "feeding a shot to your friend, he's deadly as hell on his feet, an awesome striker. I'm pretty sure his fists could break concrete."

I raised an eyebrow, watching the guy. He seemed so normal and harmless.

"That guy is a thief. That guy's a drug addict. That guy can strangle you out in three seconds. That girl's a fighter, too."

I sighed, sipping my drink. "Okay, I don't get this."

"These are my people, Alex. This is who I am."

"You're not a pimp or a drug dealer."

"No," he grunted. "But I am a fighter."

"So what?"

"So, I don't belong in your world. You're like my mother, clean and proper. I live my life fast and hard."

I felt my anger rising again but forced it back down inside me. For as annoying as he could be, I was surprised by how open he was. It was like he was trying to bring me into his world but didn't know how to do it.

And I didn't know if I wanted to see it. Part of me wanted him to just be that guy from the vacation. I wanted him to stay a faceless and nameless force that I needed to exorcise from my life. I didn't want to get to know him, because I was afraid that I was going to like what I found out.

"Then divorce me if you really think that."

"Not yet."

Before I could respond, a man suddenly loomed up in my peripheral vision.

"Cole," he said, "I'm surprised to see you here."

Cole barely acknowledged him. "Ronnie."

I looked up at the guy named Ronnie. He was tall, maybe as tall as

Cole, and about as built. He had a scar down his lip, making him look like he was constantly sneering. His eyes were so brown that they were almost black.

"Thought you ran away."

"You know I didn't," Cole grunted.

"Yeah, I know. You were busy sucking Skad's dick out in the jungle."

Cole looked up at Ronnie then, his expression completely blank. "You should walk away now."

"Nah, don't think I will. See, you're a low-life piece of shit, and I don't want you coming back here."

Cole sighed, slugged back his drink, and then slowly stood up. "All right. If that's what you want."

The two men squared off, and there was a hush over the room. I could feel my heart pounding in my chest, trying to explode out of my rib cage. I was terrified that violence was coming, violence like the kind I had seen in the ring. But I wasn't sure I was ready to see it up close.

And then Ronnie burst out laughing, and Cole grinned, and they threw their arms around each other, hugging. The room resumed talking as they laughed and embraced.

"You piece of shit," Cole said. "Jealous motherfucker."

"Jealous? Fuck yes I'm jealous. You got to train with fucking Skad."

"Alex," Cole said, looking at me, "this is Ronnie. He's my old training partner."

"Well hello there," Ronnie said, turning to me.

"Nice to meet you." I was so relieved that I could hardly form words.

"I think we scared the lady," Ronnie said to Cole. "Listen, Alex, how about I buy you a drink?"

"Careful," Cole said to him.

Ronnie raised an eyebrow at him. "What? She yours?"

"I'm not anybody's," I said.

"That's my stepsister."

"Stepsister?" Ronnie burst out laughing again. It was an infectious sound, and I found myself giggling with him. "Can't believe there's finally a girl you can't actually fuck."

Cole gave me a grin as Ronnie calmed down and sat with us. He ordered new drinks for everyone, and then Ronnie and Cole began to talk shop. I got lost in their back and forth banter about the different fighters. Ronnie caught Cole up on what had happened since he had been gone, which apparently was a lot.

I kept glancing over at Lacey. She seemed okay, though she was awfully close to that one dangerous boy, and I was pretty sure she was hammered. I didn't care if she wanted to go home with him or whatever; I just wanted her to be safe. Cole noticed me glancing at her and gave me a look, like he was reassuring me or something.

An hour and more passed that way, and the night was getting late. We finished off our third round, and Ronnie leaned back in his chair, checking his watch.

"Shit," he said. "Time to get the fuck out."

"Why? Got an early date tomorrow?"

"Nah," Ronnie said, looking nervous. "I'm just beat. That's all."

"Come on, man. One more round."

"Look, we should go."

"What's your problem?"

Ronnie took a deep breath and sighed. "Look, man, Trent is going to be here soon."

Cole got serious. "So the fuck what?"

"Who's Trent?" I asked.

"Some mindless goon," Cole said.

Ronnie gave him a look. "The last time Cole and Trent saw each other, Cole was smashing Trent's face into a wall."

"We don't get along," Cole grunted.

"Why?"

"Cole got that training gig and Trent wanted it, so Trent thought he'd fuck Cole up."

"He's an idiot." Cole paused and sighed. "There's more to it than just that."

"He is an idiot," Ronnie agreed, "but he's undefeated since you left."

"Who cares? He fights nobodies."

"Actually," Ronnie said, "he has some good names under his belt. Come on, man, let's get out of here."

"Fuck that," Cole growled. "Trent can fuck off."

Just as Cole was beginning to get annoyed, I heard something from over toward Lacey's table. I looked over and saw the guys getting up, looks of horror on their faces. There was a slight commotion. I quickly got out of my chair and ran over.

"What's happened?" I asked.

"She's puking!"

I looked over and, sure enough, there was Lacey on her hands and knees, puking all her drinks out.

"Oh shit," I said, running to her side.

"I'm pukinggggg," Lacey groaned.

"I know. I know."

She finished and looked up at me, still clearly wasted. The guys were all yelling as Cole and Ronnie waded through the crowd.

"Now we can go," Cole grunted.

"Sorry, girl," Lacey slurred. "I ruined your date."

"Wasn't a date," I said.

Cole swooped down and grabbed Lacey, slinging her over his

shoulder. "Come on."

The bartender was yelling, but we ignored him as Ronnie and Cole made a path through the crowd. Lacey's ass was hanging out from her short dress, and I did my best to keep it covered as we went out into the night.

"Holy shit, did you see her hurl?" Ronnie cackled.

"She was like a dragon," Cole said.

"Shuddup," Lacey groaned.

I stood out in the street and flagged a cab.

"I'll leave you here, man," Ronnie said.

"Good seeing you, brother."

"Same to you." Ronnie grinned at me. "Be good to your stepbrother, Alex."

"Bye, Ronnie."

Cole gently pushed Lacey into the back of the cab, and we both followed her in. I gave the driver our address.

"If she pukes," the driver said, "it's double."

Cole burst out laughing, and I couldn't help but laugh along. Even though it had been a weird night in a weird place, I had to admit that I'd had a good time. I didn't love Cole's world. But I maybe understood where he was coming from, why he felt the way that he did.

"Take us home," Cole grunted at the driver, and we pulled out into traffic.

Chapter Six: Cole

It was early the next morning, the sun just peeking over the horizon, as I finished my run. I hated getting up early, but I could barely sleep the night before. I kept thinking about her, about my stepsister, about my fucking wife.

I'd never brought a girl around my life like that before. It felt safer because she was my stepsister, but it was definitely far from safe. We were married, and I kept imagining all the dirty shit I wanted to do to her body.

I knew I could make her wet like a waterfall with just a touch. I wanted that soaking pussy to grip my cock like a vice, and it drove me fucking crazy. The run did barely anything to get her out of my brain.

Why the fuck didn't I just divorce her and be done with it?

I was a masochist and knew it.

"Good morning," Cindy said as I came into the kitchen. "You're awake early for once."

"Good morning," I grunted at her, filling up my coffee mug. I felt the two-day stubble on my chin and resolved to shave.

"How are you adjusting to the new house?"

I shrugged. "Fine. How are you adjusting to your new husband?"

"Frank is a good man. I wish you'd get to know him."

"I'm sure you wish a lot of things, Cindy."

"Don't be a brat," she spat at me. "You can at least be civil."

I took a deep breath and let it out. "Fine. Frank seems nice enough."

She nodded curtly. "Thank you."

"I'm told there's trouble in paradise, though."

"With Frank? Things are great."

"Your job."

"Ah." She nodded and looked away. "That's great, too."

I knew she was lying. My mother had only ever cared about one thing, and that was power. People sometimes called her the Ice Queen, and for good reason. I liked to call her Mussolini behind her back. She was intense and task-driven, always on to the next thing that would further her desires.

We were similar like that. I was driven to be the best at what I did, just like she was. The biggest difference was, Cindy was willing to sacrifice anyone or anything for her own personal gain.

I believed in hard work. I trained my ass off and put my body on the line. I didn't need anything from anyone, and I never would. I also didn't believe in fucking others over just because you wanted something.

"Not what I heard," I said.

She gave me a frown. "My work is not your concern, Cole."

"Please, mother. You've been trying to get me to act proper for years because of your job."

"And now you're interested?"

I shrugged, sipping my coffee. "Trying to make pleasant conversation."

She sat up and looked at me. "Okay. My marriage to Frank has caused some problems, it's true. There's talk of nepotism and other scandalous lies."

"You wouldn't marry a man to further you career," I said, nodding, though I knew full well that she would.

"Of course not," she said quickly. "It was just a coincidence."

"Of course."

She gave me a look and nodded to herself. "If you suddenly care about all this, there is something you can do."

"Maybe," I grunted.

"There's a dinner for certain shareholders and other prominent members of the company tomorrow night. I'd like you to attend with your stepsister."

"And why would I do this for you?"

"I thought you were trying to be a family, Cole."

I laughed, shaking my head. The idea of her trying to be a family again was absurd. She didn't have a nurturing bone in her body, which was probably why I had ended up seeking pain for a living.

But that was just stupid armchair psychology.

"You have no interest in being a family. If you want something, you have to give up something. You know how this works; you're a businesswoman," I said.

She nodded, thinking. "Very well then. If you do this for me, I'll give you free reign of the cars all summer."

I raised an eyebrow. It was an intriguing proposition, especially considering her fondness for vintage muscle cars. It wasn't exactly a feminine hobby, but my mother never cared much for gender stereotypes. She was something of a feminist like that.

"You have a deal."

She smiled. "Good. Now convince your stepsister to come along."

"That wasn't part of this."

"I need you both."

I grunted. "She doesn't listen to me."

"You seem to be getting along. Try."

"Fine."

She nodded again and went back to her paper. I took my coffee upstairs.

I didn't usually give in to my mother's bribes. Normally, the idea of taking something from her made my stomach churn. But I was beginning to realize that if I was staying in that house with her and Frank and Alex, I had to at least pretend to get along with everyone.

As I crested the staircase, I saw her sneak out of her room. Alex was wearing short cotton shorts and a tight tank top, her long brown hair spilling down along her back. I could see the bottom of her ass, and I felt my cock stiffen instantly.

She was the reason I was going through all this bullshit. If we weren't married, I didn't think I'd stick around. But we were, and I had to admit that I was having a ton of fucking fun with it.

I took a long drink of coffee as I came up behind her. "Good morning, sis," I said.

She whirled around. "What are you doing?"

"Going to my room."

"You scared me. Quit being a creep."

I walked up closer to her. "You look good this morning. Bedhead suits you."

"Bedhead doesn't suit anyone," she mumbled.

"Reminds me of how you look after you come. Your skin gets flushed and your hair is a mess."

"It's too early for that."

"It's never too early. Right now I'm thinking about ripping those little shorts off your incredible body and fucking you right here against the wall."

"Be quiet," she hissed. "My dad could hear you."

"So what?" I stepped closer to her, and she didn't move an inch. "They'll find out how badly I want to fuck that perfect pussy of yours eventually."

"No, they won't, because you're going to give me that divorce."

I smirked. "Maybe. Or maybe I'm going to make your body want to stay married to me."

"Whatever," she muttered and turned away. I could see the blush in her cheeks, and I knew I had riled her up. I could practically smell how soaked her pussy was, and I bet if I really did push her against the wall and press my fingers against her pussy, they'd come away soaked.

Instead, I followed her into the bathroom.

"What are you doing?" she practically yelled. "You can't just follow me in here."

"Word from the parents," I said. "There's some dinner bullshit tomorrow night. You're expected to attend."

She made a face. "Already? I hate those things."

"Been to one before?"

"Sure. It's all old people and sleazy businessmen. Not my scene. I'm amazed your mom never made you go to one."

"She tried, a long time ago. She stopped trying pretty quick."

Alex leaned against the counter and crossed her arms. "If I say I'm going, will you get the heck out of here?"

"Maybe," I said. "Or maybe I want to taste that wet pussy first."

"I'll go. Get out."

I grinned at her. "You sure you don't want me to get you off? I bet your body is begging for it right now."

"Out."

"Your loss." I turned and left, laughing quietly to myself. I couldn't help but tease her mercilessly. I loved the way she responded to me, denying in her words but begging in her body language.

My cock was practically tearing through my shorts, but I didn't care. That was the reason I was sticking around. The look on her fucking cute-as-hell face, that perfect body, those lips, those eyes, that everything. I needed another taste. I was going to get another taste.

Maybe the dinner was the perfect place to show her exactly what she wanted.

～～～～～～～～～～～～～～～～～～～～～～～～～～～～～～～～

"Car's here," I said, knocking on her door.

"Just a minute!"

I leaned up against the wall. "How are you not ready yet?"

"I said, just a minute!"

I laughed and shook my head. Finally, after a few minutes she opened the door and stepped out into the hall.

I took a sharp breath. Her dress was the perfect shade of blue, and it made her light skin and pale eyes stand out so much more. It showed just enough cleavage to have me fucking hard already, but not enough to make our parents complain.

"Not too bad," I said, looking her up and down.

"Can it," she said. "Let's go."

I followed her down the hall and out front, feeling a little stiff in my tuxedo. I hadn't worn it in a long time, but it still fit. Alex's ass swayed as we moved toward the front door, and I grinned to myself as we approached my final surprise for the night.

"Where's the car?" she asked as we got out front.

"There." I pointed.

"No way."

I nodded, grinning hugely. "Yes way."

Parked out front was my mother's 1970 Shelby Mustang GT350 in bright yellow. I had to admit, I wasn't much of a car guy, but there was something about classic muscle cars that was just so damn cool.

"Whose car is that?"

"Cindy's. I'm using it for the evening." I walked around to the passenger side and opened the door for her. "Your carriage awaits."

She smiled despite herself and got inside. I closed the door softly and walked around to the other side.

"I have to admit," she said, "this is kind of cool."

I hit the ignition and the car roared to life. "Hell yeah it is."

"Let's do it."

I hit play on the tape player and Blue Oyster Cult's "Don't Fear the Reaper" came blaring through the speakers as I hit the gas and sped out into traffic.

She laughed loudly as I wove my way toward the suburbs and the banquet hall where the dinner was being held. I was surprised that she seemed to love driving fast as much as I did. The cool night air flooded in through the open windows, and although it whipped our hair around, hers coming undone from the fancy updo she clearly had worked on, she never once complained. In fact, she turned the music up louder and rolled her window down lower.

I was in awe. Part of me had wanted to mess with her, but my plan was backfiring. Clearly, there was more to Alexa than I had thought.

Attractive stepsister slash wife at my side, we sped through the cool California night, whipping wide around slower cars, rubber screeching over pavement, the stars coming in through the past and exiting further into it.

We enjoyed the ride in silence, not bothering to try to make small talk. We got to the banquet hall much sooner than I had expected, though, and I was a little disappointed that I had to stop driving. I would have loved to keep going with her by my side, but duty called. I parked and helped her out, and we walked into the venue together. We found our place cards and wove our way through the surprisingly large crowd.

"Alexa!" Frank said as we approached, clearly surprised as we made our way to the table. "What are you doing here?"

"Cindy demanded we come," I explained.

He nodded, smiling. "Well, I'm glad you're both here."

We took our seats at the head table as Frank returned to his conversation with another old white dude. I felt completely out of place among the stuffy rich people, but Alexa seemed totally fine. In fact, she shook hands and smiled like she was born for it.

I knocked back my drink and gestured for one of the staff to bring me another. I might as well try to enjoy myself if I was going to have to endure that all night long.

"You're good at this," I grunted into Alexa's ear after a half hour. She smiled at me.

"It's easy. Just don't act like a jerk and you're fine."

"I'm being pleasant."

"Drinking too much and grunting at everyone is pleasant?"

"Is for me."

"At least try, Cole."

Before I could come up with some witty retort, my mother walked onstage and the crowd slowly quieted.

"Ladies and gentlemen," she said, "thank you for coming." The crowd applauded politely. "There have been huge changes here with Semingo, as everyone knows. When Semiotics Inc. and Blingo merged last year, nobody was sure where that would lead. What was a major producer of computer components doing merging with a software company? Well," she said with a flourish, "now you all know."

The crowd clapped louder.

"I don't know," I whispered to Alexa.

"Semingo. New company," she whispered back.

I shrugged, my eyes glazing over as my mother continued her presentation. It followed the standard formula of thanking the shareholders, the board members, and every other old and rich and important member of the company. Next she talked logistics, going over numbers and such, and finally she ended with projections.

It was all well and good but boring as hell. I tuned it out after ten minutes, and then suddenly a spotlight was shining directly on Alexa and me.

Alex was giving me a look, and I glanced up from my drink. People were staring, and Alex was standing. I ambled to my feet and raised my glass to the room, smirking.

"Our children, everyone," Cindy said. "Frank and I are so proud of them and are so happy they could be here."

Scattered applause. We sat back down. Alexa scowled at me. "You're doing more harm than good."

"Maybe," I grunted.

And the speeches continued. When Cindy was finished, she rejoined our table, shooting me looks. It was easy to ignore her when Alexa was so damn distracting by my side.

We were forced to sit through increasingly dull people talk about increasingly mindless things. Even Alex was looking a little haggard at the end of the first hour.

"Hey," I whispered in her ear. "Let's get out of here."

"We can't leave," she said. "It's not over yet."

"Won't leave," I said back. "We'll just take a break."

She gave me a dubious look. "I don't know."

"Come on. I can tell you're ready to claw your own eyes out."

I stood up as the speaker finished onstage. She had a moment of indecision, and then she quickly stood to follow me. As the people clapped and the staff bustled to freshen drinks as the next speaker set up, we skirted around the edges of the large banquet hall. We came up toward the bar, and as we passed I grabbed a bottle of whisky, pushing it into my jacket. I quickly went out an emergency exit and into a stairwell before anyone noticed.

Alexa was right on my heels. "Where are we going?"

"You'll see." I took a slug of the whisky as we climbed up the steps. I could hear the clacking of her heels on the concrete steps as she followed me.

"Did you steal that?" she asked.

"It's an open bar."

"Give it here."

I handed her back the bottle and she took a swig, making a face. "Whisky is gross."

"It's an acquired taste."

"Shouldn't things just, like, taste good? And not have to be acquired?"

I shrugged. "Sometimes the best things seem bad at first. Come on."

We reached the top of the stairs and I pushed out the door.

"Wow," Alexa whispered.

I had to agree. The door led out onto the roof, and the view of the bay was incredible. We were pretty high, and the night sky was clear, so everything was visible. We walked over to the edge and leaned up against the brick, looking out over the water.

"Beats that shit downstairs," I said.

"I have to agree with you there."

"Think your dad will be pissed we left?"

"What do you care?"

"Guess I don't."

I took a sip of the whisky. I had never loved San Francisco that much before I left the states, but I had to admit that it was pretty beautiful. Sure as hell beat the shit out of the stinking Thai jungle.

"Why don't you and your mom get along?" Alex asked suddenly. "Too much of a bad boy to be nice to mommy?"

I laughed, looking at her. "Not exactly."

"Then why?"

"Does it matter? You just want a divorce from me."

"I guess not. But we'll still be stepsiblings after the divorce."

I leaned closer to her. "I tell you something, and then you have to tell me something. Deal?"

"Fine. Deal."

"Cindy is an intense woman, but you've noticed that by now. She's been pushing me hard ever since I was a young kid. When my dad died, it only got worse. When I decided I'd rather go into fighting than business, I guess I disappointed her. She hasn't let me forget that since."

"That sounds hard. But it's not like she doesn't love you."

"Love," I snorted. "Love doesn't win Cindy any influence or power, and that's all she cares about."

"What about my dad, then?"

I shrugged, not wanting to tell her the truth, that Cindy was probably just using her dad. "Freak accident, maybe." I moved closer to her, passing her the bottle back. "My turn to ask a question."

She sighed. "Okay. Go for it."

"Why did you marry me?"

I watched her mouth drop slightly as I moved closer to her. She looked away, red coming into her cheeks. "I didn't think it was real," she said.

"That's bullshit. I know that."

She was quiet for a minute and took a swig of the whisky, making another disgusted face. "I thought you were hot, okay? And fun. Exciting. We were in paradise, you know?"

"Hot?" I whispered, practically on top of her.

"Yeah." Her lips were slightly parted, and her tongue ran over her bottom lip.

I knew what that meant. She wanted me to bite her gently, right there, and cup her ass.

"You liked the way I made you feel," I said.

"Maybe," she whispered.

Our bodies were inches apart. The only sound was her breathing deeply, in and out, in and out, and I thought I could feel the heat coming off her skin.

"You liked that I made you feel alive. You liked having my tongue slip up against your clit until you screamed."

She took a sharp breath as I grabbed her hips, pulling her against me. "I did at the time."

"You still think about it every day."

"No," she said, shaking her head.

"Don't deny it. You're soaked now, like you've been soaked every time I'm near you."

"What happened was just a vacation fling."

"I don't think so," I said. "I've had flings before. You want more of it."

My eyes locked on hers, and she tilted her head slightly to one side, practically inviting me in with her mouth. I knew what she wanted, and I wanted it too. I wanted to take every inch of her, tear off that fucking tease of a dress and stick my cock deep inside her tight fucking pussy. I wanted to make her scream out over the bay.

"It was a mistake," she said, half whisper and half gasp.

"Nothing was a mistake." My mouth was so close to hers that I could taste her minty breathe.

"All of it."

And then I kissed her, hard and fast. A buzz ran through my skull and body, and my cock pressed up against her crotch, our bodies intertwined. She threw herself into the kiss as much as I did.

And then we heard a voice. It tore us out of the moment as quickly as we had thrown ourselves into it. "Alexa?" It was a young woman's voice, and Alex threw herself away from me like I was made of flames.

"Alexa?" the voice came again.

"Over here," Alex said, trying to put herself together.

I gave her a look. "This isn't over."

She glared at me. "Yes, it is."

A young woman, maybe a few years older than us and wearing a conservative black dress, walked over. Her blond hair was pulled up into a bun, and she was wearing thick-rimmed black glasses and holding what looked like an address book. She completely ignored me, addressing Alexa.

"Your father is looking for you."

"Oh," she said, flustered. "Okay. Thanks."

The girl looked at me. "Cole."

I nodded at her, not sure who she was. She turned and walked quickly back toward the party.

"Who the hell was that?" I asked.

"Your mom's assistant. You don't remember meeting her earlier?"

I shook my head, bemused. "Nope. Not at all."

"Her name is Madison, and I'm pretty sure she saw us kissing."

I raised my eyebrow at Alex. "I doubt that."

"You asshole," she hissed and smacked my arm. "You can't just kiss me whenever you want to."

"I think you kissed me, sis."

"Oh my god. Don't call me that. Not right now." She walked away, breathing deeply. "What the fuck am I doing?" she said to herself.

"Don't get too twisted. There's no way she saw anything. It's too dark out here."

Alex turned back toward me. "Whatever. What do you even care? You don't care about anything but yourself."

I narrowed my eyes, frowning. "Okay. Sure."

She sighed. "Let's get back to the dinner."

"If that's what you want, that's fine with me."

She stormed off without another word, back toward the stairwell.

I watched her go and picked up the bottle she had left behind. I took a deep swig, sighing to myself.

The girl was a damn pain in my ass. One second she was practically begging for it, and the next she was storming off like I fucking grew a second head.

Still, that fucking kiss. It was unreal. Never before in my life had I felt something hit me like that. Her taste, her body, it all mingled in my brain like a shot of crack straight to my gray matter.

I took another swig, hard as fuck. I needed to gather myself before I rejoined the boring-as-hell party downstairs.

That girl was a problem. Although I told Alex that she hadn't seen anything, I wasn't so sure. I resolved to look into that Madison girl a little bit, find out if she harbored any grudges against my mother.

Knowing Cindy, though, I was willing to bet poor Madison had a laundry list of complaints.

Erection subsided, I walked down the steps and rejoined the festivities. Dinner was being served finally, and Alex was deep in conversation with her dad and another older gentleman. I deposited the bottle back at the bar, giving the barman a little grin, and returned to my seat next to my stepsister.

Actually, next to my wife.

The night after that was a blur of formalities. I said hello to whoever my mother introduced me to, and I smiled nicely at everyone else. I was on my best behavior, not bothering to act like a pain in the ass.

Finally, people began to filter out of the hall. Alex wasn't speaking to me, but she wasn't exactly ignoring me, either. That was fine; I was drained and didn't feel like playing games, anyway.

But as soon as we got out into the parking lot, a disheveled-looking man approach us. At first I tensed, ready to fight him off, assuming he was a mugger. But quickly I realized that he was holding a camera, not a gun.

"Cole Redson? Alexa Carter?" Alexa stopped and stared at him.

I grabbed her elbow and pulled her along. "What the hell?" she hissed at me.

"Reporter," I answered.

"What do you think about your parents' marriage?" he called out, taking pictures. "Are you aware of the allegations against them?"

"No comment," I growled at the guy.

People were staring as I hauled Alexa behind me. I noticed two big dudes in suits and earpieces walking toward us.

"Cole, do you think your mother is a cold, careerist bitch?"

I stopped dead in my tracks and let go of Alexa's arm.

"What did you say?" I asked the guy.

"Do you think your mother is using Alexa's father for success?"

"Before that," I growled.

"Is your mother a cold bitch?" he asked, sneering at me.

I stepped forward and swung my fist faster than he could think. I struck him directly in the jaw, clattering his teeth. He dropped like I had pressed the off switch on a robot.

Alexa gasped. The two security guys showed up just in time.

"Are you okay, sir?" the one asked me.

"Fine," I said, turning away. "Come on," I said to Alexa, grabbing her again.

"Is he okay?" she asked.

"Fuck him."

We got into the car and I started the engine. Alexa was staring at me, wide-eyed, obviously shocked by what I had just done. I knew that shit was going to be in the papers tomorrow, or maybe just the tabloids if I was lucky. Maybe even I was going to have some charges pressed against me.

"Why would you do that?" Alexa asked as I pulled out into traffic.

"My mother may be a bitch," I said, "but only I get to say so."

She stared at me for a second and then burst out laughing, shaking her head.

I couldn't help but grin myself, and I laughed along with her.

We sped back toward her dad's house, moving through the night.

Chapter Seven: Alexa

"Hello?" I said, answering the phone on the third ring.

"Hey. It's me."

"Hi, Lace. What's going on?"

"Nothing." She paused. "Just embarrassed."

"About the other night?"

"Yeah."

"I was wondering why you hadn't called already."

I rolled over onto my back and looked up at the ceiling of my bedroom. I was happy that Lacey had called me, even though it was still pretty early in the morning, because I'd been dying to tell her all about what had happened with Cole and me on the roof of the banquet hall.

"I'm really sorry about that, Alex. I don't normally let myself get like that."

It was true. Despite her confidence, her outgoing nature, Lacey very rarely got too drunk. Sure, she went home with guys from time to time, but that was just because she knew what she wanted and she went for it. She rarely made those decisions based on how much alcohol she'd had to drink.

I envied that about her. She had confidence, something I was lacking sometimes.

"It's okay," I said. "You should probably be apologizing to Cole, though."

"Oh god. Don't remind me." I could practically hear her cringing on the other end.

"He threw you over his shoulder and dragged you out of there," I said, laughing.

"Seriously, Al. I'm going to cry."

I laughed louder, grinning. I could imagine the look on her face, and although I didn't want my friend to be upset, it was just too funny.

"Don't worry about it. He's definitely not thinking about you right now."

"Why are you so sure?"

"Something happened."

Instantly I felt the conversation shift. "Tell me. Now."

"Well, we went to one of those dinner things with our parents last night, right?"

"How did he look?"

"Good. I mean, really good. That's not the point."

"Cole in a tux. Shit, I think I just made myself hard."

"What?"

"Lady boner. You get it."

I rolled my eyes. "Anyway, he wasn't into it, and I guess I was pretty bored too. So we snuck out."

"Snuck out? This is getting good."

"Hold on. Listen. So, anyway, he takes me out this emergency exit and up a staircase to the roof."

"How romantic."

"Yeah, well, he had a bottle of whisky."

"Where'd he get it?"

"Stole it, I guess."

She laughed. "Doesn't surprise me."

"Why, because he's an immature moron?"

"No, because he seems to do whatever he wants. It's an attractive quality in a man, you know."

"Whatever. There's nothing attractive about him."

"Sure, Al. So what did you guys do on the roof, have some deep talk?"

"At first, yeah. I mean, the view was gorgeous, and the weather was perfect. The whisky was gross, but I had some anyway."

"Sounds like a good time."

"Lace, he kissed me."

There was a pause. "Seriously?"

"I mean, yeah, and I kissed him back—for like half a second, but it was a really intense kiss."

Lacey exploded. She began talking fast, a flurry of emotions pouring out of her. At first she was all, "what are you doing are you stupid he's your stepbrother," but that quickly turned into, "he's also your husband and actually really damn hot so I guess I get it," and finally she finished with, "I knew it, I knew you would, you dirty girl, did you guys bang? I would hit that in a second, you have to tell me everything."

It was an emotionally intense ten seconds.

"Are you done?" I cut in.

"Okay, yeah. I just can't believe you!"

"I know. It's so stupid. So, so stupid. Like, I want to divorce this guy, get my life back on track. I can't be making out with him."

"I mean, it's not that big of a deal. It's not like you guys didn't bone already."

My eyes widened. "Lacey, we did *not* have sex."

Lacey laughed. "Come on, Al. I know you guys definitely had sex on vacation."

"Seriously," I said forcefully, surprised. "We didn't have sex. I thought

416

I told you that? We did pretty much everything else imaginable, but we just never had sex."

She was silent for a second. "You have to be lying."

"I'm not lying. I'm dead serious."

"But you said it was the most intense night of your life? After the fake wedding?"

"It was, but we never actually had sex."

"I don't get it. It's not like you were a virgin."

"I know! But he made me feel . . . things, stuff Bobby didn't do."

Bobby was my college boyfriend and the second guy I had ever slept with. I had thought sex with him was pretty good until I learned Bobby didn't know anything about the human anatomy compared to Cole. Bobby and I had broken up three months before I'd left for Thailand after I caught him sending nudes to some girl he met on Tinder, the scumbag. I barely ever thought about Bobby anymore.

"Holy crap. It was that intense and you didn't actually have sex?"

"Yeah, absolutely no sex." I paused, sighing, as the memories of that night came back to me. Cole's fingers, his mouth, his hands, they all made me squirm and come again and again. But for some reason I hadn't been able to sleep with him, couldn't let myself have sex. "You see the problem now?" I asked.

"Yeah. I really, really do."

We were both quiet as the truth sank in.

I hadn't had sex with Cole in Thailand, but we had done plenty of other things. He'd made me feel more with just his mouth than Bobby had made me feel in our entire relationship. Cole was a man unlike any I had ever met before, and he seemed to just intuitively know exactly what would drive me crazy. And I had kissed him again, letting all those feeling come flooding back inside me.

"What are you going to do now?" Lacey asked.

"I don't know, honestly. He's my stepbrother."

She snorted. "Stepbrother doesn't mean anything. He's not actually related to you or anything. Plus, you two were married first."

"That's true. But I can't tell if that makes it better or not."

"Probably not. Still, he's your husband."

"He is not my husband."

"Whatever. I'm just looking out for you. If you're into it, I say go for it."

"It's not that simple. Our parents are under some crazy scrutiny. Cole knocked out a reporter last night."

"Before or after you made out?"

"After."

"How did that even happen?"

"Guy came out of nowhere, taking pictures. Cole just . . . acted."

Lacey whistled. "What a guy."

"It was scary."

"I bet it was. But also a little hot?"

"No! No way."

"Oh come on, we both know Cole is sexy as hell."

"He has his moments."

"And how's his piece?"

"Excuse me?"

"His piece. His man-meat. His schlong. His ding-a-ling. His—"

"Okay, okay, I get it."

"Well?"

"Cut it out. I'm not describing his wiener."

I thought back to those nights, to his thick, large cock in my hand, to the way he grunted as I slipped it between my lips, to the warmth of his cum as he shot it deep into my throat. I felt a rush run through me as my cheeks turned red.

"Oh just tell me. Big or little? Thick? Curved? Pierced?"

"Not happening."

"C'mon. Yes or no, is he huge?"

"I am not describing Cole's penis!" I yelled loudly, embarrassed. The sound practically echoed through my empty room.

We were both quiet for a second.

"I gotta go," I said quickly. "I think he's home and his room is right next door."

I hung up the phone as she began to laugh.

I wrapped myself in my blankets and tried to pretend like I hadn't just yelled loudly about Cole's penis. The walls in Dad's house were super thin, so there was no way he hadn't heard that. I could only imagine what pervy, frustrating things he was thinking over there.

It wasn't like I was obsessed with him. Maybe he made me feel something I hadn't felt in a long time, if ever, but still. He was abrasive and cocky and everything I hated in a guy. I didn't like violence, and Cole's life was all about violence. I didn't like recklessness, and Cole was reckless.

Still, driving in that fast car with him, threading our way toward the banquet venue, I'd felt alive.

Lacey could be so pushy sometimes, but I knew she meant well. She was a good friend and always supportive. Still, I wasn't really comfortable enough with anyone to describe Cole's penis, even if that wasn't a dick move.

As I contemplated all of the awkward and horrifying ramifications of that conversation, I heard my father's voice from downstairs.

"Alexa? Cole?"

I got out of bed and poked my head out of my room. "Yeah?"

"Can you come down here?"

Cole came out of his own room and smirked at me. "Hey, sis."

"Hi, Cole." I started walking down the steps.

"Fun time last night."

"It was okay."

"You should *describe* to me exactly how much fun you had."

I turned bright red but didn't look at him. "That's okay. I don't feel like grossing you out."

He was right behind me as we marched downstairs. I could practically feel his heat pressing up against my back.

"If that assistant hadn't shown up, we both know that I would have made you come, screaming for more up on that roof."

"Knock it off. My dad is right downstairs."

He grabbed my arm, pulling me against his hard body. "I'll stop if you admit that you wanted me to keep going." We were pressed together in the stairwell, in the small, cramped space.

I bit my lip, breathing heavily as his warmth and touch flooded my body. "I was drunk and stupid," I lied.

"So you admit it."

"Fine. It was a mistake though."

"Good enough." He let me go, and I wished that he hadn't.

I started back down the steps and he followed me quietly. I was so embarrassed, and I could practically feel his triumphant smile boring a hole into my ass. I hated that I wanted him, and I hated that he knew it.

Once downstairs, we found our parents sitting together in the kitchen. It was almost creepy, and I felt like a little kid about to be punished.

"Uh oh," Cole said. "Who died?"

"Please, sit," Cindy said.

I sat down and gave my Dad a look. He just smiled and shrugged.

"I bet I know what this is about," Cole said.

"The reporter."

Cole nodded. "He survived?"

"He's fine, thankfully."

"Pressing charges?"

"No."

Cole laughed out loud. "How'd you manage that one?"

"Not your concern."

"Sure it is, Mother. What did you bribe him with?"

"Nothing," Frank cut in. "We've had trouble with him in the past. We simply told him that if he pressed charges, so would we."

Cole nodded. "Threats then. They work on spineless dickbags like him."

"Cole, enough," Cindy said sharply. "This isn't funny. You assaulted a man."

"Yes, I did," Cole said.

"That's unacceptable, totally unacceptable."

"I guess so."

"You embarrassed me."

"Not sure that bothers me, honestly."

"Cole, please," Dad cut in. "Your mother is worried."

"Worried?" Cole said, smirking. "Sure, she's worried about her career."

"Enough," Cindy said, slamming her hand down on the countertop. The whole room looked at her, surprised. I had never seen an ounce of strong emotion in her before, but suddenly she looked very, very angry. "You have embarrassed me time and time again, Cole. I want you to leave."

He stared at her hard for a second and then smiled. "Kicking me out already?"

"Yes. Please pack and leave by tomorrow."

Dad looked away, unable to meet my eye. I was completely taken aback and shocked by the fact that Cindy was so callously throwing her son out on the street. It seemed almost like it was no big deal, but it seemed incredibly absurd. She was making such a big decision without even talking to anyone about it.

"Wait," I said. "Don't you know why he did it?"

"Don't bother," Cole said. "She doesn't give a fuck about any of that. This is just an excuse to get rid of me."

He stood up.

"Wait," I said to Cole, and then I turned back toward Cindy. "He punched that guy because he called you a bitch."

Cindy raised an eyebrow. "Is that true, Cole?"

"It's true. Only I get to call you that."

She was quiet for a second. "Thank you for defending my honor, but unfortunately this isn't feudal England. You can't just punch people whenever you feel like it."

Cole looked back at me and shrugged. "Told you."

"Wait," I said again, but he had already left the room. I looked back at Cindy, anger rising in my chest. "Why would you do that?"

She sighed. "Cole has been a problem for a very long time. At a certain point, you have to be tough with him or else he will walk all over you." She paused and looked at me seriously. "That's a lesson you'll need to learn if you want to remain in touch with him."

I stared back at her, not sure what she meant. I almost couldn't believe what she was saying. "He's your son," I said.

"He's also a liability." She looked away, back toward the file of papers she had in front of her.

"He'll be okay," Dad said. "He's a tough kid. Has some money, too."

I stared at him, completely unable to comprehend what had just happened. I stood up, shaking my head in disgust. "Grow a spine, Dad.

You know this isn't right."

Before he could answer, I turned and left the room.

Anger flooded through me as I went upstairs after Cole. It wasn't fair that they were kicking him out. It wasn't right, especially since he'd been defending his mother. Sure, he shouldn't have hit the guy. He should have kept his cool. But he wasn't the type of man to just sit by and let someone insult his mother, even when his mother actually was a total bitch.

I had to admit, there was something special about that. It was old-fashioned, yeah, and maybe a little intense, but it was endearing. I didn't like violence, but I did like a man with some semblance of honor. Too many guys these days were willing to roll over and let anyone do whatever they wanted so long as they could avoid a fight.

Cole's door was shut, and so I knocked once. He didn't answer, so I knocked again. Instead of knocking a third time, I just pushed open the door.

"Cole," I said. He stopped doing his push-ups and looked up at me, rocking back onto his knees.

"I thought you might follow me up here, wife," he said, grinning.

"How are you not pissed off?"

"This happens every time."

"What, your mom kicks you out?"

"Not exactly. I do something she doesn't like, and so she finds some reason to get rid of me."

"You're okay with that?"

"I'm not some little kid, Alexa. I don't need my fucking insane, bitch mommy to be proud of me."

I sighed, frustrated. Was everyone in this house totally stupid?

"Look, I get it. But it's still not right that she's throwing you out like this," I pushed.

He stood up and stretched his arms. "I'm honestly surprised you're taking such an interest in this."

"Why wouldn't I?"

"You've been trying to get rid of me from the start. I'm sure you're excited for this."

"I don't want to get rid of you," I said softly.

He stepped closer to me. "No?" His body filled my vision, muscular and tall. "Why not?"

"Because," I said softly. I didn't want to say it.

"Go ahead. Tell me why you want me to stay."

"You did nothing wrong."

"And?" His smell filled my mind as he came closer to me, inches away. I felt my heart begin to beat fast in my chest.

"And, I don't know. You're not bad to have around."

"Not bad to have around?" he asked, grinning. "You love having me here. You want me to sneak into that room at night and lick your clit until your back arches and your hands grip the sheets."

"Cole," I said, trying to tell him to stop, but I couldn't say the words.

"Admit you want me to fuck you until you can't breathe, Alex. You want to finally feel what my cock is like deep inside that perfect, tight pussy of yours. You've been aching for it since you first saw me."

"We can't."

"We can do whatever we want."

"I don't know what I want," I said slowly.

That seemed to break the spell. He smirked again and I stepped away, putting some distance between us. "Figure it out, sis. And soon."

"Just, don't pack up yet. I'll fix this."

"You do that."

He turned away and dropped back to the floor, going back to his push-ups.

I watched him, an ache running through my chest, a desire flooding through my legs, and I knew I was wet as hell. I knew it was true that I wanted to fuck him, to finally feel what it would be like. I'd been imagining it ever since we'd met. If he could get me off with his mouth and fingers as easily as he did, then I couldn't imagine what it would be like if he fucked me deep and rough.

I wanted it. But I couldn't do anything about it, not while he was my stepbrother, not while we still had this fake, idiotic marriage hanging over our heads.

I watched for a second, his muscular and incredible body working up and down, and then ripped myself away from him. I shut the door behind me as I retreated into my bedroom.

It was wrong for his mother to kick him out, but the reason I wanted him to stay was even worse.

I wanted to fuck my stepbrother, my husband, until I couldn't walk. I wanted him to strip me down and take me, just the way he kept saying he would.

It was all so messed up. Just feet away, I could practically sense him still working out, and I wanted so desperately to rip that shirt from his tattooed chest and let him have me.

Instead, I was going to convince my dad to let him stay.

I'd worry about everything else later.

Chapter Eight: Cole

I threw my shirts into my duffel with a grunt. It wasn't exactly surprisingly

that my mother had decided to kick me out, but it was definitely a new

record. I hadn't even lasted a month in her house before she'd decided I

was too much of a liability.

That was fine with me. The whole thing had stopped being fun and

had started to feel real as soon as I'd figured out that I really was married to

Alexa. As much as I hated to leave her, it was just that time.

Still, I was going to miss having her around all the time. I had gotten

used to seeing her in the hallways, to flirting with her mercilessly, teasing

her about the way I made her body feel. But I wasn't the type to beg

forgiveness or to look back.

As I sat down on my bed for the last time, someone knocked at the

door.

"What?" I called out.

"It's Frank. Can I talk to you?"

What does my new stepdaddy want? I thought ruefully.

"Yeah, sure," I said.

He opened the door and stepped in, closing it softly behind him. I could tell that he was uncomfortable as he stood with his arms crossed, avoiding my look.

"What can I do for you, Frank?" I asked, trying not to sound annoyed.

"I just wanted to say that this wasn't my decision."

I raised an eyebrow. "Okay. Is that all?"

He sighed and looked at me. "Look, Cole, your mother is under a lot of pressure because of our relationship. I'm not sure she's thinking clearly on this one."

I laughed. "You don't know Cindy very well then."

He held up one hand, a pained look on his face. "I know what you think of her," he said, "but she's softened a lot since you last saw her."

"I find that hard to believe."

"I'll never understand you or your relationship with your mother, but I do know that she loves you."

I smirked but didn't respond. I hadn't needed Cindy's love for a long, long time. I had come to the conclusion that she wasn't really capable of it, no matter what she may have looked like on the outside. Frank would figure it out eventually. He was applying human terms and emotions and feelings to a robot. It just didn't work out.

"So," Frank went on, "I decided that I want you to stay."

That surprised me. "Does Cindy know?"

"Not yet," he said, "but I'll tell her after we're done talking."

"That's not going to go over well."

"This is my house, Cole."

"Maybe. But so long as Cindy is here, she's in charge and we both know it."

Frank laughed and shook his head. "You're not wrong there. But in this instance I'm making my own decision, and your mother will just have to go along with it."

I had to admit that I was impressed. I'd never pegged Frank for a man with a spine, but standing up to Cindy took guts, even if he hadn't even confronted her about it yet and was going behind her back.

But I didn't want or need charity. I didn't want Frank's pity, and I didn't want Cindy's scorn. I didn't need any of it. I didn't care about any of it. The only reason I was staying in the house was Alexa, but that just seemed more and more crazy.

I knew she wanted me. It was obvious. But she was so damn conflicted and so obsessed with this marriage thing that she couldn't let herself have what was clearly what she needed. I'd been up front with what

I wanted from her. There was no ambiguity in my position. Actually, there was no ambiguity in the position that I wanted to fuck her in.

So there was nothing keeping me around.

"No, thanks," I said. "If Cindy wants me out, I'm out."

"I think you should reconsider."

"Listen, Frank, this little shit between my mom and me, it's as old as time. She's a controlling shrew and I'm not a little teenager anymore trying to make mommy happy."

"She just wants what's best for you."

"Maybe, but her best isn't mine. I'm leaving. You can avoid your fight."

He sighed and shook his head. "No. I'm telling her what I've decided no matter what. You can stay or leave, but you're welcome back whenever you want."

I nodded, even more impressed. "Okay, Frank."

"Okay." He turned and left without another word.

I liked him. As much as I didn't want to, I liked him. I thought he was an idiot for marrying my mother, and maybe a little gullible, but he seemed like a decent enough man.

I finished packing and stood up, tossing my duffel over my shoulder. The house was comfortable, by far the nicest place I'd lived in a long time, but I had to be moving on. I had my bike, some stuff in storage, and some cash in savings. I was going to be fucking fine.

But for some reason I didn't want to leave. Pride or not, part of me wanted to drop my bag and take Frank up on his offer. I wanted to stay next door to Alexa, to flirt with her mercilessly until she eventually gave in to herself and her needs.

But fuck that. Fuck weakness. I pushed open my bedroom door and went down the steps.

Outside, I found my bike parked where I'd left it. I sat down on the seat, grabbed the clutch, and started it. The engine roared to life as I gave the house one last look.

And then Alexa came out the front door dressed in short shorts and a tight as fuck T-shirt. I knew I should have gotten out of there, sped away, signed her papers through the mail and forgotten the whole fucking thing. I should have concentrated on my fighting. But I didn't.

"Hey," she yelled over the engine. "Where are you going?"

"Leaving," I yelled back.

"Can you turn that thing off?"

I grinned at her. "I could."

She rolled her eyes. "Be mature. For once."

I laughed and killed the engine. "What's up, Alex?"

"I just wanted to say . . . you know."

She looked so damn uncomfortable that it was sexy. I loved how

433

sheepish and embarrassed she could get. The girl was incapable of saying exactly what she wanted.

"You wanted to say that you're desperate for me to come inside for one last goodbye fuck?"

She made a face. "We haven't even had a hello fuck, in case you forgot."

"I haven't forgotten. I haven't stopped thinking about fucking that perfect little cunt of yours since I got here."

She blushed. "Okay, well stop. That's not what this is about."

"What's it about, then?"

"I just, you know." She looked frustrated.

"Spit it out, wifey."

"I just wanted you to stay. You should stay."

I grinned at her. "I know you want me to."

"Don't be an ass. You think that's easy to say to you?"

"I guess not."

"I know my dad said you don't need to leave, and I'm saying it too."

"What's in it for me?"

She blinked at me, surprised. "What do you mean? Free room and board plus meals, I guess."

"I don't give a shit about that. What do I get if I stay?"

"Why do you need to get something? I'm just trying to be nice here."

"You want me to stay. I want something to make me stay."

She bit her lip, looking frustrated, and I knew exactly what she was thinking. She was wondering if I meant sex and couldn't decide if she would do that, if she could promise she'd fuck me if I stayed. Even though she wanted to, she knew it would be weird, or bad, or whatever she thought.

"What do you want?" she asked finally.

"Come to my fight. It's in a few days."

She looked surprised at that. "Wait, you just want me to come watch you fight?"

"That's it. Come watch me fight and then decide if you want me to stay or not."

"I can do that."

"I'd be careful, sis. You might not know what you're getting yourself into."

"I've been to a fight before."

"Maybe, but you've never seen someone you know put their life on the line."

She shrugged, not sure what to say. "Well, fine. I can do that."

"One more thing. Come alone. Don't bring your friend."

She opened her mouth, shut it, and nodded. "Okay."

"I'll text you the details."

"Okay."

I grabbed the clutch and started the engine again. She stepped back away from the bike, blinking.

"Later, wife," I yelled.

"Stop calling me that," she called back. I began to pull out into traffic. "And sign the papers, you asshole!" she yelled as I roared away.

I smirked to myself, tearing up the road. Maybe I would be moving back home after all.

~~~~~~

I liked it when the locker room was empty.

It was a few days after I'd moved out of Frank's house. I hadn't seen or spoken to Alexa, though I did send her the fight details. She hadn't gotten back to me, but I wasn't letting that distract me from what I needed to do.

The last few days had been dedicated to training and watching tapes of the guy I was fighting. He was young and aggressive and strong, but I was confident. I was always confident.

I liked it when the locker room was empty. I could sit there and meditate, get my mind right, empty my brain, and get ready for what I was about to do.

And I was about to fight for my life. Every time I entered the ring, I knew that I could die. I was risking life and limb in there, risking my future, my career. One wrong move, one false step, and I could easily get beaten, broken, or worse.

It had happened before. It happened to guys like me. In a sport as brutal and fast-paced and violent as MMA, it would keep on happening.

That was what we wanted. The rush of bodies breaking bodies, of the possibility of defeat, or victory, or serious injury. It was all there and it was right.

It was what I lived for.

And then the promoter came in, and my manager came in, my trainer, some media guys. I didn't like the locker room as much when I wasn't alone, but it was part of the gig. I answered questions, I talked strategy, but mostly I worked on keeping my mind right.

And then there was the roar of the crowd as the announcer said my name. I walked through the tunnel, heart beating slow, slow, and my whole body loose and calm, radiating a deadly calm. I had learned how to control my emotions and how to enter into an empty, mindless fighting state at my whim. Skad had taught me that and much, much more, stuff nobody knew that I could do.

It'd been a long time since I was out in front of people, but for some reason my usual pre-match jitters weren't there. I couldn't even remember the name of the girl I had been thinking about over and over ever since I'd gotten back to America.

There was only the ring and my opponent, an intense focus I hadn't felt since the Thai jungles. Hours of training in incredible heat and humidity had hardened me to distractions.

Once in the ring, I stripped down to my shorts, my hands wrapped and ready. People spoke words, but I couldn't hear them. I couldn't see them. I could only see my opponent. Time ceased to flow, and I felt nothing but my heart beating softly.

Then we were faced off, circling each other. Somehow the round had started. His hands flashed out and I blocked them.

I dance back, testing his speed with a few jabs.

He swatted them. He was angry, a snarling bull. He wanted to make a move, to see what I was made of.

I floated back. The crowd was screaming, but I couldn't hear them.

He feinted. I didn't fall for it.

Then he made his move. He juked forward, trying to grapple me, but my feet snapped out quicker than he could have realized.

I caught him right in the face.

Blood splashed from his nose.

It was all fury and excitement as I lunged.

He stumbled back, shocked, in pain, his eyes wide. He thought he was fast.

But I was faster.

My fists found him then. Pummeling him.

I wanted to break him. Kill him if I had to. I was ready to smash his skull into pieces.

Fury and intensity rolled through me as my fists snapped out, again and again, pounding and destroying. I forgot that the thing I was beating was a human, an actual person. He was just a bag of meat to me then, an enemy that needed to be destroyed.

And then the ref was there, pulling me back. I realized that my opponent was down on the ground and the bell was ringing.

The night came rushing back in a cacophony of sound and emotion.

～～～～～～～～～～～～～～～～～～～～～～～～～～～～～～～～～～～～

People were pressed in on all sides in the locker room. It was packed, promoters everywhere, everyone congratulating me.

"Fuck, man," Ronnie said. "When did you learn to move that fast?"

"Thailand," I grunted at him, grinning.

He laughed. "That shit was crazy! You made that kid look like a fool!"

I basked in my victory, in the crowd, but my eyes kept scanning for her. For Alexa.

I'd come back to myself as soon as I had won the match. It was always a shit show after a knockout, especially a fast and brutal knockout like that. People were screaming and cheering. I scanned the crowd, trying to find her, but people kept getting in my face, congratulating me, wanting something from me. I had nothing to give them.

But I was elated. Nothing felt better than a victory, especially a victory you needed so desperately. And I needed to show everyone what I was still made of. That I was still a threat.

"Hey," Ronnie said. "Isn't that your stepsister?"

And then I spotted her, standing across the room, looking lost and shy. She was wearing a low-cut dress, all tight and fucking sexy, making her tits look incredible. She looked out of places standing among the fighting crowd, almost as if she was pure and everyone else was tainted. I quickly walked through the crowd, elbowing my way toward her.

Her whole face lit up as soon as she saw me. I felt something right then, something that was almost as good as the fight itself.

"Hey, sis," I grunted.

"Hey, yourself. Congrats on your win."

"Thanks."

She stood close to me, and I could sense exactly what I expected. Behind her smile, there was a tinge of fear. Subtle, but it was definitely there. She was uncomfortable, but I couldn't tell if it was because of the crowd or because she had just watched me beat a man to a pulp.

I had known she would respond that way. I had known it would scare her to see me fight like that, to see me really let loose and try to destroy another person. She wasn't used to it; it wasn't a part of her life like it was a part of mine.

"What did you think?" I asked her.

"It was . . . exciting."

"Liar," I grunted, standing close.

"I'm not lying."

"I can see right through you."

"What do you want me to say?"

"The truth."

She sighed. "Fine. Okay. It was intense. It was easy when I didn't know the guys fighting, but watching you like that was a totally different thing."

"And now you're a little scared of me," I said, smirking at her.

"No, I'm not scared."

"You should be, sis."

"Why?"

"Because now you know what I'm capable of."

"Yeah. That's true. But there's something else, too."

"What?"

She looked embarrassed. "I can't believe I'm saying this, but it was also a little . . . you know."

I grinned and felt my cock stir as I looked at her. She was clearly uncomfortable, and I knew exactly what she was going to say. I could see it in the way her chest rose and fell quickly, her breath coming in deep and fast. I could see it in the dress she was wearing, the dress that screamed sex, and the way her eyes lingered on my body. I knew what she wanted.

"It turned you on," I whispered in her ear. "You thought to yourself, if I could fight like that, imagine how I could fuck."

"Yes," she breathed.

"And now you can't decide if you want to run away or if you want to go all in."

"Maybe."

"I'll tell you this: I fuck better than I fight. You only got a little taste of what I could do to that dripping pussy of yours."

"I'm not dripping."

"Don't lie to me again. I know if I reached under that dress, I'd find you soaked through your panties."

"Cole," she said, pushing me away. "Look, I just wanted to say that you can come back, okay?"

She was blushing like crazy, and I could practically smell the desire rolling off her in waves. My heartrate was up and my cock was hard, so hard that I was worried someone might notice.

"Come on," I grunted at her. "Let's get the fuck out of here."

She blinked at me and then nodded. "Okay."

I grabbed her by the hand, nodded at Ronnie, and then led her out of the locker room and down a series of hallways. The venue was old and full of a bunch of different dressing rooms. I chose one at random, ducking inside.

I flipped on the light. There was a couch against one wall and a vanity on the other. I grabbed her hips and pressed my body against hers, kicking the door shut behind us.

She knew what I wanted. She could feel my dick pressed against her core. But she didn't move, didn't say a word, as I slowly slid my hands up her legs and grabbed her ass, pushing her dress over her hips. She gasped as soon as my palms pressed against her panties.

"Sure you want to be alone with me?" I asked.

"No, not at all," she whispered.

I kissed her, deep and hard. She kissed me back, and I knew she was lying.

I knew she wanted to be alone with me more than anything else.

Head over to Amazon right now to finish this story!
Thanks so much for reading!

Step Bride

Made in United States
Orlando, FL
31 July 2023

35629514R00245